# City of Pillars

## By Dominic Peloso

**The Invisible College Press, LLC**

**Arlington VA**

Publisher's Note:
This is a work of fiction. Names, characters, places, and incidents
are either the product of the author's imagination or are used
fictitiously, and any resemblance to actual persons living or dead,
events, organizations, or locales is entirely coincidental.

ISBN: 1-931486-00-1

Cover Art ©2000 Juliana Peloso
Cover Design ©2000 Michael Yang
First Printing

The Invisible College Press, LLC
P.O. Box 209
Woodbridge VA 22193-0209
http://www.invispress.com

Please send questions and comments to:
editor@invispress.com

This novel is dedicated to:


Phil R., who sparked my interest in the subject

Fred S., for providing daily inspiration

Teressa W., who was the only one who believed in this book

# Prologue:
# (Daat)

Let me say one thing straight off the top. I am not writing for your amusement, to ensure historical accuracy, or to get across some sort of philosophical metaphor. This document is my confession. I am writing down my experiences because I can no longer stand their weight on my soul. I need to relieve myself of the burden of my years and my actions. This is my last chance, my last desperate grasp onto the final traces of my sanity and my humanity. If only I can objectively recall what has happened to me, what I have been through, what I have done, then perhaps somehow I can find some loophole, some way to stem the inevitable tide of events that threatens to completely consume me. Deep down I know that I am kidding myself. I have no faith in this endeavor. In my heart I know that there is no hope left for me, but still I must try, must struggle against my inner demons one last time, one last gasp before the end.

I fervently hope and desperately pray that no one will ever get a chance to read what I am about to commit to paper. They'll be coming for me soon, and I am almost certain (for reasons which will become apparent later) that I will completely destroy all evidence of this manuscript in the next few hours. Once that happens there will be nothing left to tell my tale. No one still alive knows enough of the pieces to understand the horrific whole. There are no records of my travails. Without maps (which for the reader's safety I will not provide), there is little chance of finding any of the objects and sites scattered around the world that could validate my words. If by some strange twist of fate this document does somehow get into a reader's hands, I urge that reader to immediately destroy the copy before proceeding any further. The words written down here can be the result of only two things. Either I have gone completely mad, in which case the following is just gibberish and ravings, unworthy of review; or second, that I have been the victim of an organization that does not wish to become known, and possesses such power and influence that even having the simple knowledge of their existence could be a significant danger to the health and sanity of the reader. In either case, no mention of this manuscript should ever be made, and no part of it should ever be allowed to see the light of day. The information contained within can be of no benefit to the reader. I am a man who looked too closely at the inner mysteries, and it has only resulted in my downfall. Retain your innocence.

\*\*\*

# Chapter 1:
# Kingdom

My name was Mitchell Sinclair. I say 'was' because it has been over eight years since that name last meant anything, since it was valid in any meaningful sense. I was born and raised in the better part of San Francisco, California to a set of dull yet caring upper middle-class parents. As a child I was small for my age, which led me to develop academic skills over athletic ones. I was accepted to several Ivy League schools after graduation. I had become a successful lawyer by the time my hunting began. I want to point out that I was a normal rational person in every way up until I was mistaken for the wrong man. I had never believed in any of the strange conspiracies that were rumored about in the alternative press. I never had any inclination toward magic or hermetic sciences. I played golf on the weekends. I was not interested in aliens or ghosts or any of the things that live beyond mankind's normal definition of reality. I had a wife of four years then, and we were expecting a baby girl. I can't say that we didn't have our problems, but I was sure we would work them out. My wife was normal if a little materialistic, and we lived in a plain, but decent house that was far enough up in the Marin hills to be enviable, but not enough to be pretentious. Business was good, and I was rapidly moving up the ladder at my law firm. I expected to make partner in another three years. Although I was not rich, my finances were in good shape, and I had just purchased a classic car. It was a 1958 Cadillac Sedan (the one with the giant tailfins) and I was very happy with the vehicle. It performed well, and its shiny black exterior was the envy of all the little people I drove past on my way to the office each morning. I spent a lot of time polishing the chrome, and it always looked almost new.

I mention my car specifically, not because of vanity, but because my particular choice seems to be the initial cause of the stress and horrible events that have taken place in my life since its purchase. The horror started one morning on my way to work. If you are unfamiliar with the geography of the region, let me just say that one must cross the Golden Gate Bridge in order to proceed from my home in Marin to my office located on Montgomery St. in San Francisco. As you can imagine, traffic backs up on the bridge during rush hour, and I was caught in the daily traffic jam in front of the tollbooths. I'll admit that I was not a patient man at the time, and I was eager to get to the office so I wouldn't have to stay as late. In the law firm hierarchy, every hour billed counts in the competition for promotion. I was in one tollbooth line that seemed to not be moving very rapidly. Apparently the toll collector had something else on his mind. I noticed that the line directly to my left was moving slightly faster, and I decided to make my move. I noticed a space and took it, much to the chagrin of the driver that I just cut off. I looked in my rear view mirror to give the driver the insincere wave that we all do when we've just screwed them, when I noticed that the car behind me was also a Cadillac, very similar to my own. Being a car snob as I was, I was saddened to see that I had just cut off someone with the same style and good taste that I had, but on the road it's every man for himself. The driver behind me honked his displeasure.

I maneuvered my way to the front of this new toll line and went to hand my three bucks to the operator. Three ple. As for what the paper said, I would have no idea. It was covered, front and back, with a strange writing. I had never seen such script before. It looked a little like Indian, but I didn't think that it was. I had to admit that my knowledge of foreign cultures at the time was minimal, and had taken a back seat in my education to my main goal of greed. The text was handwritten, which was odd since the document was over a hundred pages in length. There were no paragraphs, punctuation, or pictures to break up the writing. In fact, someone had even written sideways in the margins of the pages, in what I could only assume was an attempt to stuff as much information as possible into a limited space. I sat and pondered the document for a while, flipping through the first few pages. It was very beautiful script, and someone had obviously taken a long time to create it, but why would a toll collector throw it into my car? Was it a joke? Was he getting rid of some old junk cluttering up his booth? I honestly did not know. One possibility that crossed my mind at the time was that the toll collector was an amateur writer, and this was an attempt at a screenplay. With my hot car and my fancy suit, perhaps he thought I was some sort of movie executive. When lunch was done, I meant to throw it in the trash, but I must have accidentally gotten it caught up in with my newspaper, which I usually brought back home at the end of the day for my wife to read. I returned to the office though the crowded mid-day streets.

When I returned to work, I was greeted with quite a shock. I opened the door to my office to find a man inside, rummaging through my desk. He was evidentially a foreigner of some sort. He wore an ill-fitting dark business suit that seemed to have been dragged through the mud. He immediately looked up at me in shock. He ran around the desk and pushed his way past me. "Hey you, stop," I yelled, but he was already halfway down the corridor. I followed him, but the last I saw of the man was as the elevator doors closed in front of me. I walked back down the hallway and asked my secretary who the stranger was. She responded that she had been sitting there since I had left, and she swore that no one had entered my office. I called down to security and reported the incident, and they said that they would look into it, but there was not much that they would be able to do. I searched through my office. Some files were in disarray, however none of my legal papers were missing. Strangely, it seemed that the man had taken only one object from my office. A generic mug that I had used as a pencil holder was gone, the pencils spilled on the desk.

The rest of the day passed without incident. I resumed my duties as an attorney, and actually made some progress on one case I had been having trouble with. I grinned at the thought of how much money the settlement would net our firm. By the time the afternoon was over, I had completely forgotten about the odd events of the day. At 6:30 I left the office, absentmindedly picking up my briefcase, newspaper, and coat. I drove home to my wife, my unborn child, and my unused ham sandwich. On the way home my car was passed on the highway by some nut who must have been doing a hundred and ten miles per hour. Seconds later a police car with lights flashing came into view. A few miles down the road, I passed the pair as they sat on the shoulder. The man looking agitated as the officer sat in his car writing a well deserved ticket. I felt a lot safer knowing that maniacs like that guy were getting tickets. Hopefully they'd revoke his license.

Once home, my wife and I ate some of the rubbery roast that she had prepared for dinner, and after which I retired to the den to go over some reading I had brought home from work. I could hear my wife washing the dishes in the kitchen as I began pouring over some contracts. A few minutes after the water stopped, I could hear coffee percolating. A few minutes after that, my wife appeared carrying a steaming mug and cookies for me. She returned to the kitchen to get her cup, and then sat down on the other side of the den to read the ketchup stained newspaper I had been carrying with me all day.

"What's this?" she said, holding up the foreign manuscript that had been passed to me that morning. She paged through it curiously.

"I don't know what that is," I replied. "Some tollbooth collector gave that to me this morning on my way into work. I think that it's a movie script or something."

"Why you?"

"I don't know. Maybe he was impressed with my style."

"Why is it written in different languages?" I looked at the passage she had pointed to. I was uncertain what the language was, but there definitely seemed to be some sort of change after the first ten pages. It switched from what looked like Indian to what looked like a Romance language. Then Hebrew, then to what could have been Arabic. Flipping through the document, it was obvious that there were a number of languages represented, including some hieroglyphic languages. There were even some strange pictures and incomprehensible line diagrams, as if from a geometry textbook. It seemed to be written in many different types of handwriting, and both my wife and I were impressed at the skill of the author. "Maybe it's some religious nut? You know trying to convert people to Hare Krishna or something?" I started telling her about the tollbooth collector and his strange appearance, when I realized that the toll collector and the man in my office were very similar looking. "Do you think that the two incidents could be related?" I said.

"I wouldn't know, but I'd be careful if I were you. San Francisco is known for its religious nuts and vagrants. I just hope he didn't get your license number." With that she dropped the yellowed paper down onto my pile of case law.

Her attention turned to her hobby of the month, which was collating our old photos. The floor of the study had been a mess with photo albums for quite a while. There wasn't much conversation after that, except a heated debate about the allocations of our mutual funds and our daughter's budding college savings account.

A strange dream. It was a nighttime world. Leaves around my face, a stick in my ribs. I was kneeling in the brush, hiding in the woods. There was a low hill with a clearing at the top. Rough-hewn, stone obelisks ringed the clearing. Dark, ominous men stood around a wood pole at the center. The top was carved like the head of a bird. Its long curved beak cast a shadow across the glade like a black scimitar. A man was tied to the pole. A dusky man, stripped to the waist. Lackeys brought sticks, twigs, kindling. They placed them all around the man tied to the pole. Oh no. What were they doing? Drums were beating, boom, boom, boom. Torches were set, boom, boom, boom. The glade was ablaze with light as the man burned silently. Oh god no! A strange but familiar scent was in the air. Rivulets of melted human fat ran down the branches at the edges of the pyre. Rivulets of sweat ran down my cheek as I watched. The burned man made no sound as the flames ate him.

With a start I awoke in the darkness, wrapped and tied in a knotty mess of blankets and bedclothes and sheets. It was hot that night, too hot. I needed a drink. I went downstairs and poured myself some Scotch in the darkness. Back then I went through two bottles of single malt a week. A noise at the window. It was dark out here on the suburban street. A shadow moved past the window. Only a shadow, nothing more. I returned to bed, visibly shaken from my dream. I still had to go to work in a few hours.

That morning I stopped off at my secretary's desk on the way into my office. She handed me my messages for the day. "Oh, by the way, a Mr. Jones came here to see you."

"I don't know any Mr. Jones. What firm is he with."

"I don't know if he is with anybody. He just said that he had an appointment. I tried to get him to go to the waiting area, but he said that he didn't want to wait. He left you this envelope." I took it and went off to my office. "By the way, when you see him, tell him that he didn't return my pen," my secretary shouted to me from down the hall.

Inside my office, I put my things away and opened the envelope. Inside was a single slip of paper with children's writing on it. It said simply, 'You have something we want'. I didn't really know how to take that. Was it some sort of a joke? I considered the strange note for a few seconds, only to be interrupted by my phone. It was Bill from down the hall. He wanted me to stop by his office. I absentmindedly threw the strange note in the trash. I didn't have time for games.

Bill's office had a few other mid-level lawyers in it. Bill was sitting with his feet up on his desk, twirling the keys to his new luxury car around on his finger. He had placed some brochures on his desk to let people know what a great car he had bought. He had just been elevated to partner, and was showing off with his new purchase. That made me really jealous. I mean, I had a cool car, I liked my car, but I didn't have what he had. Couldn't afford what he afforded. Why wasn't I a partner yet? It's kind of silly actually, worrying about those sorts of things. I was so preoccupied with the materialistic aspects of life in those days. Worrying about how my house and possessions compared to other people's houses and possessions. Worrying about how my career was going compared to how others careers were going. Was Bill younger than I was? He was already a partner. He was a bit of a backstabber, perhaps I should be more aggressive as well. I really wasn't happy for him. I should have been, but I wasn't. I was jealous.

15

In the hallway back to my office, I was given a pat on the back by one of the senior partners. He had liked the work I had done on a recent contract negotiation. He predicted big things for me, big things. I blushed with false modesty and told him that I was only doing my job, that I was just happy to help the firm win. Then I made a backhanded compliment about Bill, subtly implying that he wasn't pulling his weight. As soon as I turned back to my office, my false smile changed back into my jealous scowl and I ran back to my desk. I needed to work harder. I needed to succeed. I needed to become a partner. The only way I would do that was to be even more impressive than I already was. I didn't have time for anything else. I didn't leave my desk until well after dark.

That night during dinner I told my wife about Bill's new car. She was able to verbalize a "that's nice", but she seemed sad through most of dinner. "What's the matter honey?" I asked.

"Why is it that we don't have all the things that everybody else has?" I furrowed my brow in puzzlement. "You know, a bigger house, a fancier car. Why is it that we have to stay in the cheap hotels when we travel? There are things I want, products I want, but we're always struggling."

"Don't I make enough money? We're not destitute. I'm a corporate lawyer for goodness sake. Hell, I'm clearing six figures, and that's not even counting bonus!"

"But there are so many people who have more. I'm tired of being embarrassed when our friends come over. Your boss has a fancy mansion, and what do you have? I just want what they all seem to have."

"What 'they', I make at least triple what the average American family makes. I'm trying my best you know. It isn't easy."

"Well, maybe you should try harder. There is so much more out there that we could have. We could live so much better than we do now. That's all that I'm saying. We're doing ok, but we could be doing better. We'll always be well off, but we'll never be rich will we? We'll never have a maid and a butler and a chauffeur and all those things that you see on television."

"We're doing fine. All those things you see are an illusion. No real person has that, except maybe a few movie stars. Trust me, we're at the top end of the food chain here. There isn't much more that we could have." Of course, I'm really misrepresenting myself as I write about this conversation all those years ago. Deep down, I guess that I agreed with her. I wanted the same things that she did. But I knew the amount of work it took. I was the one out there busting my hump twelve hours a day so she could have the gold jewelry and name brand merchandise she did have. Since I guess that subconsciously I knew that I would never be as rich as we both dreamed, I tried to placate my desire by convincing myself that we were already as rich as we could be at that point in our lives.

"Then why do I feel so poor. Why do I see people on television who seem so happy, while I need antidepressants. Why do they have grand adventures all the time, when the only adventure I get is a week-long trip to Egypt, and you were sick half the time."

"What the hell do you want me to do? I work 70 hours weeks already. I can't do anymore."

"I suppose, but it is frustrating to see how happy we *could* be, if we just had a little more. Its like there are some people out there that are doing, living, but we just sit here. Wouldn't it be great if we could live like that? Isn't that the American dream? Every little schoolgirl wants to be a princess and live on a yacht. That's what I want. Wouldn't it be great if we could find a way to have it?"

"I'm trying my best dear. We'll get there eventually. It doesn't happen all at once though. Be patient." I left it at that. Didn't she think that I wanted more? Didn't she think that I worked? I push harder and harder, but it's slow. There is always someone standing in your way. You have to push them aside, but even then, the best you can hope for is to break even. I was caught up in the rat race. What other way was there? I assumed that if I worked hard enough I would get ahead, had gotten ahead. I wasn't rich, but I knew that if I just worked a little harder, I could be there, I could keep up with the Joneses. That's what was great about our country, if you worked hard enough, no one could stop you from succeeding…someday.

I had brought home a lot of work to do that night, and I needed to get started on these contracts.

# Chapter 2:
# Foundation

The next morning my alarm didn't go off on time. Looking back on the past from today, I wonder how my life would have been different if I had gotten up earlier. If I hadn't been so rushed that morning. If had paid more attention to the pile of papers I swept up in my rush to get to the office before the morning traffic became unbearable. Although I suppose now that it wouldn't have made much of a difference. I have my theories about that morning, but I won't go into them just yet. You need to know more. This day would become very significant for reasons that will be apparent shortly. My life was about to take a considerable turn.

Other than being late, my commute to the office was typical. I didn't interact with any more disgruntled drivers or receive cryptic messages from strange tollbooth collectors. I got to the office about a half-hour later than I normally did. I expected that by the time I arrived, all of the other lawyers would already be in their places, reading their morning mail, telling obscene jokes around a half-filled coffee pot, and making more money than they honestly deserved. Nothing was different about the parking garage. The electronic gate greeted me the same as usual. The cars were all parked in their assigned spaces. The elevator came quickly when I pushed the button. I traveled straight up to my floor without incident. No one even got on at the lobby, which was a little odd, but I assumed that I was just lucky that day. The floor indicator lights changed rapidly, 1... 2... As the elevator rose I began to notice that my fingers felt a little sticky. 3... 4... I looked down to see that they were wet with what looked like blood. I immediately began a mental check of my body to see where I was bleeding from, did I cut myself shaving? I was ok. 5... 6... 7... I looked at the elevator buttons and some of them seemed to be smeared with a bloody handprint. 8... 9... 10.... "Great," I said aloud. "Now some sicko is bleeding in the elevator". 11... 12... There was also some blood drops on the floor of the elevator, but they were easy to miss with the rug patterns. I hope I don't catch some disease I thought. The elevator doors opened on the 13th floor.

I immediately headed for the hallway bathroom and washed the blood off of my fingers. Quick check to see if any was on my Italian suit. No. I was still drying my hands as I walked down the hallway to my office. "Jane," I said to my secretary as I walked in, "Call building maintenance and tell them that there is blood or something in the elevator." I walked past her without looking more than peripherally. She did not reply. I stopped to see if she heard, but it was apparent that she hadn't. My secretary was dead. She had had her throat slit from ear to ear. There was blood all over the place. All over her beaded blue dress, all over the desk, all over my papers and correspondence. Oh my god, I thought. I ran down the hall. Help! As I turned the corner to the other attorneys' offices I saw that there would be no help here. The hallway was strewn with more bodies. Bodies and blood. I checked several offices to be sure. Everyone was dead. All had been slashed to death in some gruesome manner. And recently too. Blood still dripped. Blood doesn't drip for very long after it is exposed to air. I ran back to my office to call the police. Call the building security. Phone was dead. No answer. Tap tap tap on the receiver. No answer. Dead, like all the people. My office had been ransacked. Papers everywhere. Papers splashed with blood. My filing cabinets had been emptied and overturned. I didn't realize it at the time, but in later reflection I believe that no other office had been disrupted like that. Whatever they were looking for, they were looking for it in my office alone.

There was a good reason for not paying attention to the state of my office at the time. And I mean besides the dead bodies lying limply on the floors and against the walls. On my desk there was a device. It was rather large, made of wires, putty, metal bits, and a timer. My heart began to beat faster as the shock of recognition set in. It was a bomb. Someone was going to bomb my office. beat. beat. beat. Why would someone bomb my office? The timer was set to go off about five minutes from now. I put the phone down slowly, as if in some way my dropping the receiver would set off the charge, and began to head to the door. beat. beat. beat. By the time I was in the hallway I was in a dead run, stopping only to notice the fact that there seemed to be several more bombs placed in other offices. The whole floor was going to go up in four and a half minutes. I got to the elevator and frantically began pushing the call button. Doors began to open. beat. beat. beat. 4 minutes and 10 seconds. This must have been a different elevator from the one I came up in. On the floor of this car was a crumpled body. A woman lying face down. Arms and legs twisted. Blood. beat. beat. beat. The elevator began its descent. Must get to the lobby. Evacuate. beat. beat. beat. 3 minutes and 50 seconds, beat. beat. beat. The elevator reached the lobby. The doors opened with a pleasant ding. beat. beat. beat. 3 minutes and 20 seconds. I rushed to the guard desk, but he would be of no help. The guard was dead as well. I ran to the front entrance. At least I would get out alive. beat. beat. beat. I got to the door and looked outside. There were police cars rushing in from all directions. Lights flashing. Several skidded to a halt near the door. beat. beat. beat. Car doors opening. I rushed outside. Someone had called for help before the slaughter. 2 minutes and 50 seconds. Three police officers knelt behind their car doors. Shotguns pointed. Pointed at me. beat. beat. beat. Pointed at me! Stay where you are! Said the cops. Firing. They were firing at me. Shotgun pellets began to fly by. beat. beat. beat. 2 minutes and 30 seconds. I panicked. I ran back inside the building. Bullets shattered the glass door behind me. Ran through the lobby. beat. beat. beat. I slipped on the marble floor in a puddle of fresh blood. Blood was everywhere. There was blood all over me. beat. beat. beat. I reached the stairwell and headed towards the parking garage. Why were they firing at me? 2 minutes even. I headed toward my car. beat. beat. beat. Keys. I needed keys. I fumbled around in my pocket for them. 1 minute and 45 seconds. I pulled out some keys along with change that fell to the floor. beat. beat. beat. I flipped through the ring to get my door key. beat. beat. beat. The key ring fell to the floor. Fell under the car. I got down on my knees. Where were they? I reached under the car. Grease, oil, rocks. 1 minute and 15 seconds. There they are. I opened the door of my car. Hands fumbling at the ignition. beat. beat. beat. Car starts to turn over. beat. beat. beat. The car started pretty quickly. If it hadn't, it would have ended right there. beat. beat. beat. Sometimes I wish it hadn't. The car is in gear. 50 seconds. I drove the car around to the entrance. 20 seconds. I reached the gate. Where was my pass? No time for that. beat. beat. beat. I floored the gas and the car broke through the gate. 10 seconds. 5 seconds. beat. beat. beat. The car cleared the garage and exited to the street. 0 seconds.

The entire 13th floor of the office building exploded, right on cue. Window glass rained down below. My car swung out into the street behind the waiting police cars. What the hell was happening? Balls of flame shot out of the windows high in the air. The explosion rocked the street. Some people fell over with the shock of the blast, others began to duck. A woman screams. The police officers were momentarily stunned by the blast wave, and struggled to dodge the pieces of glass, metal, bodies, papers, that were descending from above. The law firm was no more. I didn't wait for the police to recover. The flight reflex was still strong. Adrenaline pumping away. I brought the car about and took off down the street, running a light. Some police saw me driving off, but they didn't have time to follow before I was out of sight.

You may have seen a lot of movies in which there were explosions and murders and horrible gory death scenes. It's easy to daydream yourself into a similar situation, isn't it? You may even think that you would be able to remain calm and cool throughout the experience. You would be able to defuse the bomb. You would be able to remember everything that happened clearly as you threw yourself out of the window, guns blazing, cradling the starlet with one hand while you plug several enemies with unerring blasts of hot lead. You may think that you know what a dead body looks like. You've seen them on television thousands of times. You've seen the war movies, even the 'realistic' ones. Well, let me tell you something. No matter how much you think you're ready, you aren't. Dead bodies don't look anything like they do on TV. Blood is not ketchup. Corpses don't fall in picturesque poses. People don't die quietly and stately, whispering one last cryptic message. Their nervous system sends them into spasms. Blood separates when it congeals. Dark black spots floating in clear yellow ooze. People piss themselves when they get their throats cut. It is revolting. If you have anything resembling a normal reaction you will run in horror from the sight. No time to light up a cigarette. No time to make sure your clip is loaded. You just run. The site of a real bomb ticking away will make you run, no matter how much of a man you believe yourself to be. It's a built in reaction. Fight or flight. And it never gets easier, never gets better. No matter how many bodies you see.

I mention this because I want you to understand my actions in fleeing the police and the scene of that gruesome incident. Sure, I probably should have stayed and given a report. I should have told people what I saw. But I didn't. I ran. I wasn't thinking clearly. I was not thinking at all. My mind was awash in smeared blood and flying broken glass. All I could think was, "Just drive, just escape. Just get somewhere safe, away from the reality of death." Not until I was already back over the Golden Gate Bridge and halfway back to my home in Marin did I regain the capacity for conscious thought. I didn't even stop to wipe the blood off my face.

I didn't really know where to turn. I didn't know where to go. Why would someone do this? What the hell was happening? I drove home. Undoubtedly my wife would be watching the news bulletin. It isn't every day that a major San Francisco skyscraper explodes in a ball of flame. She would be worried sick, rightly thinking that I was in that building. Imagining that it was my blood that was smeared all over the office walls. As I turned the corner onto our street, I noticed two men exiting our house. They wore plain black suits and hats. Were they notifying my wife of my demise? As I drove up, they were getting into what appeared to be an authentic 1950's Cadillac. Were they investigating the bombing already? By the time I had pulled into our driveway, they had begun to speed off in the opposite direction, so I didn't get a good look at them. I got out of my car and headed indoors. My wife was waiting at the door, still watching as the black sedan drove off. She had a concerned look on her face, but she appeared glad to see me. She was so beautiful. Only four months pregnant, she had that glow of expectation. She would make a wonderful mother. "Honey, I'm ok, don't worry, I wasn't in the building." I shouted as I ran up the walk.

"What building dear? What are you talking about?" She brought me into the house, apparently oblivious to the fact that I was a bit more rumpled and bloodstained than usual.

"The building. My law firm. There was an explosion. Isn't it on the news?" I looked over to the television in the living room. It was on, quietly playing some soap opera or other. Its warm, comforting glow filling the room. There didn't seem to be a special report. I looked around for the TV remote, but it was nowhere to be found. I walked over to the set and began flipping channels manually. There was no mention of anything. Just talk shows, soaps, and the rest of the pap that makes up daytime TV. No news bulletins, no reporters on the scene, no shaky helicopter shots of a burned out building, no interviews with the fire chief. Wasn't this the sort of thing that the media lived for? How many times did they interrupt the evening sitcoms to bring a special report on some 2.0 earthquake out in some meaningless suburb? But now nothing. My wife took me by the shoulders and brought me into the kitchen.

The phone is ringing. It seems only natural to answer it. I sit down at the table, hands still shaking and sweaty. My wife picks up the receiver. "Hello? Yes. Yeah, he's back here. No, I understand. Ok, I'll see you soon." I was off in my own world. I wasn't even listening.

The receiver goes back on the hook. "Tell me all about it dear. I'm glad that you are all right. What exactly happened now?" She pats my shoulders for a moment until the shaking stops. Then begins to prepare some coffee. She did not seem too upset or shaken at what was happening. In fact, she was smiling, almost radiant. At the time I chalked it up to her ignorance of the severity of the situation. I would fix that right now. I animatedly began to tell her about my morning's ordeals. I explained the dead bodies, the ransacking, the bombs, the police and their shotguns. The more I described the scene the more nauseous I became. Images of that gruesome display involuntarily flashed through my brain (a process that continues even to this day). My wife continued to listen with a look of concern on her face as the coffee percolated and she set out the cups. "Well, what a day you've had. I'm glad that you are all right. Here, have some coffee, then we'll get you changed out of those dirty clothes and into a nice hot bath." She handed me a cup. Two sugars. "That is strange dear. Why do you think that the news wouldn't be talking about it?" We continued to chat about my incident. I began to calm down and to recover my wits. I began to feel more and more at ease. I guess that once the ordeal is over and everything is safe, the adrenaline glands take a breather. Relaxation began to set in. The hot steam of the coffee began to nudge the drying blood and C4 out of my olfactory memory. My mind, which had been a conflagration of thoughts and images, began to calm and grow steady once again. After a while I began to regain the ability to think about other things. The two men in my yard came to mind.

"Honey, who were those men at the house today?" I said as I reached the bottom of my first cup.

"Which men do you mean dear?" She smiled at me lovingly. Her eyes moved back and forth across the room.

"There were two guys walking across our lawn as I drove up. They both had black suits on."

"Oh, those men," she said with a nervous giggle, "They just came to get their document back. The one they accidentally gave you the other day." My head began to swim a bit. I felt groggy all of a sudden. "They were really very charming people, actually. They don't want to hurt you. If you would just give it back to them, I am sure that they would go away. They're going to make us rich dear, I'll have everything I've ever dreamed of. I'll have everything that you've been unable to give me. Look, they already gave me this as a retainer." She pulled a black velvet cloth from her pocket.

When opened, several karats of diamonds sparkled. "They promised to make my wildest dreams come true. All I have to do is get their document back. Where is it honey? What did you do with it?" She smiled apprehensively and shook her head in a 'yes' motion. I began to feel faint. I looked down into the coffee cup I still held in my hand. There was a residue at the bottom. Drugged? The screen on the back porch begins to rattle. Someone was trying the door. I stood up, but immediately fell back down to my chair. My legs felt like rubber. "Where is the package Mitch. They just want their package back. Give it to me before it's too late." I tried to get up again. Using the wall for support I was able to get to my feet and began leaving the kitchen. There was a bang at the back porch. Someone was trying to break down the door. Flee. My wife tried to grab me. "Don't you understand you jerk, we can live in luxury. They just want their document back. They promised that they wouldn't hurt us, wouldn't hurt the baby, why are you always standing in the way of my dreams." Her friendly demeanor turned angry. Betrayed, I pushed her aside and moved into the living room. She fell to the floor. I heard the front door to the house being opened. Someone was in the entryway. Flee. "They promised! Damn you! They promised. I was going to have a butler! A real butler, and a yacht. I knew you'd screw it up!" My wife sobbed, still sitting on the hallway floor. The sound of rushing blood was in my ears. I shut the door to the foyer. Put my back to it. Someone was on the other side. Bang, bang, they began to push against the door. Bang, bang, I heard the back door being forced open. I picked up a lamp and threw it through the bay window in the living room. It shattered the glass. A bullet came through the foyer door, narrowly missing my shoulder. Shattered glass was falling. The back porch door was open. The sound of hard footsteps resonated from the kitchen. A woman screams. Bang, my unborn child dies within its mother's womb. The sound of blood spattering against wallpaper. With what strength I had left I ran to the window and jumped through it. I hit the front lawn headfirst. Flee. My reflexes had taken over now. There was not much conscious thought involved. The drug weighed me down like lead. I ran to the car. Two men in black suits and dark sunglasses stood inside the broken window, inside my house. Blood on me. Broken glass. I somehow got the door open and fumbled for the key. The men pulled out weapons and began to shoot. Their sharp black suits, white starched shirts, stained with red. Smash, the front window shattered as the engine turned over. The men began to climb out of the broken window. The car was in reverse, I exited the driveway. Flee. The men ran across the lawn shouting and firing their weapons as I drove away.

Looking back on this incident, I can't understand how I was able to get away. Most of my memories of that day have been degraded into a drug-induced haze. I could barely walk, never mind drive. If there were any pets or children in the street that day then they were undoubtedly flattened. I don't know where I was headed, or how I was able to get as far as I did before passing out. I am sure that they must have tried to follow me, but I must have lost them. Over the years I have constantly been surprised at my ability to rise to any occasion. Fear is a great motivator I guess. Some people, such as myself, seem to be fairly average, but due to high potency adrenal glands I guess, they are able to push themselves beyond their limits when the need arises. Perhaps that is the trait they were looking for. I can't say that I didn't panic that day, that I don't panic every time people are shooting at me. You would have to be inhuman not to panic at the thought of imminent death. I guess what has set me apart from others is that panic leads me to take actions that are advantageous. I don't just fall to the floor and cover my ears like my wife did. I don't jump to my death to escape the high-rise fire. Even in shear, blind terror, I was able to get away from them that afternoon. That weird ability, that strange quirk was what has helped me survive all of the travails that I have faced over the past eight years. But I am getting ahead of myself.

My next clear recollection was of the next morning. I awoke with my head on the steering wheel of my car. The vehicle was stopped, with the front end half buried inside a large tree. I seemed to be in a wooded area, perhaps a park of some sort. Cool, green shade surrounded me. The place seemed quite deserted. Apparently the drug that was given to me had worn off. There was a bit of blood on my forehead from a small cut. My muscles were sore, from either the drug, the accident, or sleeping in the car with my face mashed against the steering wheel. Birds were chirping. The sun was just coming up. I was still a bit groggy, but I tried to gather my thoughts of the previous day. Bombs, death, mysterious strangers, betrayal of those closest to me, foreign languages. What was happening? Had my life turned into a bad movie? This didn't happen to normal people. I had always been taught that the world moved in mundane and predictable ways. Running gun battles and mickeys only happened in stories. But then how do I explain what had gone on in the last few hours? My car would never be driveable again, but the radio still worked. I turned it to the news channel, but there was no report on the building explosion. Maybe people thought it was a gas leak. Maybe they had already played the story to death and had moved on to something else. Since my pre-programmed stations still came in I concluded that I was still somewhere near San Francisco. Maybe it was all a dream? Maybe the lunch boy slipped me some acid in my coffee for a joke. Maybe all of this was unreal. It was the only rational explanation. I had heard of those things happening to people before. The only thing I knew for sure was that it was 7:04 am, and that I had apparently rammed my car into a tree.

Then I saw the briefcase. I could feel a knot of fear rise in my throat. I don't know how I still had it. I know that I brought it with me into the office on the morning of bombs and blood. I guess that in the panic of trying to get out of the building I had simply forgotten to let go of it. I reached for it with dread. It contained the only piece of evidence that could prove that all of this *was* really happening to me. The document from the toll collector! If it existed, then it should still be in my briefcase from two nights ago. Was I delusional? I opened the case with trepidation. Was I just being paranoid? Inside were some papers relating to cases that no longer mattered, a few pens, a two-day-old lunch, and the yellowing document whose existence I dreaded. I paged through it again, trying to discover some meaning to the jumble of hieroglyphs and strange lettering. No answer was visible. It must be some sort of code, but what does it say, and who would be willing to kill a whole office full of lawyers for it? The distant echo of a car horn resonated in my ears. Perhaps it was the bump on the head that started me thinking about things in a different direction, but pieces began to fall into place. I thought back to the man in the car behind me at the tollbooth. He was angry. The toll collector gave me a package. He must have had instructions to give the package to the man in the other Sedan. It's a rare car, how would they know that another one would be on the road at the exact same time? The echo of a car horn resonated in my head. The toll collector was supposed to give a package to the man in the Sedan, and I drove up and he gave it to me. The man behind me was angry, followed me. Lost in traffic. They must have gotten my license plate number and, and...

But who could it be? Who passes documents except spies? I didn't know much about real intelligence work at the time, but I had seen some TV shows and was well versed in movie fantasy. This was some sort of 'North By Northwest' scenario. Foreign spies had accidentally passed me a coded message, and were now trying to retrieve it. There was only one thing to do. I had to get to the authorities and give them the information. Who exactly are 'the authorities' when it comes to something like this? You couldn't exactly look up the local CIA office in the phone book. I decided to go to the police. They would be able to help. That's what they're there for, right? Plus, they would probably be interested to get some information on the bombing of the office building downtown. The driver's side door was slightly bent out of shape, but I managed to push it open. The car was dead, totaled. My pride and joy, an American treasure was lost. The rear license plate dangled, swaying in the wind. Goodbye 'California YHV-2323', goodbye old friend. I stuffed the document into my shirt and began walking in the opposite direction my car was facing. I figured that there had to be a town around here somewhere. I needed a phone.

I walked for several hours before spotting any sign of civilization. Not even a car passed me by as I traveled down the road past stand after stand of old growth trees. Somewhere a bird is singing. The world looked different somehow. The morning light filtered down through the green canopy. A breeze is rustling leaves above my head, the scent of pine. Eventually I came out of the forest near Point Reyes, a few miles from the Golden Gate. I must have driven around in a circle the night before and wound up in the park just north of Mount Tam. Reyes is a beach that caters to locals who need a quick getaway, but not this early in the day, and not this early in the season. The sand-covered parking lots were empty. Peeling signs for fresh seafood swung and creaked in the wind. I could hear the ocean current in the background. An old black car approached, slowly. I moved off the side of the road, behind some brush. The driver was a wooden man in a black suit. Was the car driving too slowly? It might have been nothing. The man didn't even turn his head towards me as he passed.

I walked down the main beach road until I found a convenience store. It was one of those independent places. A sign in the window advertised ice cream on a stick in a variety of unappetizing colors. There was a pay phone located near the front door, on the old wooden porch. I walked across the street towards it, feeling in my pocket for change. The proprietor stepped out from behind the rickety mesh door. He was a tall dark man, and he watched menacingly as I crossed the street. I am sure that he was just an old man, surprised to see such a disheveled character such as myself meandering incoherently towards his store. For some reason though he scared me, standing as he was with his arms crossed, defending his store like a border guard defending his post. I walked right past, hoping that his eyes weren't following me as I continued down the lonely road. I told myself that prudence had gotten the better of me and I decided that I should make a copy of the document first, just in case. As a lawyer I knew that evidence and documentation are your best friends when it comes to proving your story. It would be better to not call the cops right away. I should probably take the time to get my story straight and make sure that I had some evidence to back me up. There probably weren't any copy machines up here in the woods, so I started to think about calling a cab to take me back into town. It was then that I realized that I didn't have my wallet with me. I must have left it at home when the men attacked me. I didn't have any money or credit cards. I didn't even have any identification. With my rumpled appearance I probably could be mistaken for being homeless. There was only one thing left to do. I would have to hoof it over the bridge into the city. It was only a few miles, and hikers did it all the time. Plus, it was reasonable weather, the sea air was clearing my mind. I started off down the road.

I made it as far as the middle of the Golden Gate Bridge without stopping. Did you know that the Golden Gate is the most popular place for suicide in America? They don't put up a big fence for aesthetic reasons, and when you are up there you can tell how certainly fatal the drop would be. It is more than that though. Standing up there gives one a sense of perspective. You can see how small you are. The combination of the water, the mountains, the tiny buildings of the city off in the distance. It is the perfect place to have your last look around. My left hand wouldn't stop shaking. One last glimpse of life before diving into the icy beyond. It's full of tourists too. Little children scamper back and forth across the pedestrian walkway. Asian travelers snapping pictures of each other holding onto the russet cables. Hikers and bikers making their way up to the park north of the city. Why won't my left hand stop shaking? Everyone is so happy. You can sense your loss. Standing there by yourself makes you feel so alone. The giggles of a child make you feel so melancholy when you know that they are not directed toward you. My wife was dead. My unborn child would never grow up to inherit that large college fund. I gripped the rail tighter and tighter. My livelihood was disrupted. I couldn't stop my hand from shaking. Most of my co-workers were gone. Even my precious automobile had been wrecked. Hell, I didn't even know where my sunglasses were. I thought about it you know. I thought about taking that one final leap. There was little left for me. I was at a nadir at that time. But something stopped me. Some part of my brain would not let me give up. Some part of my psyche told me that I had to fight on, that I had to expose these people. I would have to rebuild my life true, but my revenge would be sweet. I would stop these murderers in their tracks and make them pay for what they had done to me. I would sue the pants off of everyone and everything. Visions of dollar signs and lethal injections replaced those of bloody horrors and shattered glass. After almost an hour staring off into the East Bay and listening to the tide banging against the rocks, my resolve strengthened enough to move on.

I wonder now, looking back with perspective, why I was really upset. When I try to understand my mood that morning on the bridge, I can't decide if I was more upset at the loss of my wife, or the loss of my car. I suppose it doesn't matter now, does it?

Once I got over the bridge, I started looking for someplace to get a copy made. There are plenty of 24 hour copy places around town, so it didn't take me long to find one. I carefully undid the strings and staple holding the document together and placed them on the feeder. The machine hummed away, getting caught once or twice on the old heavy paper, but eventually copying all one hundred and thirty-two pages, front and back. The copies were three cents apiece. As the machine pushed out pages I reached into my pocket and counted my change. I only had about a buck fifty on me. I reserved a quarter of that for later and laid the rest down on the copy machine. As the young clerk shifted his attention to a young co-ed who had entered the store, I ran out the side door, clutching the copy and the original.

I then walked over to the bus station in the eastern part of town. I needed to put the copy in a safe place, and I knew that there would be lockers there. On the way I passed Montgomery St, and I stopped to take a look at my old office. From a block away I could see that the entire 13th floor had been gutted, as well as the floors above and below it. The place was cordoned off with yellow plastic police tape. I was surprised to see that there were construction workers already working on the damage. They even had a crane up. I had thought that it would take a while to hire a contractor, and that the police would have wanted more time to search for evidence. Had they even identified all the bodies yet? But, what the hell did I know. There were several policemen standing around out front, watching the work, so I guess that it was all being done with their ok. The whole place still gave me the creeps though. I began to shiver slightly before I even got close. A man in a dark suit walked down the street in my direction. Something about his eyes bothered me. I decided not to tempt fate, and I turned off onto a side street before I got too near the wreckage.

The bus station wasn't far. I had stopped shivering before I arrived. I stuffed the copied version in a box, inserted my final quarter, and took the key. Box 47B, located in Terminal A of the San Francisco Bus Station. It was an orange locker that had bits of paint flaking off at the time. The key was orange too. Perhaps I could use the copy as proof of my story when I started negotiating my book deal. From the terminal, it was off to the police station. They might even be looking for me now. I was now missing from the scene of three separate incidents (the car, my house, and the office), and could potentially be wanted for photocopy theft.

There was a police station on Pine St., not too far away. I had been there once a few years ago when some vandal had broken one of the windows of my car. Nothing had been taken, and the police never found who did it, but all the same, I went down and made a statement for insurance purposes. Like almost all the other ones in town, out front of this police station there were some concrete containers filled with dirt. In many places, government offices are worried about car bombs and they put concrete barriers around their entrances. Since these are not aesthetically pleasing, they are often filled with bushes, trees, and plants, so that their true function is obscured by the pretty leaves and flowers.

I had always had a deep sense of love and respect for the police. From childhood it had been taught to me that they are the defenders of the population. Others might complain about incompetence and brutality, but all I remembered were the lollipops they always carried for lost children, their shiny silver badges and sharp blue uniforms, the comical characters they brought to my grade school to warn us away from candy-bearing strangers. I never had any fear. That is, until that day. As I approached the station, I passed by several officers leaning up against a barrier waiting for something or other. They were wearing their sharp blue uniforms, their shiny silver badges, leather boots, steel guns. Steel guns. Steel Guns. Steel GUNS. It had never occurred to me before, but any of the people surrounding me could, on a whim, fire a shot and end my life, just like that. They all had killing machines strapped to their hips. Killing machines. Of course, there were laws that prevented misuse, and there were the teachings of common morality and social responsibility to protect me, but these things are ephemeral. These things are not a bulletproof vest. If one of these people really *wants* to, they could end my life and there was not a damn thing I could do about it. Power; right there, on the hip. I became afraid.

I walked past the entrance to the police station, over to the other side, where there were more barriers and less cops. I rested up against one of the concrete planters. There was a squirrel darting through the branches overhead. Breathe. I gave myself a few seconds to calm down. Breathe. One of the first things that they teach you in the law business is that you need to completely trust your partners, but you also have to take precautions against their betrayal. You never know when a friend is going to become an enemy. Breathe. It was this sort of double-speak that led me to what happened next. I completely trusted the police to help me in a courteous and thoughtful manner. However, I took the locker key out of my pocket and placed it in the dirt of the barrier. Then I covered it with a few leaves. It was hard to fully cover owing to the fact that it was a bright, neon orange object, but I did a good job. I hoped that the squirrel wouldn't move it. I didn't know much about the habits of squirrels, maybe they collect shiny objects. I looked down at myself. I was torn, ratty, a bit on the dirty side, no ID, no money. Nothing to back up my story. Except of course the document I had from the toll collector. It had to be some sort of secret code. I had no doubt in my mind that once I spoke to the police, they would contact the terrorism unit of the

FBI, and the counterintelligence unit of the CIA, or whoever, and this would get all straightened out. Then I would
go get my car out of the woods, grieve a while for my de-
ceased wife, and spend the next few weeks fielding job
offers from law firms impressed with my ability to break
open this international terrorism ring. My resolve strengthened, I lifted my head, and I walked straight through the
front doors of the police station.

The entrance to the police station looked like a bank.
Old marble walls, creaky wooden floors, faded and cracking
plaster filigree on the ceiling. People's footsteps echoed as
they meandered about the large hall. Individual soft conver-
sations were being transformed into a collective din of noise.
There were several open windows, and a series of tellers in
blue uniforms were politely answering the concerns of a
number of citizens. An officer yawns. I stepped up to him
and asked him to direct me to someone in the anti-terrorism
unit.

"Who are you, and what crime would you like to report?" said the officer mechanically. His badge said 'Frank
Daly'. He had been working a long shift and was a bit tired.
He had manned the desk for almost a year now and had
heard it all. His main function was to stop all of the nuts
from bothering the real detectives. He resented his job.

"I said, 'I need to talk to someone in the anti-terrorism
unit'." Did the SF police even have an anti-terrorist unit? "I
have information that might be important to that bombing on
Montgomery Street yesterday." I reached into my coat to
pull out my yellowing sheaf of evidence.

"What bombing on Montgomery Street?" replied Daly.
He looked over to the officer at the next window. That officer was helping to process a woman in a long curly gold
wig, hot pants, a neon tube top, silver platform boots, and
carrying a orange fur muff. Or maybe it wasn't a woman.

"Hey Phil," said the officer, "Did you hear about a bombing on Montgomery St. yesterday?" The other officer shook his head and went back to processing forms. "I don't know what to tell you big guy." Officer Daly said, addressing me again, "It doesn't seem like anyone here knows about a bombing on Montgomery St.. Why don't you go home and sleep it off."

"You don't know about the bombing on Montgomery St.?" I replied, stunned at the officer's incredulous statement. "It blew out the entire 13th floor. A lot of people were killed. The police were there, a lot of police, maybe it was in a different precinct." I became more confused and agitated. These things simply didn't happen in a normal life. What, was I on TV? How could my office explode, my co-workers be killed, and my wife try to poison me? This made no sense. And now no one even knew about it? The police were ignorant of a large explosion right in the middle of the city? I began, for the first time, to fully understand the weight of the past days events. I began to lose control, which is something that never happens to me. Lawyers are specifically trained to maintain composure at all times. I became more animated. I became belligerent. I started to yell and scream at the officer. I told him that he was incompetent, and that there were things going on in this city he wouldn't believe. How could a city function with such poor performance from its designated protectors? I told him that an army of men in black was out there, killing people. I waved the document at him and told him that I had all the answers. Sure it looked like gibberish, but they were in there somewhere. The answers to the all of the questions that the local government was not even competent enough to ask.

The officer listened to my ranting for several minutes with bored restraint. He had spent many hours at this job listening to drugged out wackos who had all sorts of paranoid delusions. Just twenty minutes before I arrived he had listened to a similar monologue from an insane war vet who thought that he could hear the North Vietnamese tunneling under the city. The officer just sat there with his head in his hands, occasionally nodding with feigned interest. "uh-huh, uh-huh." He understood that the worst thing to do in these situations was to have a hostile attitude. He was just waiting for some of the other officers to step in from behind and restrain me. They would take me down to a drunk tank where I could calm down and get a hot meal. It was the best that he believed he could do for me. He was not an unsympathetic man.

What happened next was a bit of a surprise to both myself and to Officer Daly. A police officer did approach me from behind, but it was not a blue with some handcuffs, it was a plainclothes detective. He stepped up from behind me and introduced himself, "Hello Mr. Sinclair. I'm Detective Abraham M. Smith, with the anti-terrorism unit. If you'll just come with me, I will be happy to take your statement."

Detective Smith was a small man, only about 5'4," which I think made him a anomaly for the police department. He was dark, possibly of Indian origin, and he spoke with a slight accent. He was impeccably dressed in a fancy Italian suit that looked a bit too good for someone on a detective's salary. He also wore a sharp hat, which was a little odd for this day and age, but not too out of place. He had a shiny new badge that identified him as a member of the SFPD. He put his hand around my waist and led me through a door to the right of the windows full of tellers. Officer Daly was slightly confused at the detective's interest, but shrugged it off, thanking his creator that this issue was no longer his problem. He turned to the next customer, who was a homeless man who believed that aliens were about to destroy the city with an atomic bomb. Officer Daly listened calmly with his head on his hands.

Detective Smith led me through several brightly-lit hallways, down into the maze that was the police station interior. We traveled down a flight of stairs into the basement, then through more, not so brightly lit hallways. He brought me to a hospital-green door with a large safety-glass window. He pushed the metallic handle and motioned for me to enter. Inside was an old, metal desk and three matching chairs. On one side of the room was a large, poorly disguised, one-way mirror. A small table against the wall held a stained coffee pot. He told me to sit down, and asked if I wanted something to drink. I told him no. I just wanted to get rid of this thing. Wanted to make it someone else's problem. Wanted to get back to my life, what was left of it. Detective Smith was very calm and friendly. He asked if he could have some coffee, and he poured brown liquid into two smallish Styrofoam cups, handing me one. He asked me to tell him my story. I began with the strange tollbooth collector. I explained the discovery of the mysterious document. I went into detail about the strange people that I had met along the way, and how now, with 20/20 hindsight, I could see how they were trying to get the document back. If I had only known that at the time I would have happily given it to them. It was really none of my concern. I didn't want to be a part of any of this. I wasn't playing their game. I told him about the massacre at my office building. I told him about the incident at my house and how they had done something to my wife. I told him about the mysterious men in black that seemed to be following me. Detective Smith listened to all of it with attention and care. He agreed with me at certain points, and pointed out some of the apparent inconsistencies in my story. He was nothing but friendly and helpful, which in my naiveté I thought was expected of all law enforcement.

Finally I got to what was at that time the present. I pulled the document out of my coat and put it on the table. It lay there, dusty and cracking. Yellow parchment paper peeling flakes onto the table. Detective Smith thumbed through it. He agreed with me that this all looked suspicious, and that it was probably best to get this thing to the proper authorities as soon as possible. Lives could be at stake.

"So, what do you think it is?" says Smith, flipping past pages of hieroglyphs and curlyiques.

"I couldn't even begin to guess," I reply. "It looks like some sort of code. It's all just gibberish to me. The best I could figure out is that it isn't all the same language. There are a bunch of codes in there."

"You don't have any idea why someone would give this to you?"

"No."

"And you don't have any idea what significance this document has?"

"No."

"Who else have you shown this to, besides your wife I mean."

"No one. I didn't think that it was important until everybody started ending up dead. Then I came here." Smith nodded.

He told me that he would take this to the FBI office in the other wing of the building. I was to stay here. Then he would come back and take my formal statement about the bombing, the home invasion, the car crash. They would give me police protection, and they would have an officer take me home. He even offered me the services of the station bereavement councilor.

That was all a great relief. It was good to know that something was finally being done about this. I could finally stop looking over my shoulder. I pushed the document towards him and he stood up. He told me not to worry about a thing. He claimed that he would be right back. That I should just relax. He picked up the document and left the room, closing the door behind him gently. I sat for a few minutes thinking about the events of the past few days, and how it might change my life. Perhaps I had thwarted a terrorist attack? Maybe this was the key piece of information that the FBI needed to crack a spy ring? How many lives would be saved by my courageous actions today? Maybe I would get a reward? Maybe even a medal. I sat and daydreamed about receiving a medal from the president of the United States of America. I had always had delusions of grandeur. I was a bit sleepy too. I guess that with the excitement and all I had forgotten to sleep. I looked over the desk I was sitting at and noticed that Detective Smith had not touched his coffee at all. My teeth were biting playfully at the rim of my mostly empty cup. I stood up to get a refill from the pot.

A refill? Why was I drinking this first cup? I remember distinctly saying 'no' when Detective Smith offered me some coffee. And he poured some anyway. And I drank it without thinking about it. My mind was elsewhere. And he didn't drink his coffee at all. And he was the only one who believed my story. None of the people outside of Smith had even heard of the explosion downtown. None of the officers knew anything about it. Even the desk watch officer. It wasn't on the news. Detective Smith was the only one who seemed to know anything about it. Smith is such a common name. Smith was so friendly. Ready to believe me. Maybe too ready to believe me? Where was he? He had the document. He had the proof. He had what they wanted. What they wanted. What does Smith want? Who was Smith? Why is the room starting to spin?

I took the pot over to the garbage can and slowly poured out the remaining liquid. There was a white, solid powder revealed, half dissolved. What was happening? You can't trust the police? Who are these people? Where does it go? I thought that I was being paranoid. I thought that I was seeing things that weren't there, that I was still caught up in fantasy. I went to the one-way mirror and tried to look through it. Was anyone there? I couldn't see through it. I went to the door. I tried it. It was locked. Locked from the outside. Why would Detective Smith lock the door from the outside? Who were these people? Must get out. Can't stay here. I grabbed one of the chairs and threw it against the large window in the door to the interrogation chamber. It bounced off. I threw it again. It crashed the glass. The window had a metal mesh reinforcement that held most of it in place. I pushed through the mesh near the handle. Reached my hand out and opened the door from the outside. Red. Red. All over my hand. No time for that. Must escape. Must get out. Must survive. I looked down the hallway. A surprised Detective Smith stood there. He had been talking to two men. Men in the same black suits that I had seen all over the place. Men in black. They had no badges. They had no uniforms. Men in Black. Detective Smith cried a warning to stop. I ran in the other direction. "You don't understand," cried Detective Smith. The two men with him both reached into their jackets. Pistols. Glint of metal. Pop. pop. pop. Shots rang out in the hallway. I ran. A police officer stood in my way. He was confused. Scared. I grabbed him and pushed him up against the wall. My hands were at his waist, on his holster. His gun was in my hand. I ran down the hall behind him. Thud. thud. I heard the sound of two stray bullets hitting flesh. Have you ever heard the sound of a bullet hitting flesh before? In the movies, you always hear the sound of the shot, but you never hear the sound of the reception. The police officer went down. He had had no idea what was going on. "Stop! Police!" shouted Smith. He had a gun too. I pushed through a door as more bullets zipped past. I was in a stairwell.

I went up a flight. I could hear commotion behind me. More police officers began to flood the lower hall to see where the shots were coming from. They got in the way of the dark men. I pushed through a door on the floor above, and found myself in an old corridor. Dark, wooden trim on everything. Tile floor. There was sunlight streaming in from a window and the beams of light reflect on the millions of motes of dust. It was warm. I bet the floor was warm. Warmed by the heat of the beams of light. I used to lie on the floor of my parent's living room so many years ago. The beams warmed the carpet. I shook myself out of it. The white powder was having an effect. I can't believe I let them do it to me again. My legs felt week and my feet and hands were numb. They wanted to get rid of me. They had the document. The cop's gun was still in my hand. The report is what they wanted, but they needed to get rid of me. I was the one who knew about them. I was the one who could interfere in whatever they were planning. I was the thing they feared. I ran down the hall and through an open door that led right to a back alley. I took the opportunity. No one had come up the stairs yet, at least not to this floor. It was far easier to get out then it was to get in.

Maybe they didn't need me. They had what they wanted. I was just a footnote. Without the document I had nothing that could hurt them. I thought about these things as I ran from one alley to the next. The cop's gun was still in my hand. My other hand was wet. I had no evidence of my admittedly hard to believe story. Maybe they were satisfied with that. Each step became harder and harder as the drug took effect. I should probably get to a hospital. I need a doctor. They might be there looking for me. Better hide out. I kept running. I could hear sirens in the distance. I looked down at my left hand. It was covered in blood. I must have cut myself deeper than I thought during my escape. I need antiseptic. The cop's gun was still in my hand. I put it in my coat. My feet carried me a bit further. Then swoon. The floor was not where it should be. I passed out behind a dumpster.

# Chapter 3:
# Honor

I was standing in a field of red poppies. The sun was shining down from the heavens. The clouds were moving overhead. Impossibly fast. In the distance was a city. It was growing as I watched it. Buildings sprouting and forming. Growing skyward. Pyramids of stone erupted from the earth. Flashes of light. The sun moved overhead in arcs. Faster and faster. Light dark light dark light dark. The clouds moved across the sky. New patterns formed. The city rose. Pillars reached to the sun. A city of pillars. The poppies withered at my feet. I stood motionless. Time moved on. Impossible time. The stars weren't right. The city grew in the distance. Pillars. The stars weren't right! The clouds dissipated. No rain fell. The field became scrub. The scrub became dirt. Parched dirt. Sand. The city began to sink. Sink into the sand. The stars weren't right. The sand blew across the barren plain. The clouds became thinner and thinner. The last pillar sank beneath the sand. You could still feel the heartbeat of the city vibrating through the ground. The city was still breathing, living, hidden, beneath sand, beneath time. The city was still alive, still sending its vibrations out across the infinite desert plain.

The first thing I noticed was the smell. That was what brought me back to consciousness. Light behind my eyelids. Red. A shaking. "Hey buddy, you ok?" A voice from above.

Shadows moved in front of the light. I opened my eyes. I was lying on my back in a dirty alley. The sun shown almost directly overhead. 12:00. You could see a slice of the sky between two dirty brick walls. A fire escape snaked up the side. A face moved into view. The clouds had stopped moving so fast. The face was bearded and dirty. Green ragged coat. The stars were right. What stars? The man shook me again. The floor was moving. The drug was still in my system. Dizzy. The man shook me again. Leaves in his hair. I came back to what I still considered to be the real world.

"I'm ok," I said, sitting up. I leaned against the wall. My head throbbed at even this minor effort. "I'm just feeling sick that's all." The harsh reality of the alley struck me. A breeze blew some discarded papers, others just rustled.

"Your hand's pretty cut up there buddy. You gotta see a doctor or something. You wanted by the cops or something? They been driving around all morning." The man smelled of fish and cheap liquor. "You lucky that you passed out where you did." I looked down the alley. The dumpster had effectively shielded me from the street. The cops must have underestimated me. They must have thought that I would run down the main street and pass out there. Or make it to a hospital. Couldn't go to a hospital. My hand hurt, although not as much as my head. Blood was caked on my sleeve.

"You look like you could use a belt buddy." The bum pulled out a half empty bottle of some cheap liquor from his coat. He opened the cap and rubbed the top with the dirty sleeve of his stained flannel shirt. He pushed the bottle towards my face. Bottle. Liquor. He wanted me to drink. Take a sip. He was right. I could use a belt right now. I took the neck of the bottle with my shaky right hand and moved the rim to my lips. "That's right buddy. Take a big slug." The man smiled at me. The sweet stink of cheap liquor filled my nose. The glass of the rim touched my lower lip. The coffee had white powder at the bottom. The coffee had white powder at the bottom! Was this man trying to poison me also? Was this man in on the whole deal? What the hell was happening? I had been drugged twice in as many days. They weren't going to get me again! I pushed the bottle aside and got up. "Wait buddy, I want to help you," said the bum, still sitting in the pile of wet newspapers and old wrappers that he had found me in. I pulled the cop's gun from out of my coat and pointed it at him. It was cold and heavy. I started running down the alley, out to the street. They weren't going to get me again. I was smarter than that now. I ran into the street, directly into the street. A car came screeching to a halt as I ran in front of it. I bounced off of the hood. I was ok. The man behind the wheel honked. I left some fresh blood from the opened wound on my hand on his windshield as I rolled off. Keep running. Don't let them find you. Don't let them catch you. Had to run.

I continued my flight from the police station and the hideous things that they had in the basement there. I went from one alley to another. Watching for police. I avoided them. Watching for the dark men in the black suits. I didn't see them. They were around though. I could feel them watching me. I ran blindly through the streets. Must have been for an hour or two. Several 'concerned citizens' tried to stop me. Offered me soup. The coffee had white powder at the bottom. I need to be more careful. The drug that Detective 'Smith' had given me was still in my system, and I have to admit that most of my flight was a blur of terror and alleys and dreams of the desert. I eventually stopped running on the other side of the city, near the Mission District. The people here were dirtier and the streets were sloppier than the San Francisco that I knew. In my disheveled state I fit in ok. I could feel the heavy steel inside my coat, bouncing against my chest. Bouncing in time to my heart. The pounding in my head subsided, leaving only the pounding in my left hand. It was all wet. Sticky.

As the veil of fog finally lifted itself from my fevered brain, I eventually found myself inside of a laundromat on 16th Street. It was one long room, washers on one side, dryers on the other. In the middle picnic benches sat on the cement floor. There was a small room for the manager to sit, but no one was there. The place was left to run by itself. One wall held a disconcerting mural. It was meant to be a large panoramic view of San Francisco as viewed from the East Bay. But the artist had added in several space ships shooting lasers at one another. A giant one-eyed monster stood on the Bay Bridge. Several washers hummed. A large, scary looking bearded man sat at one table, drinking a latte and reading the paper. A young girl sat at another table, doing homework out of a biology text. I had no laundry to do. I sat at the table farthest from the door. Occasionally a police car would drive past. They were still looking for me. A door led to a back alley near my seat. I could get out in a hurry if I needed to. I looked at my hand. A few deep cuts. Not too bad once I had wiped most of the blood off. I held the wrist gingerly with my right hand and felt the blood pulse. I sat and considered my situation. I was alone. No money. No identity. They were after me. I didn't even know who 'they' were. It no longer made sense that they were representatives of some foreign power. They wouldn't have the ability to infiltrate the police like that. Could it be my own government? That was a good possibility. It could be the CIA or something like that. They were known for this sort of cloak and dagger stuff, weren't they? But what then? If I couldn't trust my own government then whom could I trust? I could go to the newspaper. Would they believe my story? Probably not. I no longer had the manuscript that the toll collector had handed me. No proof. The media had seemingly ignored the blast in the office building downtown. Were they being controlled too? That seemed likely. If they could infiltrate the police, they could easily infiltrate the San Francisco Chronicle. What was the next step? I couldn't go back to work, that no longer existed. I couldn't go back home, that no longer existed. I couldn't go back to my car, that was just crumpled metal. I'm not really sure where it is anyway. I needed some guidance. I decided to call my older brother, Alan. He would be able to help me, he would be able to make sense of this. He would be able to reassure me that everything was going to be all right. I went to the payphone, made a collect call, and prayed that he was home.

He answered the phone after a few rings. He seemed overjoyed to hear who was calling. "Mitch, where are you?"

"I'm calling from a payphone in the Mission, you've got to help me Alan, nothing is making sense anymore. Everything's gone nuts. I'm hurt and I need help."

"I know, I heard. The police paid me a visit this morning. They are looking for you. They found your car. Where are you? What is going on." I started to explain what had happened. I must have sounded like I was completely off my rocker. I was ranting about men in black and giant, secret conspiracies, secret codes and handfuls of diamonds. It all sounded so crazy. No wonder Alan didn't believe a word I said. A few days ago I wouldn't have believed a word I said either.

"Look Mitch. They found your wife's body. Your house burned down. It was arson Mitch. They think you did it. They think you burned down your own house. Are you on drugs Mitch? Have you been taking drugs?"

"Damn it Alan, you're not listening, they're after me. They've set me up. You've got to help me."

"I'm trying to help you. Look, the police are looking for you, they need to talk to you. Go to them, we'll straighten it all out. I'll get you a good lawyer. We'll fight this thing together, get you some medical help. We'll plead insanity. But look, you've got to get some help. Give yourself up to the police, I don't want you getting killed in a shootout."

It wasn't working. Alan was taken in by their aura of authority. He was more willing to believe the police than his own brother. He thought that I was insane, that all of my actions were the result of cocaine or manic depression or something. But I knew I was lucid. I knew that what was happening to me was true, was real. Going to my brother was a bad idea. He wouldn't be able to help me. He might even get hurt in the crossfire like my wife did. I couldn't involve him. Alan continued, "Stay where you are Mitch, I'll call the police and tell them to pick you up. We'll fight this together. It'll be all right. You say there's a conspiracy, then sure, there's a conspiracy. We'll fight it together. We'll find some evidence to back up your story, just..."

Evidence, I didn't have any evidence. They had destroyed all the evidence by now. The house was burned, the building was repaired, and they had confiscated the document in the police station. I had nothing. Except the photocopy. Wait, I still had the photocopy! I felt around in my pocket for the locker key. A bolt of panic shot up my spine when I couldn't find it. Then I remembered that I had buried the thing. It should be safe there. The copy should still lie safely in that locker. They wouldn't have known about that. They hadn't been following me. They must have known that I would come to them eventually. That is why Smith was waiting in the station. They had underestimated me.

I hung up the phone. Hung up on my brother. They could have his house bugged. He wasn't going to be much help to me anyway. Even if I showed him the copy, he would still try to bring me to a hospital or a police station or something. Then they would get me, disappear me. Alan only had my best interests at heart, but this was something outside of his bounds. I realized that he wouldn't be able to provide the help I needed and that he would only get hurt if I involved him further.

I knew that the copy was not of much use as evidence. It wasn't the original. There was no way I could prove where I got it. The paper only had my fingerprints on it, if they even left fingerprints on the original. I was glad for the copy though, if only to prove to myself that I wasn't crazy. Maybe I could decipher it. Maybe I could use it to figure out what was going on. A new found sense of strength came to me. My life had always been geared toward being a cog in the great societal machine. I had always been a part of the greater whole. I never had to depend on myself for anything. But now I was alone, no longer part of society. I had no identity or history. I would have to work out my future on my own. The idea both exhilarated me and terrified me. The first thing I needed to do was take care of my hand. The laundromat had a sink. I washed my left arm as best I could. Cleaned the blood and bits of glass. The hot water hurt a lot as feeling returned to my numbed fingers. It hurt more when I put some soap on the wound. I hoped it would be an effective antiseptic. The girl was folding her laundry. She had several dishtowels in her wash. She leaned back into the dryer to get out another armful of whites. I quickly ran past her and grabbed a towel. I was out the door before she could protest. I ran down the street with my bounty in my right hand. Back down an alley. I lost her in the shuffle of people on their way to and from lunch. I wrapped the clean towel around my left hand and tied it tight. That would help keep it clean. I felt terrible. I had never really stolen anything before. My need was great though, National Emergency and all that. She could get a new towel. They only cost a few bucks.

I went most of the way back to the police station, then, as I approached the block, fright rose in me. My feet became lead. They were looking for me now, I had no doubt of that. Was I crazy going right back there? It had only been a few hours. They were still sensitized by my escape. Hell, I bet that they hadn't even washed the blood off the wall in the basement where the cop was shot. If there was an APB out with my description on it, it would be almost impossible for me to get away with what I wanted to do, walk right up and root around in the bushes in front of the station. Steps became slower, slower, stopping. I stood on the street corner motionless for quite a while. I needed the key to get the manuscript, but how? I suppose I could have just broken the locker open at the bus terminal, but that would hold risks as well.

There was only one thing I could do. I had to just walk up and take it. If I didn't look too suspicious, then the cops near the station wouldn't notice me. They had other things on their minds, right? Those coming or going were getting off work, going to lunch, responding to an actual emergency. None of them should have any reason to think that I would be anywhere near there. I looked around, it was still mid-afternoon in a major city. There were a lot of people about. I could blend in, be invisible. I straightened my tie, hid my damaged hand, and walked right up to the station door.

I could feel my heart beating stronger and stronger as I approached the barrier with its hidden treasure. I had to act fast, yet nonchalantly. I felt the gun, heavy in my pocket. It was a last resort. I felt its cold steel with my fingertips. As I came down the street, two uniformed officers walked towards me. I began to panic. As I said, I was not used to this cloak and dagger stuff. I glanced around me. There were people all about. These guys wouldn't try anything out in the open would they? In front of all these people? Of course they would. They are police (or at least dressed like them). I looked like a vagrant. Of course they could try something. They could do anything they wanted to me. The populace has been trained well. If they grabbed me and hauled me off, who would come to my aid? Who would hear my pleas? No one. Everyone assumes that the police are doing their job, that they are here to protect and serve. That they are here to keep vagrants and miscreants off the street, away from decent people. But if they just cuffed me and carried me off, no one would know what they were really doing it for. Sweat came down my brow. I knew that my only chance was to act like I belonged here, act like I was not nervous or suspicious. That I was the same as everyone else walking down the street. I straightened myself, walked purposely ahead. My heart was beating faster than it ever did on a treadmill, but outside I kept my cool. I had been trained as a lawyer after all. As they passed I even managed a 'good day officers'. The cops nodded a reply and kept walking. My gambit had paid off, I was going to be all right. I smiled as I brushed the dirt off my key and walked calmly out of harm's way.

I traveled back to the bus station through a fairly circuitous route, just in case. I was less worried about the police now. It was near dusk and there were a lot of other people on the streets coming home from work. There would be more people later, going out to dinner. I could blend in. I started to get a feel for the shadows. The darkness beckoned to me. I stayed mostly to side streets. There wasn't any trouble. A few times I thought that I saw one of them, but no. Black suits were very common in the financial district. My adversaries were around, but they weren't everywhere. I tried to stop myself from thinking that everyone I passed was somehow in on it. They were just living their little meaningless lives just like I did before, before...

I made it to the bus station without incident. I walked straight to the terminal that my locker was in. I felt the key with my right hand. It was still in my pocket, cold and orange. I stopped down the hall a-ways and sat. I began to scan the crowd, looking for someone looking for me. If they had been following me all this time then they would know that I had a copy here. They would know that I would come back here soon. Everybody seemed to be going about their business. People got on buses. People got off buses. Sad farewells and bright hellos. Balloons. The sound of a child crying. I sat for a long time. I watched until I was sure that everyone in the vicinity had either left or arrived while I was sitting there. I assured myself that no one was waiting for me. Then I moved to the locker. The key slid into the lock smoothly, but it wouldn't turn. It wouldn't turn. It was a trap. They had done something to the lock. I jiggled the key. Should I run? Should I get out of there while I still had the chance? They were coming for me. I jiggled the key. Beads of sweat began to form on my brow. The key clicked. The door opened. I looked inside cautiously. A bomb? This would be a great place to put it. Tie up the last loose end. Inside was just the sheaf of papers that I had left there. They didn't know about my little sheet metal hideout. I had beaten them. At least this battle. Many lawyers had underestimated me in my last life. They were sorry. Now these people had underestimated me. They thought that I had no inner strength, that I lacked the capacity to fight. They would soon learn. Soon they would be sorry also. I grabbed the papers and closed the locker. I moved quickly through the crowd while flipping through the pile. No bugs or tracers or anything besides freshly copied papers. I moved to a bathroom and locked myself into a stall to think of my next move.

I spent several minutes with the document. It was still a mystery. What did it say that was so important? What the hell language was this? People entered and left in the bathroom. There were buses to catch, loved ones to see. I undid the makeshift bandage on my hand. The bleeding had for the most part stopped. It was likely to be a nasty scar though. I could really go for some alcohol or something. I retied the bandage. I needed to get out of town. As long as I was here they could find me. I needed to get to a new city. It didn't matter which one, if I was outside of the city limits I could get lost in two hundred and sixty million Americans, not just four million city residents. But how? I had no money. My clothes were a mess. I hadn't shaved in a while. I was far too conspicuous. There was only one thing to do. I left the stall and took a seat on a bench just outside the bathroom. I waited for about fifteen minutes. Men came in and out of the restroom, oblivious to me. One guy threw me a quarter. Yeah buddy, that's going to help me. A young guy came in. He was about my size. He was going somewhere. He had a rolling suitcase. I followed him in. He stood with his back to me, relieving himself. He never even saw my face as I grabbed his bag. I was out the door before he could zip up. He chased me, but I lost myself in the crowd. I was getting good at that. I took a back exit and found myself on the street. It was dark already. I walked down half a block to a fast food restaurant. I entered the bathroom there and again locked myself in a stall. I opened the suitcase and examined the booty. There were several sets of clothes, a shaving kit, a camera, and some other items. I took the opportunity to change into some fresh clothes. Then I used the bathroom mirror for a quick shave. I cut myself a few times, but it was a reasonable job. I stuffed my old clothes into the trash, and the photocopy into the suitcase. Then I left the bathroom. I still needed some money. Across the street from the restaurant was a pawnshop. I went in and pawned the camera. I got a good price for it too. I took the film out first. I thought that someday I would mail the film to the address on the suitcase, with some money, when this was all over. I went back to the restaurant and ordered some food. I hadn't eaten since yesterday. I was still worried about the potential for poison, but I thought that if they had known where I was, they would have grabbed me by now. The meal made me feel a lot better. I had been pretty queasy all day without really being conscious of it. I stayed away from the coffee.

The camera had given me enough money to get out of town. I calmly walked back down the street to the bus station and bought a ticket for the first cheap place I could find, which was Sacramento. The bus left at 11pm, which gave me enough time to stop and buy a small bottle of rubbing alcohol and a large bottle of drinking alcohol. It wasn't the single malt that I was used to, but beggars can't be choosers.

I stepped out of the station into the night air. Things felt clear for the first time in days. Had my liver finished metabolizing the drugs? I felt alive for the first time ever. That feeling scared me a bit. My life was changing. The fog that I had lived under for the past thirty years was lifting. Everyone is raised with certain limits placed on their personality in order to function in society. Things such as stealing suitcases and running from the police were never actions that I had even considered. I could understand them on an intellectual basis, but a wall existed within my psyche that prevented me from ever considering the performance of these actions to be possible. Just as I know that people climb Mt. Everest, and I might dream of one day climbing Mt. Everest myself, my unconscious self image cannot believe that it can ever happen, and I am consciously prevented from ever taking any actions to get closer to the hike. But here I was, breaking down those walls inside my mind. Here I was actually doing. Becoming. I was not watching life from my comfortable sideline, I was living it. I am not a cog! I was in motion. Fright? Adrenaline? Loss of blood? I couldn't explain it, but something was changing within me. I was no longer the same person that was just trying to pay a toll all those days ago. Maybe it was the loss of my support system. As a white, male, American I had a great support structure. My office sent me a check every other Friday, regardless of job performance. My wife gave me unconditional love regardless of sexual performance. The police and social services kept the bad things away from me and gave me freshly paved roads, sent me tax forms right on schedule, and kept me as an engaged member of society without my ever having to think about a thing. Now all of that was gone. My office destroyed, my family, dead. My faith in legal protection, shattered.

My new found awareness came with a clarity of purpose and a clarity of vision. Instead of just performing actions the way they were expected to be performed, I was actively and consciously looking out for my best interests. I was no longer doing what I was told to do, or living my life as a performer reading from a script. From the shadows, I carefully watched everyone else get on the bus. No one looked particularly suspicious. You never know with these people though. I only expected to encounter something I didn't expect. Only a few people got on the bus. Sacramento isn't a popular destination I suppose. The bus driver got on. He was a fat black man, older, slower. Didn't look the type to be involved with anything past getting the bus to its proper destination. At the last minute I stepped from the shadows and slipped through the closing doors. The driver motioned to me that I should stow my stolen suitcase in the storage rack under the bus. I ignored him and rolled it to the seat next to me. There was plenty of room. The bus started off into the darkness. I was getting out of town. Whoever these people were, they weren't going to get me easily.

The trip up to Sacramento took several hours, owing to the darkness and the mountains. I lay in my seat in the blackness, looking out the window at life passing. Houses, telephone lines, farms. No animals were out this late. Fences. You couldn't see that much from the highway, but you could see enough. The monotonous passage of the streetlights was hypnotizing. I slept for a little while, and dreamed perhaps of a great city. I was standing in an alley. Stone cobblestone floor. Walls made of stone slabs and mud bricks, impossibly tall overhead. It was hot. Oppressively hot. Some people shuffled by in long green robes. A hum was in the air. They spoke a strange language. They didn't seem to notice me. A chicken clucked. From down the alley footsteps came. Loud, hard. No, that wasn't footsteps, it was a heartbeat. A heartbeat so strong that it shook the ground. The beat of a living city. A man approached. Not in a robe.

57

A police uniform. It was the policeman who was hit by the stray bullets. There was blood on his uniform. His gun was missing. He came up to me and just looked. Looked into my soul, with his eyes asking the question 'why?' I told him that I didn't do it. He shouldn't haunt me. It was the detectives. The men chasing me. I looked down. I held the policeman's missing gun. It was heavy in my hand.

I was jolted awake by the bus coming to a quick halt. The road was deserted. Were we in Sacramento? This didn't look like a bus station. I could only see out the right side of the bus, but blue, white, and red lights were alternately lighting the fences and telephone poles there. Police lights. The door was opening. A policeman in uniform got on the bus and began speaking to the driver quietly. Were they looking for me? Did they know? My heart began to beat faster. This was it, I thought, I have nowhere to run. They can take me off this bus and bring me out into that field and shoot me dead. The officer took out a flashlight and began walking down the aisle. Slowly shining his light on each person as he passed. Groggy, confused faces stared back at him. He walked slowly down the aisle. Pace. Pace. Pace. My hand reached into my stolen jacket. I felt for the gun. My heart beat hard in my chest, beat, beat, beat. My hand was on the handle. Finger on the trigger. The cop came closer. My fight or flight instinct had kicked in. I was prepared to kill this guy if I needed to, without regard to what would have happened next. He turned towards me and shined his light at my eyes. I kept focus on his free hand. Watching his gun. The glint of blue metal. I would see when he went for his gun. He turned the light from me and passed on to the next sleeping traveler. My hands were sweaty, rusting the gun in my pocket. My breathing didn't return to normal for fifteen minutes.

The cop made his way to the back of the bus, turned and left. A "Thank you folks" accompanied his departure. It was nothing. As the bus drove off, the bus driver explained to no one in particular that there had been a jailbreak nearby that night. They were looking for some escapees. It had nothing to do with me. I tried to remind myself that despite the appearances in San Francisco, not everyone was in on this thing. At most, it was only a handful of people. Most of the people I would meet would be as comfortably oblivious as I used to be before the mistake. Intellect does not always conquer fear though, and I remained alert the rest of the way to Sacramento.

# Chapter 4:
# Victory

The bus pulled into the main terminal of the Sacramento bus station just after 1:30 am. I was tired, but adrenaline coursed through my system, making sleep an impossibility. I had to figure out what to do next. I needed a place to think, a place to breathe. I stood on the street a few steps from the bus doorway, clutching my stolen suitcase, feeling the weight of the gun in my pocket. Despite my years living in San Francisco, I had never ventured into Sacramento. To me, it had always just been an exit to get gas on the way to Lake Tahoe. I didn't know my way around. Didn't know where to go. The smell of soot and gasoline filled the air. A neon sign beckoned from over the rotted wood fence that surrounded the bus terminal. It was a hotel of some sort. It looked cheap enough. I only had a few dollars left from the pawnshop. I proceeded through the station and onto the street. Let me tell you, the bus station in Sacramento is not in the best part of town. Cars drove past, on their way to who knows where. People walked the streets, scary people. Dark, dirty people on their way to some nefarious business one could only assume. I fingered the gun in my pocket as I walked down the street to where I thought the hotel sign called. It would be very ironic, I thought, to be killed in a simple robbery attempt after surviving such an organized effort against me. I wondered if any of the people

I saw had something to do with what was going on? That bum, half passed out by the station doorway, could he be an informer? Did he have a cell phone, ready to call home base if a person of my description came out of the station? The homeless are so faceless. They are so hard to see that they would be a good choice. A whole legion of homeless, all working together to bring about the master plan.

What was the master plan?

I arrived at the hotel. It was one of those places that mostly catered to the 'rent by the hour' set, but they did occasionally see an exhausted bus traveler or two. That was fine by me. It looked like the sort of place that wouldn't ask you to sign a ledger. The man behind the counter was so stereotypical of the sleazy motel owner. He was fat, balding, wearing a dirty t-shirt. His whole body oozed grease and muck. The hotel was cheap, but I didn't have much money. I was able to get a room for the night, but I was left with only a few dollars. He took my money and gave me a key and a set of sheets. He also tried to imply that he could provide other services if I needed them. I ignored him. I didn't have time for that. I went up the stairs and down the hall to my room. It was not as bad as I would have thought, although the sudden light erupting from the bare bulb caused several roaches to dive for cover. I put down the suitcase and locked myself in for the night. The room was beige and dingy. It contained a bed, stained and sheetless for the time being, an old television, and a night table with a lamp. The bathroom was dirty, but sufficient. I realized at this point that I was feeling pretty grimy from my recent ordeals. I took off the stolen clothes and took a long, hot shower. There are few things that make one feel better and more focused than a good hot shower. I suppose that is why they are so popular in the mornings. The shower was not as relaxing as I had hoped though. The walls of the room were thin and I kept hearing bumps and voices from outside. In my psychological state I thought that they were coming from inside my room. I was fearful that a knife would suddenly come swinging through the shower curtain, and that would be that. I had judiciously placed the gun on the top of the toilet, but that was still an arm's length away, and I had soap in my eyes. I felt naked and vulnerable and I kept shivering, no matter how much I turned up the hot water. Fortunately, I was able to make it through without having my room invaded by thugs or psychotics, and I felt clean and clear as I dried myself with the rough towel.

I came back into the bedroom with the towel wrapped around my waist. After putting the moderately clean sheets on the bed, I sat down and began to go through the suitcase I had 'acquired'. It contained the standard stuff that you would expect to bring on a trip. Several pairs of clothes, all casual, various toiletries, an American passport in the name 'Joshua Vorhees', a dog-eared book whose title I can't remember. In a zipped pocket I found the ultimate prize. There was almost a thousand dollars of cash hidden away. Apparently Mr. Vorhees didn't think that his wallet was safe enough. This cash would help a lot, once I figured where I was going. I put everything back in the suitcase and reclined on the bed. I turned on the TV. It was mostly dead air at this time of night, but I found some reruns or something. I started to think more about my situation.

It was obvious that I had stumbled upon something big, I knew that much. It was obvious that the people in charge of this thing had tremendous resources that they could direct toward me. Could it be the mob? Organized crime? That didn't make a lot of sense. What I knew about gangsters was just what I learned from the movies, but it didn't seem like their style. I don't ever remember hearing about secret codes and fake police. From the size of all of this is seemed like it could be a ring of spies. That had the right M.O., but it doesn't explain the police reaction. If it was a bunch of foreigners blowing up buildings and passing secrets, it seems to me that the FBI would want to know about it. They would have shown my destroyed office all over the place instead of hushing it all up. Was the media part of all this too? It seemed that they would have to be, wouldn't they? There was really only one conclusion that one could draw from all of the recent events. It had to be something within the US government. Maybe what I had was some CIA document. Since the Vietnam War people have accused the government of plotting against them. The army poisons thousands of unwitting people with LSD. The CIA sells crack in Los Angeles to fund a secret Central American war. I had never given much credence to these sorts of things before. I had always assumed that no matter what their job was, every CIA agent was still an American. They still went home to their wife and kid at the end of the day and watched baseball on TV and ate apple pie like everyone else. I couldn't imagine that there was a faction that was so callous as to actively try to kill innocent citizens such as myself. I certainly never thought that this group would have the power to cover up something as big as that office building explosion. But, here it was. There was no denying the evidence in hand. I was sure that I had not gone crazy, and I still believed in the things that I saw before my own eyes, so I took the facts at face value and evaluated the evidence that I had. Sherlock Holmes said that once you have eliminated the impossible, what is left, however unlikely, must be the truth. There was only one conclusion that made any sense at this time, that my own government (or at least a faction thereof) was actively trying to kill me to reclaim a classified document that came into my possession by mistake. This is the theory that I came up with that night, and it was the premise that I would operate under for some time to come.

I lay there for a long time, thinking about these sorts of things. Thinking logically, rationally. Linear steps of thought. I was thinking in Binah consciousness, not the

Hockamah conscious that can produce real intuitive leaps. I hadn't learned that yet. As such, I was stuck in my mindset and although the boundaries of reality had begun to bend, they were still in place and I was unable to truly comprehend the gravity of what was going on. I would, in time. Perhaps if I hadn't focused so hard, hadn't strived for an understandable solution, I would not be in the place I am in now. I was so far removed from the za-zen and the Taoists and the others who could have led me away from the path I was about to choose. I should have destroyed the copied manuscript at that time. I should never have made it in the first place. I spent an hour or so going over it that night. Page by page. It was filled with hieroglyphs and strange symbols. Letters that made no sense. Pages of English letters that repeated, with no breaks for words. I was not a master of languages, but I thought that I would be able to recognize something. But no, it was all just gibberish to me. Why would someone want to kill for this? It was obviously of no use to anyone without some sort of key.

I put the copy aside. It had nothing that I could use. At least not now. I needed to come up with some sort of plan. Who could I go to? The police would be a risk, even in other cities now. The FBI? The media? Should I go and find some sort of linguistics professor? I didn't know where to turn. I was in uncharted territory at the time. I looked over to the night table in the alternating flash of the television. It had a drawer. I opened it. My first steps towards Hockamah. Inside was a bible. I should have expected it. They are in every room (although at that time I didn't know the true reason why). I was not a religious man. I was a man who was taught to believe and trust only in that which you can see and feel. If you wanted to change a situation you could only do it through your own actions. Some higher power was not going to be there to pat you on the back and make everything all right just because you ask nicely. But now, lonely and cold in this hotel room, I needed a higher power. They say that prayer is the last refuge, well I needed a refuge, and I didn't have anywhere else to turn. Maybe it was because I needed guidance, maybe it was because I knew that people gain strength from the bible, maybe it was sheer curiosity. But for whatever reason, I picked it up and began reading. Genesis 1:1, ' In the beginning...', and so on and so on and so on.

I made it as far as the first book of Exodus;

Exodus 1:13, *And the Egyptians made the children of Israel to serve with rigor. And they made their lives bitter with hard bondage in mortar, and in brick, and in all similar manner of service in the field.*

My mind flashed back to our honeymoon touring the old monuments of the Giza plateau. A tour guide's voice echoes in my mind. "Now you can see here how this arch was put together. It consists of several stone slabs, held in place with nothing but pressure. The Pharaohs didn't need cement and mortar like today's buildings do." I ran my hand along the hairline gap between two slabs.

The Bible passage struck me as odd. I mean, the Egyptians didn't use bricks. They used big stone slabs, but they had no bricks, no mortar. I thought that I might have just misinterpreted the phrase, or it was an error in translation, but later on was a similar passage;

Exodus 5:6, *And Pharaoh commanded the taskmasters of the people, saying, 'Ye shall no more give the people straw to make brick, let them go and gather straw themselves'.*

The Egyptians certainly had no straw and mud bricks in their constructions. All the Egyptian buildings were made of stone, at least all the ones I saw, and believe me, my wife had made us look at every prehistoric painted rock and recently-unearthed antiquated latrine they have in that hot sandy wasteland. Why would the Pharaoh have made his slaves make mud bricks? Was this an error in the text? Was there another purpose for the bricks? Where were they taken? Why hadn't archeologists found them? Why wasn't it on the tour?

Dark space. Infinite, dimensionless. Ein sof. Before the world, before the heavens, before even the concept of distance was formed. Ten crystal spheres stand before my eyes. They are in parallel, they are in series, they are each inside the others. A vibration approaches. You can feel it coming through the void like a stampeding herd. A heartbeat from under the firmament. The spheres are being filled, filled with the divine energy, filled with the divine word of God himself. I stand in awe at the display, as the divine spirit vibrates and resonates down through the spheres. But something is wrong. The harmonics fail, the voice is too strong. The crystal has not been annealed thoroughly. The vibration increases. The din is too much to bear. The sound of shattering crystal. The shards are falling. I hear the final cry of my unborn daughter.

I awoke with a start. I must have fallen asleep while looking through the bible. It still lay on my chest. Light was streaming through the window. A bird chirped vainly. The television was still on. 'Tomorrow's weather, sunny, with a high in the mid-60s', said the news. I watched for a while in a half dream. What was there? What were they not saying? How many others like myself had been removed. How many other buildings exploded? What was the hidden message behind the news?

I turned the TV off. There was nothing for me there. I no longer trust what the reporters said, and the fiction was just a distraction. I sat up. As I did, the bible that I had been reading fell off the bed and onto the floor. It opened to a page. A page that gave me the hint that I needed to proceed. A shiver ran up my spine. The Gideon's Standard Bible is the one that comes in every hotel room. It contains both the new and old testaments, as well as the Psalms. It also has one thing that most other bibles don't have. In order to show

how worldwide and universal Christianity is, the Gideon's had translated one of the most famous bible passages into every language they could think of:

John 3:16, *For God so loved the world that he gave his only begotten Son, that whosoever believeth in him should not perish, but have everlasting life.*

Right in the front of the book, there are several pages of this verse repeated again and again. First in English, then Dutch, then Sinhalese, then Tamil, etc. The book opened to one of these pages. The first language on that page was Devenagari, Tibetan. Devenagari is a beautiful language consisting of whirls and straight lines, slightly similar to Hindi. I had seen Devenagari only once before. It was the first part of the document I had gotten from the toll collector.

A-ha! Here was my first clue. Perhaps this document wasn't all gibberish and codes. It was just filled with very obscure languages. Who the hell speaks Devenagari these days anyway? Were the agents who originated this document from Tibet? Chinese communists perhaps? No, that still did not make sense, considering that most of the document was not in Devenagari or Chinese. But why speculate? I now had the key. I now had the ability to figure out what the document said. All I had to do was find someone who spoke Tibetan. But wait. How hard would that be? There were not that many people around who would know such a thing. The men in black would have to assume that if I still had a copy of the document I would eventually figure out that the first part was Tibetan, and of course the first thing I was likely do would be to find a Tibetan translator. There were not that many people like that around. It wouldn't be too hard to watch them all. At least all the ones I could get to easily. No, I couldn't go there. I would have to do it myself. How hard could it be to translate a few paragraphs? I'm a college graduate. I would just get a dictionary, learn the letters and I should be able to get the gist of it in a few weeks.

I thought that I should move on this information immediately. I jumped out of bed and got dressed in some more of the stolen clothes. They actually fit pretty well. I stuffed everything else into the suitcase except the gun, the passport, the money and the copy. Those I put in my coat. I even took the bible. At best it would provide some spiritual guidance, at worst it would provide me with a quick reference to some obscure language. Maybe I could even sell it if I got desperate. I didn't want to leave anything in the hotel room when I went out. It could be searched, bugged, or who knows what. I thought about going down to the manager and staying for a few more days. I did have a thousand dollars after all. But I thought that it might not be a good idea to stay in the same place for too long. Who knows how far behind me they are? I grabbed the suitcase and went down to give the manager the key.

There was a new guy on duty that morning. Obviously the fat, greasy, night manager had gone home. This guy was tall, thin, and young. He had a small name tag that said, 'Hi, my name is MITCH'. Hmm. Same as me. He asked me if I had a good night and took my key. He told me to come back again next time I was in town. I turned to leave. "Wait a sec buddy," he said. "You got a message." That surprised me. No one knew that I was here. It must have been a mistake. He turned around to the little message bins and pulled out a small sheet of paper. I was going to tell him that he must have the wrong room, but before I could really react the paper was in my hand. It was small and white, on motel stationary, folded neatly in half. I unfolded it to see what it said. Written particularly sloppily, as if written by a child, were two small words.

Turn Around

I broke out in a cold sweat almost immediately. I slowly raised my head and turned around as the note instructed. My gut tensed up in anticipation. Sitting on the lobby couch behind me were two men. They wore dark sunglasses and old fashion black business suits, with black fedora hats. *They found me!* The one on the left smiled, or maybe bared his teeth in anticipation of feeding. The fight or flight instinct kicked in immediately. The two men began to stand up and reach into their coats. A gun. I still had a gun. I tried to pull it out from my jacket, but it got stuck. Then it came out. I pointed it at the two men with both hands. I fired four or maybe five shots at them. They were only a few feet away, but I missed, or at least I think I missed. The two men dove for cover. They didn't know that I had a gun. They were unprepared for this. They expected me to be easy prey. I took advantage of the situation by running right past them out a back door into an alley. It seems spent a lot of time in alleys back then. I ran down the street. The gun was still in my hand. I had the presence of mind to try to put it in my pocket. It burned. They don't tell you that guns are real hot after you fire them. I suppose that it makes sense if you think about it. I had never thought about it. Anyway, I could feel it burning in my hip pocket as I ran down the street. I heard the hotel door being opened again, and then footsteps. I didn't look back. Pop, Pop. Shots were being fired. I ran around the corner out into the main street. It was morning rush hour now, and there were a lot of people about. The bus station was filling with people starting the day's journey to who knows where. The men didn't follow me out into the street. Typical. They like to work in secret, in the shadows. There were a lot of taxis around, waiting for people who didn't get as far as they wanted on a bus. I jumped in one and told him to go. He asked me where. I said anywhere. He stepped on the gas and the cab moved into traffic. I looked out the back window and I saw the two dark men standing at the entrance to the alley, flanking the clerk with my name. They didn't try to follow the cab.

After a block or two the driver insisted on a destination. He was a dark, bearded man. He wore a turban. Sikh. I told him to take me to a mall, it didn't matter which. He drove on. Luckily he didn't talk during the trip. I hate talking to people, especially people who are just trying to make conversation. I reclined in the back seat and tried to relax a bit. These men had proved fallible. Again and again I had been able to get away. I saw them duck when the bullets went off. They were scared just like me, human just like me. I could beat them, at least on an individual basis. That gave me the confidence to continue. But how did they find me? I needed to be more careful. Were they just playing with me? The note they left made them seem like cats toying with a mouse before finally crushing its throat. I needed to be more careful. They could have had me if they wanted me. They were not expecting me to have so much fight left. Likely they were expecting to see a pathetic wretch, cold, tired, and scared out of his wits. That was their mistake, underestimation. I assumed though that they were smart enough to not make that mistake again. Next time I would get a bullet in the back instead of a note. I needed to be more careful in the future. Perhaps the hotel right by the bus station was not such a good idea. I needed to cover my tracks more. Move around more. Keep looking behind me. I would also have to get out of Sacramento as soon as possible. But I needed some information first.

The cab pulled up to a mall. I got out and gave the cab driver some money and he went away. I went inside and proceeded to the nearest bookstore. I needed a book on Beginning Devenagari. I searched the shelves in vain. Spanish? yes. French? yes. Tibetan? no. A clerk came over to me as I was squatting between the shelves. "Do you need some help?" she asked.

"I need a language book, Tibetan," I replied, after a pause. The clerk gave me a confused look.

"Um, I don't think that we have anything like that. Let me check the computer." She went over to the register. I looked around cautiously. They could be here any minute. They knew that I was in the area. They knew what I was looking for. No wait. That isn't true. They have no idea that I'm looking for a book on the Tibetan language. They don't know that I have a copy of their document, and even if they did, they shouldn't be assuming that I know what language it is in. I told Detective Smith that it was all just gibberish. Wait a second! They don't know. Can't tip them off.

I ran over to the cashier and told her to forget it, to forget the whole thing. She was typing into the keyboard. I grabbed the cord and pulled it from the wall. The screen went blank. I pushed her away from the keys. They don't know that I know. That is my secret weapon against them. Who knows how powerful they are? Who knows what resources they might have? I know that they already control the police, and seem to have informants all over. It would be easy for them to check computer requests. All they would have to do is look for stores that are inquiring about Tibetan books. Then they would have me. "Sorry, sorry," I said, "Don't worry about my request. Thanks." I left the store in a hurry. I didn't know what she had typed in, but it could be jetting towards my enemies at the speed of light right now.

I left the mall through a different entrance than where I had come in. I had intended to stop off and buy myself some clothes, but I didn't want to risk staying around here too long. The mall was a mistake. They wouldn't have the books that I needed there. It was all bestsellers and science fiction and cooking. I needed someplace that would have a more diverse, more academic selection. The nearest college was University of California, Davis. They must have a library there. That would be the best bet for getting the books that I needed by the end of the day.

I went across the street to a convenience store. They had maps of the area there. Davis wasn't that far. Only a few miles from downtown Sacramento. There were buses of course, students shuttling back and forth from campus. I decided not to take them. They might be watching. They knew I was in town. They knew that I would be trying to leave town somehow. They knew that I was likely to travel by bus. I decided to hitch a ride. It worked. I had never done anything like that before. As a child, my parents had told me that it was dangerous, that you could get raped or mugged or knifed. In the back of my mind I believed that every single person who picks up a hitchhiker is a psychotic murderer looking for victims. Ridiculous once you think about it. I guess that I never questioned my early conditioning. A man in a red truck picked me up. He said that he was going that way and that he could take me all the way to the campus. I sat in the cab nervously at first. Looking up and down for traces of a black suit. He was not in on anything, as far as I could tell.

"You a student?" said the man as the truck barreled down the highway towards Davis.

The radio droned on quietly. Country station.

"um. Yeah. A student." There was no point in explaining myself to this guy.

The song ended. Commercials...

"What are you studying?" I was too unnerved by the morning's antics to have much of a tolerance for small talk, but I needed the ride, and I didn't want to give this guy any reason to remember me.

News report.

"Law. I'm a law student." It was mostly true.

'In local news today…'

"Law student huh? I didn't know that they had lawyers up there. You thinking of working for the *government?*" You could tell that this guy was just a yokel from out of town. He was most likely anti-government.

"No sir," I replied.

'…A UC Davis student was shot to death early this morning. The man, identified by police as Mitchell Theremin, was working as a clerk at the SleepAway Motel…'

"You look a little old to be a student. You ain't one of them slackers are you?" the man said with a bit of a sneer. I told him this story about how I had to work for years to save up the money to pay my tuition. I knew just what he wanted to hear. You don't get as high up in the legal hierarchy without knowing how to suck-up flawlessly and seamlessly.

'…this morning, guests found him on the floor in a pool of blood. Police have no suspects for now, but robbery appears to have been the motive.'

The news story shut me up for a while. Mitchell. That was the clerk at the motel I stayed at. He was the one who witnessed my altercation with the men in black. They must have gone back and shot him dead. It was my fault. He was just an innocent bystander. My resolve to get these people was strengthened. Another death to avenge.

We got into a discussion about firearms, and, although I had to fake my way through it, I did learn a few things that helped me later. The trip was not too long, and the man dropped me off a block or so from the main campus, wishing me luck. I traveled up the road, pretending like I knew where I was going. It took me a while to find the place. Eventually I saw a campus map posted.

As it turns out, the library at Davis isn't all that extensive. The school is sort of a satellite campus and they just don't have the facilities that a lot of larger campuses might have. In addition, the school isn't that big on either languages or Asia. It turned out that they didn't have any books on Devenagari. The clerk was rather helpful though and explained to me that the Davis library didn't normally keep a large stock of obscure works. They just ordered them from the Berkeley campus when needed. He offered to order the books for me. Only two days delivery time, but he needed to see a valid student ID. I told him to forget about it. I went and got something to drink. I needed to think about my next move.

In a local pub I sat sipping beer as college jocks with the day off watched football and ate the brand of chips that the TV told them had the best taste. The Berkeley campus is located right across the bay from San Francisco. The belly of the beast. That is where all of my troubles began. That is where they were. It would be sure suicide to go back there now. I should run to someplace like Idaho or Rhode Island, or Fiji, somewhere far from the city by the bay. Of course, they were everywhere, or at least here in Sacramento. Who knows how far their grasp reaches? Maybe they could just as easily be found in Idaho or Rhode Island or Fiji. If my theory holds that 'they' are US government agents, then anywhere in the country would be their domain. It doesn't really matter. Plus, they expect me to run. They probably staked out the Sacramento bus station because that was the quickest way to get out of town. I played right into their roadblock. They were probably setting up in Tahoe, which is the most likely destination from Sacramento. They think that I am a scared little boy. They think that I am running from my life. Even the shooting incident that morning shouldn't really change their opinion of me, I was acting from shear panic. They should still think that my main objective is flight.

But what was my main objective at that point? Not to flee, but to prevail. They didn't know I had the copy. They didn't know I would translate the Tibetan. They didn't know that I intended to unravel their little plot. I didn't know how to do that just yet, but I knew that it was going to happen. I didn't know how I would alert the people of this country to the sinister machinations that were occurring, but I would somehow. I was on a quest. It was a challenge. It was terrifying yes, but also, …fun. My life had lacked excitement for so long. Every little schoolboy wants to grow up to be a hero or a spy or an astronaut. Someone who *does* things, as opposed to someone like the person I was, who let things happen. In my old life as a lawyer, there was no excitement. Nothing happened. I was a just receptor for things to happen to. Every week my retirement fund got a little larger, and every week one more contract for something that no one cared about was written, only to be placed on a shelf, unread. Every week a few more products got consumed. I had no effect on the world, and the world had no effect on me. Life went on, but nothing *happened*. Here was my opportunity. An opportunity to *do* something, to *be* something. Descartes said, "To do is to be." Now I would start doing, start being.

And why not go back to the Bay? That was the last place they expected me to go. Those little bastards thought that had me on the run. I would show them. Dive back into the maw, that's what I would do. I guess that I had been taken in by all of the movies and television programs that they show to subtly put into your head that the noblest thing is the single wronged man, working alone against the system. All of that programming is there to make everyone think that they themselves are the hero of the show, that they *alone* will rescue the princess and return the rightful heir to the throne. What a great scheme. Discourage the disparate elements in society from joining forces against you. Why didn't I go to the police? Why didn't I go to my friends and relatives? Why didn't I go to other underground groups of people that may suspect the things that I now had evidence of? Simple. I was the star. I had been well programmed by four hours of television a night and I naively believed that I, one man alone, would be able to bring down the whole plot by myself. I was incapable of believing otherwise. I had no idea how I would do it of course, I didn't know what would happen once I cracked the code. I figured that the document would somehow solve itself. I had $1000, a loaded pistol, and a mystery encoded on one hundred and thirty-two sheets of paper. Let the adventure begin!

The best way back to Berkeley was to hitch. It wasn't really that far after all. My pursuers would undoubtedly have the bus stations and airports staked out. They might also have connections with local cab companies. There was no way though that they would be able to find me if I just hitched a ride with random people. They couldn't watch everyone all the time, could they? Well, however many people they were watching that night, they didn't find me. I got a ride with some students that were headed into San Francisco for a night of fun.

The main library on the Berkeley campus is a huge thing. It has eight stories of books, supposedly one of the largest collections anywhere. If they couldn't help me there, I would have to go to Tibet itself. I entered the main hall. It was a tall room, maybe fifty feet in height. The walls were paneled in dark wood, and there were colorful frescoes on the ceiling, gilded in gold foil. Obviously this place was built before labor got so expensive. I walked around for a bit trying to figure out how to get to the stacks, but the librarian told me that the place was so big that they didn't let customers in. You had to go and look up the book you wanted and give the number to a librarian, who would get it for you. Luckily, the library had several books on beginning Tibetan. I handed the slip of paper to the clerk and she disappeared into a doorway. I went and sat on an old wooden bench and waited. Students came and went, living their little lives. They were too young, and hadn't realized yet that the world outside was full of disappointment and monotony. They still believed that they would make a difference in the world, somewhere, somehow. After their spirits were crushed they would make nice cogs in the great societal machine. I sat nervously, eyeing everyone around me, looking for the dark men. A lot of kids came in dressed in all black, but more than likely they were just philosophy majors rather than conspirators.

A few minutes later the clerk returned and I picked up my book. It was hardly used. I guess that a lot of people aren't interested in a half-dead language on the other side of the world, even in this bastion of multiculturalism. I proceeded to another room where there were desks and tables for research. I pulled out the first sheet of the document and laid it on the table along with the book. I opened the book to the first page and started reading. The spine crackled as it opened. I had never been that good with languages in school, and I didn't know how long it would take me to get anywhere, but I really didn't have anyplace else to be. The first step to learning any language is to learn the basic letters. At least that was what the book said. I took Spanish in high school but I already knew those letters. The book went on to give descriptions of the letters of the Devenagari alphabet and how to pronounce them. They don't all match directly with English letters, but there is some similarity. I practiced saying the letters quietly, and as I got a few pages into it, I began pronouncing certain words of Tibetan. I didn't know what those words were exactly, but I could verbalize them.

After about an hour I felt pretty confident with the majority of the letters. I took a look at the document and I could definitely see that the letters there were the same as the ones in the book. They broke out into patterns that, while I couldn't yet understand, I was pretty sure I could verbalize. I took a stab at the first sentence of the document, which appeared to be some sort of chapter title. To my surprise, when I said the letters out loud, they did not come out like some strange foreign language. It sounded like English. The chapter title was not actually in Tibetan, it was English words transcribed in Devenagari letters. It was short. Just three words. Three scary words.

FEAR THE FORGOTTEN

I have to admit that that was not what I expected to read. I was hoping for something that explained what the document was, or who wrote it, not a warning. I also have to admit that I was not expecting the title to be in coded English. That gave me some hope that it would be possible to quickly figure out the rest of the manuscript. Unfortunately my luck ran out with the title. The next few sentences proved to actually be in Tibetan. Except of course for a few proper names here and there, most notably 'Peru'. I spent several hours in the large hall trying to learn the words I needed. I was able to translate a few words here and there, a fragment of a sentence. "Excuse me sir." The problem with the Tibetan language is "excuse me sir, the library is closing." A clerk was tapping my shoulder. "Would you like to check that book out?" I didn't have any ID.

"No, not today," I said. She shrugged and pointed to the return rack. I walked over there and put the book down. I had really had a groove going, it was a shame to have to stop for the night. The clerk returned to her business. I stood at the return rack fingering the book. I didn't have time to waste on this. I needed to work more. I was getting a few words here and there out of the text. I was unable to quite get the gist of the first few paragraphs, but it had something to do with Peru. I couldn't stop now. Whatever this document was telling me, it was something important. I was sure of that. The crispness of the pages in the Tibetan primer told me that no Berkeley student needed this particular volume. It wouldn't be missed at all really. I slipped the book into my coat and started to walk out. There was an alarm to prevent this sort of theft. When I reached it, I just ran through it. The bell started to ring, and the few remaining patrons looked up, but I was already down the hallway. One of the clerks had time to vocalize an "excuse me sir," but I didn't heed. They didn't really care anyway. The clerks were all students on work-study. No one even bothered to chase me as I made my way out of the building and across campus.

I wandered the streets of Berkeley aimlessly for a while. I was not very familiar with the place, and it was beginning to get dark. I pulled my jacket around me and looked about for a hotel, eventually locating a cheesy dive on University Ave. Most of their clientele were moms and dads coming for graduation, but since it wasn't that time of year they were pretty empty. I checked in under the name Josh Vorhees, and flashed the stolen passport at the clerk. The picture looked nothing like me, but the clerk apparently didn't care and gave me a key. Room 1935. I paid in cash. He asked me if I had any bags. Any bags? No. I had had a bag, but in the commotion trying to get away from the men in black I had left it at the last motel. That had my fingerprints on it, and it was not only stolen, but was found in a murder scene. I hope that wouldn't get me in trouble. Of course, the people who could hurt me already knew all about me, so it was doubtful that an incriminating suitcase would matter any more than anything else would.

I spent the next few hours reading and studying, and made some significant progress. Around 10pm my hunger started to become more important to me than my quest. I packed up my meager things and left the hotel in search of food. In what was one of the most ironic instances of my entire journey, I found that directly across the street from the hotel was a Tibetan/Nepali restaurant. I certainly appreci-

79

ated the coincidence, and I decided that I should not tempt fate by ignoring such a harmonious event. Besides, I always appreciate a good curry. However, as I waited for the light to change so I could cross the street, apprehension set it. Perhaps it was just too obvious. It was a little too convenient. It occurred to me that they might be staking out nearby places that might have Tibetan speakers. Wouldn't a Tibetan restaurant be one of the most obvious places to go if I was looking for help in translation? I instead hurried down the street and got a burrito.

On my way back to the motel I was careful to look at who might be hanging around the Tibetan place. My caution was well founded. On a bus stop bench just down from the restaurant's front door was a man dressed in a black suit with a black fedora hat. I stood on the corner and watched for a few minutes from behind the safety of a few newspaper boxes and a telephone pole. He held a cigarette in his left hand, but it didn't appear to be lit. He tapped his foot, as if along to some music, or beat that only he could hear. A bus pulled to the stop, but the man waved it by. He just sat there. Waiting, tapping. He must have been looking for me. Waiting for me to come to one of the few places in the area that might have some people able to translate their document. There were three things that scared me about that man. First, he implied that they knew that I had retained a copy of the document. Second, he implied that they had anticipated my coming back to the San Francisco Bay area. And third, his presence implied that they had the manpower to dedicate an agent to each place I might be found.

I had left nothing at the hotel. They might search it, but I wouldn't be there. The room was registered to Joshua Vorhees. They might know who that was if he filed a police report in Sacramento. I retreated back around the corner and started walking in the other direction. Luckily most of the back streets of Berkeley don't have lights, so I was able to get away into the darkness without the man ever seeing me. I wandered over to the other side of campus. It was nighttime and that side was filled with students taking out their frustrations on pizza and beers. It was easy to lose oneself in the crowd. In my shabby clothes and unshorn face I looked like a lot of the graduate students who lurched down these busy streets this hour. I could also be mistaken for one of the city's many homeless, although many of them were younger; runaways. Trying to survive on meager handouts and copious amounts of drugs.

I walked down Telegraph Avenue for about an hour. Stopping in different stores, pretending to shop for music, or trendy clothes, or drug paraphernalia, or other sorts of hippie crap. I initially thought that I was just trying to be careful. That I was trying to blend in with the crowd that I was trying to throw whomever off my trail, but to be honest there was no one following me. At least not actively, not now. I was wandering back and forth because I didn't really have anywhere to go. I couldn't go back to the hotel. I assumed that the bus stations might be similarly guarded, if I even could figure out where they were. My feet were tired. I was tired. I sat down on the street corner, up against a building, and did the only thing that I could do, continue my studies.

I didn't last very long. There was too much noise and commotion on the street to make any study productive. I got into a conversation with several street urchins who were sitting nearby. They had come to the streets willingly to 'live the lifestyle'. They had parents who loved them and homes with heat and beds and hot soup, but they chose the streets. I couldn't understand that. I was still in the mindset that there was a goal in life. I was not sure exactly what that goal was, but it was generally in the area of go to school, get a job, get married, have kids, live in bigger and bigger houses, and retire to Florida with your hard-earned savings. I knew that other people had not made the progress that I had made towards that goal. A lot of my classmates from high school didn't end up with the success that I had had. But I had always been sure that they had always been striving for what I had been achieving. These kids taught me a valuable lesson. Different people have different goals in life. These kids were willingly not following that which they had been taught; by school, by parents, by television. They had decided not to be consumers. They lived without the safety net.

They did something else for me that night. They shared some of their marijuana with me. They smoke it there, right in the street. I have to admit that I had lived a sheltered life, and had never been exposed to drugs before, not even during the wild college years. I remember being a child and seeing all sorts of warnings against drugs and how to say no to all of the pushers that would try to force you into joining them. No one ever forced me into anything. If anything, the kids who I suspected of doing drugs shied away from me. There were no drugs to say no to. Even if I had wanted some I wouldn't have known where to find any. This was another way that these kids were different from me, they took the risks that I never took, they did the things that I never even thought possible. I know how I was back in high school, I couldn't even get by without mom packing my lunch, never mind living on the streets in a permanent drug induced stupor. Of course it all took its toll, on their health, on their minds, on their souls, but what price freedom?

I didn't smoke enough that night to have any of the hallucinogenic effects, or the mind expanding effects, or the paranoid effects. Although maybe the paranoid effects of the drug just come from having your eyes opened and mind expanded enough to actually see what is happening? I just had enough to be giggly. It was a real departure for me, but my old walls were breaking down and I was entering a new stage of consciousness and life-experience. People say that drugs diminish capacity. I wouldn't say that. From this experience I learned that drugs *alter* capacity. Sure, you can't do complex math while you are on them, but you do learn to see things in a different way. Connections are made that you hadn't been able to make before. Leaps of creative logic appear as if out of nowhere. That is not to say that every drug induced dream and joke makes sense, many don't. But the fact that all of it *does* make sense during the experience became proof to me that there is more than one way of looking at life, at reality.

I spent a few hours with them, there on the curb. We had our backs up against the window of a record store. Loud tribal rhythms pounded out of the store's internal speakers, boom, boom, boom, boom. The glass was shaking, vibrating in synch. Was that from the music? In my stupor I imagined that it wasn't. That it was the beat of the city itself, that it was the heartbeat of the world. You just couldn't feel it when you were straight. I shared this with my comrades. Some nodded in agreement, some only giggled.

As the evening progressed deep into night, the crowds began to thin. The freaks and non-conformists who travel only in the darkness replaced the last remnants of tourists and students. I decided to leave my new friends. I needed to find some place to go for the night, needed to keep moving. As a parting gift I gave them the key to my hotel room. It had been paid for already. They took it eagerly. It was only much later that I realized that the men in the dark suits were probably waiting for someone to show up at room 1935. No telling what horrors those wild yet innocent youths might have experienced that night. But, they were strong, street savvy kids, I am sure that they knew how to take care of themselves. I wandered off into the darkness, stopping once at a 24-hour liquor store to get a small bottle of cheap booze. I wandered the dim streets of south Berkeley for what was most likely several hours. Thinking incoherently about my situation, Tibetan consonants, and life in general. It might be wise to get out of town, but how? How much did they know about my movements? How much did they know about my intentions? The sight of the man outside the restaurant had awakened me to the fact that they were more wily than I had previously thought. I needed to be more careful in the future. But how to get out of town? Walk? Hitchhike? I didn't think that I could take public transportation safely.

Then, an opportunity presented itself. An opportunity that only a desperate drunk would take mind you, but an opportunity none the less. As I walked in my addled-brained haze I stumbled upon a curious sight. A young man staggered out of a fraternity house and began walking across the street. He was clearly out of his head. The street lamps were not working well on this block, and so I am sure that he did not see me approaching as our two paths crossed. He came across the street to my side and fumbled around with his keys. He was attempting to open the door on a late model blue car. He was not having much success. In my more civic-minded days (which had only ended less than a week ago mind you) I would have stopped the young man from trying to drive off, instead calling him a cab, or at least guiding him back into the house where his friends were likely snuggling into unconscious dreams. But now, in my desperation, resolve strengthened by a good belt of gin, I had a different plan for the young drunkard.

It wasn't something that I had been pondering or intending. It wasn't something that I had considered myself capable of doing. It was an action that had no preceding thought. It was there, so I took it. I crouched behind a parked car and watched the guy play with his keys. I waited until the just the right time, when the key was being turned in the car door lock. Then I made my move. I jumped up from behind the car and ran over, pushing the drunkard out of the way. The key remained in the door as he fell to the ground. I pulled it out and opened the door. The drunk took a few seconds to recover, but he was able to get back on his feet before I was able to start the ignition. The sharp blow must have restored some of his sanity, because he realized at once what was going on. Fortunately for me he must have felt that he could handle the situation by himself, and he did not call out to his neighbors for help. He opened the door to the car and grabbed me by the collar. I fumbled with the key in the ignition. He grabbed me with his other hand. I have never been one who was into brawling. I preferred to win my battles intellectually and legally. But I did have one advantage over this guy. I had a bottle, which I promptly smashed over his head. He fell like a sack of potatoes. I am not proud of the way I beat him, but in the feral reality of that night, the important part was that I beat him. The car was mine. I drove off before he could recover.

I tooled down the streets of the city, across to the Bay Bridge and onto the 101 North, out of town. I had the last thing I needed, my freedom. With this car I had unrestricted freedom. I could go where I wanted without having to look over my shoulder at every bus stop for a man in black. At least for a while anyway. The cops would catch up with this car, but I would dump it somewhere. It would eventually get back to the kid. Serves him right for driving drunk. I decided to go north, up to the wilds of Oregon. Driving that distance on the lonely highway at night gave me time to think about the full implications of my actions that evening.

I had actually stolen a car. Me. I had done some illegal things in the past. Stealing photocopies and such, but that wasn't big stuff. And before my adventure I had done even less wrong. Certainly nothing that one could ever go to jail for. The cash in the suitcase was a fortunate accident. But this! This was a deliberate felony. My walls were breaking down. I felt less restrained by the social fabric that I had been brought up in. I felt a newfound sense of liberty. At last I could do what I wanted, when I wanted to. Before, I thought that the police, the bureaucrats, the social web was there to protect me, like a womb. It kept me safe and warm. And that was a good thing in my childhood. But now I was ready to break free. I didn't need safety, I needed freedom. I sped the car ahead in a subconscious display of my new-found disrespect for the law. 55 miles per hour my ass! This car could do a hundred, easy! I laughed heartily as I drove northward. They wouldn't get me now. Even if they did find this car somewhere, I would be long gone. And all I needed was for them to make one misstep, to make one wrong move and I could disappear forever. Well, not forever, but long enough. Long enough to decipher the document. Long enough to figure out what they were planning. Long enough to learn who I could trust and who I couldn't, and long enough to come up with a way to stop them and make them pay for what they had done to me, my family, my life.

I came back to my senses as I realized that the car was doing almost 120. I didn't have a license remember, and I was driving a recently stolen car. I slammed on the brakes, bringing my speed down to the requisite limit. This is why they get caught, I thought. You always hear about crooks being pulled over and caught for speeding or something. A quick check of the trunk revealed the dead body and the pound of coke. I always thought that was strange. The police never pulled me over, nor my wife, nor any of my friends. How was it that so many crimes were stopped/discovered by police accidentally stumbling upon a criminal with a taillight out? Now I understood. Once you make the decision to commit a felony, once you decide that you are no longer go-ing to play by the rules of society, once you take that giant leap into murder, bank robbery, grand theft auto, you lose all respect for the little laws. These criminals drive the streets thinking, "Look at me, I am free, I am liberty, I live my life the way I want to, need to, and the police and the bureau-crats and the social web can't touch me." Then they get sloppy. Most criminals will actively plan their crimes, they know how to get rid of the knife, they know how to open the safe, but they don't plan on the little things. If I can get away with robbing a bank, how could I think of getting caught for running a red light? That is the trap. That is how they are caught. Maybe that's why the speed limit is set at 55. Maybe that is why those damn red lights are so long or they make you come to a complete stop. It isn't safety they are worried about. It is a trap. They want you to flaunt their little laws. It is easy to catch violators. People who flaunt the little laws are often the ones that also flaunt the big ones. Was the entire highway police system there for a different purpose than what we think? They claim to be there to stop accidents, to stop deaths, but look at other countries. Look at other systems where the government isn't as 'civilized' as the US. They have anarchy on the streets and highways. There are cars everywhere. No respect for yellow curbs or red lights or speed limits. Look at their accident statistics. Are they that much higher than the US? No. Not really. Not an amount that justifies the huge expense of maintaining a force to ensure order and give out large fines. No. They weren't there to keep me safe. They were there to pick the troublemakers out of the pile. On the road the criminals are separated from the meek like gold and dirt are separated in a sieve, and the police are there to make sure that each nugget of gold gets a thorough examination.

This is what I was thinking about, as I drove northward, no specific destination in mind. Just trying to get out of town and lost in America somewhere. I told myself that I needed to stay in control. I couldn't make the mistakes that they wanted me, expected me, to make. There were at least 100 million cars in the US, thousands of them had been stolen. I knew that if I got out of the immediate area, and obeyed all traffic laws, there was no way that the police would catch me. The troopers in Oregon had better things to do. There was no way that they would have the license plate number of every stolen car with a California tag memorized. Most police officers were pretty dim bulbs. They had their little on-board computers to tell them whom to arrest. If I didn't do anything suspicious, there was no way they would even bother to check. I drove northward, into anonymity, into the vast American continent.

# Chapter 5:
# Fear

I won't bore you with the details of the next few weeks. My time is short and your attention is limited. To be honest I'm not sure that I could put together a coherent picture of those days. Suffice it to say that I spent my time on the road, staying at different hotels, sometimes under my name, sometimes under that of Josh Vorhees. Sometimes under a name made up from the concatenation of whatever thoughts were in my head at the time. No one ever bothered to check. Clerks don't care. No one cares. If you have money and seem to be confident of who you are and why you're there no one bothers to question your actions. That was the most important thing that I learned over that time. As long as you seemed to know what was going on, no one will want to put in the effort to contradict you. As I moved further and further north, I found my grip on reality was slackening. I became wild, feral as the days went on. Desperate. The man with unkempt hair and darting eyes. Depression set in. Anxieties set in. I felt that I was still being pursued. I slept little, even in hotels whose security I was sure of. The doors were double locked. I slept in my clothes, meager belongings packed and ready to get out at a moment's notice. Monomania set in. I read and translated. Eyes red and blurry from too many long hours in dim lights with small text. Mind blurry and unfocused. I accomplished little in that time. A few words here, a few words there. Not much real value considering all the time I had put in. Money began to run low. I couldn't live like this. I couldn't keep running. I had to find a place I could hide in for a while. Regain my bearings, my objectivity, my sense of self.

Funny. With all the paranoia I was feeling in those days, with all the looking over my shoulder and sleepless nights and running and hiding, I can't recall ever actually seeing a single one of my pursuers during that time.

I drove from town to town as I went in a generally northward direction. I wound up in Eugene, Oregon. Eugene had the things I was looking for. It was small, quiet, private. It was out of the way, and off the beaten path. It also had the Oregon State University library which, while not as extensive as the one back in Berkeley, did have some of the resources I needed to continue my efforts. I wound up settling there for a time. After a quick trip to the YMCA for a shower, and the mall for some new clothes, I was able to land a job at a coffee house near the campus. I was friendly to the people I worked with, but kept my distance and remained private. There was nothing to indicate that any of the people working there were informants, but it's always good to be on the safe side. I let my hair grow out and grew a beard, to help with the anonymity. I still had the stolen car. Surprisingly no one ever asked about it the whole time I was there.

It was all a big change for me. Perhaps a good change. A growth, a liberation. I slowly got over my fear of coffee. For the first time in my life I was living for today, at least with regards to my career. I lived from paycheck to paycheck. I never considered how I would get ahead, how this step was just one point on the ladder that culminated in CEO. I had no retirement plan, I had no ambitions to rise to management or partner or president. I didn't look at my co-workers as competitors in the race for that extra 1% raise. I just did my job and went home to my work learning and translating.

I worked in the evenings of course, when the shop was filled with students socializing and copying each other's homework assignments. That left my days free to do my research. To my surprise I got pretty good in Tibetan in the four months or so I spent in Oregon. In school I had always thought that if I could devote a lot of time to one subject it would be a lot easier than taking six classes at once, and now that hypothesis was proving to be true. My Devenagari handwriting improved, and, although I had never had a verbal lesson, I felt that the words I said at least sounded right. The document proved to be harder to translate than I had originally hoped. There are some intricacies with the Tibetan language of course, but the main problem was that the document wasn't so much of a story as it was a set of directions. Many of the words, it turned out, were Devenagari transliterations of Peruvian landmarks. Since I had never been to Peru, I wasted hours on some words that didn't appear in any of the available dictionaries.

Somehow, Eugene had given me a sense of belonging, a sense of community. I had grown up in larger, more anonymous cities, so I was not used to having these feelings. Here I walked the streets, I waved to the people. I breathed the fresh air and basked in the green pine that surrounded me. I could have been happy there. I could have stayed there, not worrying about the future, living day to day, moment to moment. It would have been fulfilling. There was even a pretty girl who worked at the coffee shop with me. A student. The overheard gossip was that she thought that I was cute. I never pursued it though, always kept my distance, my privacy. I told myself that it was because I didn't want to involve anyone else, endanger anyone else. Was that true? Maybe I was just not quite ready to live yet. My entire life had been filled with planning and working and learning and striving, but never living, never just living. My guard was up, my defenses were on alert. To have stayed in Eugene would have meant becoming something that I wasn't, something I didn't know how to become. Sure, I could watch it from the sidelines, I could get insights into how to live by interacting with the people of the town, but I couldn't reach out and touch it. It was forever behind glass.

After months of work, I was able to translate most of the first few paragraphs of the document. It was essentially directions to a specific point on a specific mountain that was located in the wilds of the Peruvian cloud forest. It was in very flowery, archaic language, filled with euphemism and imagery. A lot of the directions were so vague and colorful as to be debatable, with phrases such as, 'travel for four days in the direction of the creation of Viracocha'. I interpreted this as west, since my studies had shown that Viracocha was an Inca god who created (among other things) the sun. As I said, I had spent a lot of time with this.

As I was able to fill in more and more words from the translation, I got myself some maps of Peru and did a little calculation of where they were talking about. Loosely following the directions that were given would put you in the general vicinity of the mountain of Machu Picchu, which I understood was some sort of forgotten Inca city/modern tourist attraction. That area was known as the holiest part of the Inca Empire. It was full of deserted, overgrown ruins dedicated to lost gods. The document implied that there was some sort of secret base or outpost up there in the mountains. Did that make sense? Were these people some sort of Peruvian terrorist group? I knew that they had a lot of rebels and drug lords and whatever down there. Maybe this was all wrapped up in some sort of South American rebellion. I remembered that 'Detective' Smith was a small, darkish fellow. I could believe that he was originally South American. But questions still abounded. It couldn't be that simple.

What were they doing in the US? How did they gather enough influence to do what they've been doing to me? Was this a CIA inspired rebel movement? Maybe it was a drug thing. Those guys make piles of money, they could easily buy influence where they needed it. It would only make sense for them to have people on the inside at the local police stations. At the time, some people were saying the CIA was involved in drug smuggling. It all started to fit into place. For the first time, I started to believe that I had a reasonable idea of what was going on. I wished that I could have translated more, but the document changed after the directions were given. A new language. A new secret code. I suppose that I should have been patient, that I should have taken the time to decode the whole manuscript. Oh, how things would have turned out differently if I had. I probably would have thrown the thing away, thinking it was a bad joke, I might have found myself less and less drawn to the mysteries inside it if I had only read about them, instead of experiencing them firsthand. I could have found something else to distract me; love, work, life. But I decided that I couldn't be patient, that I couldn't wait. Now was the time for action. I needed to strike before the trail was cold. I had the location of their secret hideout. The place where they were making all that cocaine. I see now that I was reading a lot into the document that wasn't there, and jumping to conclusions that may not have reflected reality, but I had something to grab onto for the first time in months. I finally had what appeared to be an answer to the craziness that I had been living. Only one question remained, only one thought nagged at me, why Tibetan?

But I couldn't let that tiny inconsistency bother me. I knew what I had to do. I had to go down there and get the answers for myself. I had to go to this 'drug city' in the Andes and get some hard evidence. Then I would go to a third country, in Europe maybe, and send my information anonymously to as many press sources as I could find. One would print it I'm sure. Then the US government will have to go and look, no matter how much these gangsters were paying. Then they would all get arrested. The cartel would be smashed. Then I could go home again. Then I could come back and reveal myself and get to meet the President and win a medal or something.

The first step was figuring out how to get down to Peru. It was easy enough to cruise the highways and byways of backwoods America unnoticed, but it would be a different thing altogether to try some international travel. There are borders to cross and customs officials to pass. It would also take money, a lot of money. I had been slowly depleting the last of the $1000, and the amount coming in from the coffee place was not quite what I needed to make ends meet. I had no credit, I hadn't seen my gold card for months, and I was sure that they had the numbers traced anyway. I couldn't use that to get a ticket. I thought about taking the cash out of the till. The place cleared a few hundred a day, I could easily cop enough for a ticket. But I decided against that course of action. Not because of any moral compulsion, but because I knew that airlines were required to report cash purchases of tickets. The US government is concerned with smugglers and other riff-raff coming and going without an easily followed paper trail. No, cash wouldn't help. I settled on stealing a credit card. I waited until someone used credit to buy something from the store, then I palmed the carbon. I called an airline and booked two tickets to Cusco Peru, one in the name of Josh Vorhees, and the other in the name of the credit card owner. I did that so it wouldn't look so suspicious. I made the reservations for the next day. Then grabbed about $500 from the till and left work, packed up my things, and drove up to Portland to catch my flight.

On the way I stopped to pick up some gear. I ran into a mall and used some of the stolen cash to get a pair of hiking boots and some other camping equipment. I also bought a suitcase, so that I would look like a legitimate traveler. That blew almost half of the money I took. I got to Portland and slept in my car in the airport parking lot. I say my car. It had been mine for the last four months. This was the last I would see of it. That morning I put a note on the dashboard advising the parking attendants to call the Berkeley police department, and left her sitting there. I had intended to leave some money in the car as some sort of compensation, but I didn't have any to spare. I really didn't feel that bad about it. I wanted to. I should have. Everything from my background told me that I should feel bad about stealing this guy's car. But I didn't. Maybe my emotions had been blown out by the events of the past few months. There was too much stress. There was too much fear. There was too much ennui. I didn't realize it until later, but that seemed to be the point in my life when I started to fully live for myself, and fully supplant the needs of others with my own needs. Ethical egoism. The car was only one part of it. What about the credit card fraud? What about the money stolen from my employers, who had done only good things for me over the past few months? I felt nothing. I just took what I needed and I left.

I entered the airport with several hours to go before my flight. I only had one obstacle left to clear. How do I get on the plane and past customs without any ID? I approached the counter and picked up my ticket. No police around. The credit card people had not figured out my scam yet. Good. I handed my suitcase to the woman at the ticket counter to get it checked. It held the gun I had been carrying since San Francisco. I know that they x-ray carry on luggage, but I was under the impression that they just put checked luggage through a bomb detector. She took the case and I watched it disappear down the conveyor belt. I proceeded to the gate. A bubbly airline worker was standing around, assigning seats. I handed her the ticket for a boarding pass. She stamped it in a few places and put some information into the computer. I was sweating a bit. She asked me some questions about seats and strange gifts.

"Now, this plane is going to Peru, so I'll need to see your passport." I handed her the Joshua Vorhees passport. This was the weak link in my plan. Josh looked nothing like me, and the passport was stolen four months ago and had probably been reported to the police by now. I looked around nervously to see if agents were coming in. It could have all been a set up. There could have been people looking to see if/when Joshua Vorhees got on a plane somewhere. "Thank you, have a nice trip." The attendant handed me back the passport. I learned a valuable lesson that day. People don't care. I could have handed her a hand-written slip of paper with the word 'passport' written on it and she wouldn't have cared. The key is this: people don't want trouble. If I had been caught using a fake passport it would have caused all sorts of hassle and trouble and even maybe danger for this girl, so she chose to ignore a possible discrepancy in order to make it to her next cigarette break on time. As long as I seemed confident and looked like I was not expecting trouble, she felt no compulsion to make it. I think that this woman, like most other people in our society today, believed that if there really were a problem, then somebody else would have noticed it already.

I went to a seat and quietly read a magazine until boarding time. I kept an eye out for anyone who might try to stop me from boarding. I sat a gate over from where my plane was leaving, just to be sure that I would see anyone looking for me before I was spotted. A few times I saw men in black suits, but they seemed to be just businessmen with no special secrets to hide. I guess, looking back, it was silly for me to get so upset at a certain type of dress. It would have been perfectly reasonable for their agents to be dressed up in jeans, a Hawaiian shirt, or even a ball gown, but for some reason that possibility didn't occur to me at the time. The people that were chasing me were a certain breed, always identical, always suspicious, never quite fitting in with the rest of the masses, faceless, nameless. I felt that I could spot them a mile away. Perhaps it is some sort of Jungian ancestral memory.

After boarding the plane, an announcement came that there were some mechanical difficulties and that the aircraft would be an hour or so late into Los Angeles. The flight made a stop in LA before heading out to Cusco. There was nothing that I could do about the delay, and I was pretty much trapped on the plane, so I sat back and tried to relax with an in-flight magazine. The plane eventually took off and after a turbulent trip, touched down in LA an hour or so late. This meant that the plane leaving from LA to Peru had left without me. I had missed the connection. An attendant met me at the gate and they handed me a free meal coupon and a plane ticket for a later flight to Peru. At the time I suspected that the mechanical difficulties were caused by my adversaries in order to disrupt my plans, or that it was part of a sting to corner me in the Los Angeles Airport. I couldn't have been more wrong. I didn't find out about it until later, but the original flight that I had been booked on crashed into the Pacific Ocean, all aboard were lost. A cause for the accident was never found, but I knew what happened. What sort of people would crash a jetliner full of innocents to try to stop me from learning their secrets? And what secrets were so worth hiding?

Of course at the time I was blissfully unaware of what was going on in the air a thousand miles south, and so I waited quietly at the airport, munching on bad airport pizza and keeping a paranoid eye out for anyone showing undo interest in me. The plane I eventually got on was mostly filled with tourists, either Americans vacationing south or Peruvians returning from the north. The plane disembarked at the airport in Cusco, the highest airport in the world. It had been a long flight and everybody on board was a bit cranky and excited to reach their destination. There was the typical crush as the passengers moved through the airport. I was disturbed by something that I saw while deplaning, albeit briefly. As I said, most of the people on the plane were tourists and were dressed in typical tourist clothing. However, I caught a glimpse of one passenger, far ahead in the plane's corridor, who seemed to be wearing the same dark suit that I had come to fear so much. I tried to push my way ahead to get a closer look, but I was held back by the throngs of people pulling large luggage from the overhead bins. By the time I reached the airport runway the man had disappeared from view.

Unlike planes in the big airports, planes in the third world don't pull up and attach themselves to the gate. I got off the plane and had to walk down the tarmac a way to a bus that was waiting to drive us to the proper terminal. I pulled my luggage along and jumped into the waiting bus, which was covered in soot, and spraying carbon monoxide fumes everywhere. It was very crowded on the bus. There is never enough room to take everyone in one trip, and no one wants to waste precious vacation time. I was pushed up against a small Peruvian man. He was dark and greasy. He wore a tattered, blue, plaid shirt and dirty jeans. An old, red baseball cap sat on his head. He looked up at me and smiled with a mouth filled with half rotten teeth. I smiled back politely and turned, trying to retain some modicum of personal space in the hot, overrun bus.

There was a tapping on my shoulder. I turned around to see the man smiling up at me again. The bus jerked and I almost fell against him. I tried to back up, but there was no room. Other passengers owned that space now.

"Have you accepted Jesus as your personal savior?" said the man, with a thick Spanish accent.

"I'm a Christian, yes," I replied. The easiest way to deal with zealots is to agree with them. Then they have no compulsion to convert you. The man leaned in and stared at me intently. Trying to decide if I was telling the truth.

"It is an easy thing to say, but it means nothing. You have to live it. Otherwise it is nothing." He tapped a thick dirty finger against the side of his head. Tap, tap, tap. Then he shook his head up and down slowly, apparently pleased that he had passed on an exceptionally contemplative piece of information. He smiled.

"This is for you. Go with God." He handed me a pamphlet of some sort. I took it and pushed it into my pocket without looking at it. The bus jerked to a stop in front of the terminal. The man giggled a bit and tapped his head a few more times. Then the push of passengers separated us in the rush to get to the customs gate.

The inside of the airport was a bit of a zoo, people all over the place, luggage all over the place. The intercom shouts instructions in unintelligible Spanish. A baby is crying. There were long lines of people waiting to have their passports stamped by officials. One line was much smaller than the others. Almost no one at all. I saw the back of a man passing through that gate. He was wearing a black suit and a dark, fedora hat. I pushed through the crowd to get a better look. Making my way towards the empty gate.

"Diplomats only," said a guard in Spanish. He blocked my path and pointed back toward the longer, tourist lines. "Diplomats only sir." The man in the dark suit had disappeared into the crowd on the other side of the customs gates. I guess it was nothing. I walked back to the end of the tourist line. It went faster than I had thought it would, and I got to the customs official in a few minutes. She asked me for my passport. I fumbled through my pockets and pulled Mr. Vorhees' passport out. This would be the harder test. The clerk at the Portland airport was just an airline employee. This woman here was an actual government official. My passport was in the same pocket that I had stuffed my tickets and the pamphlet from the Christian, and it all came out together. I extricated the passport from the other papers and handed it to the official. She took the passport and looked at it. I began to put the rest of the stuff away when I noticed a cord. On closer inspection, the man had given me more than a pamphlet, folded inside of it was a necklace. I pulled it out. On a plain black cord was a small metal cross. It wasn't like any other cross I had seen. It was plain, but right in the middle was a circle with a carving of a flower. A rose. I looked nervously at the official while I fingered the necklace. She looked at me. Then she looked at the picture. Then she looked at me again. It was obvious to anyone that I was not the person in the picture. I was trying to sneak into Peru on a fake passport. She looked at the picture again. Then she looked at the necklace that I had dangling from my hands. She was going to call the police. They were going to cart me off to jail. Peruvian jail. Beads of sweat started to form on my forehead. She looked at me. I had told myself that this was all a confidence game. That as long as I looked like I belonged, no one would question me. She looked at the passport. She looked at the necklace. My left hand started shaking. They were going to send me back. Send me back to the US. I knew it was going to happen. They would forward the name on the passport to the police. The men in black would get a hold of that for sure. They would be waiting. Waiting at the airport. They would disappear me for certain. They would

"Thank you sir, move along," said the woman in Spanish. She stamped the passport with an entry visa and handed it back to me. I shook off the panic and moved along. I paid my 'entry tax' and went to wait for my luggage. My bag made it down the conveyor. I grabbed it quickly and moved towards the exit. I didn't want to waste any time. There was another line to wait in of course. At first I didn't know what it was for, but as I approached the front I could see. It was a random baggage search. People were told to press a button that was hooked up to a randomizer. For most people a green light flashed and they passed without incident, for some people though, a red light flashed and they had to empty their bags for the customs men. I watched as the people in front of me took their chances. Green, green, red, green, red, green, green, green, green. The panic that I had been able to hide at the visa desk came back. If they found the gun in my case who knows what would happen. I could make a break for it. I didn't see any armed guards around. But who knows what lies outside? Three people to go. Red light. Two people to go, green light. One person to go, green light. I stepped up to the button. The customs man looked at me, trying to guess from my appearance if I had anything to hide. I reached out towards the button. This could have been the end of my journey. I pushed the button. It was only a second for a light to go on, but it felt like a lifetime. Green. I quickly grabbed by case and moved on. There were taxi drivers waiting, pushing each other, for a chance to drive, for a chance to gouge. One put his arm around my shoulders and asked where I wanted to go. It was too easy. I shrugged him off and left the terminal. Outside there were other cab drivers unloading. I grabbed one and told him to take me to a hotel near the city center. I thought that it was safer that way. If I picked a driver who hadn't noticed me yet, then the chance of him being involved in anything besides driving was lessened. Even so, I took the extra precaution of leaving the hotel he brought me to and walking a few blocks down to another place.

It was early morning in the city. Peasants were coming down from the hills in ones and twos, leading their llamas, carrying their packs. These people made a good living on the tourist trade. Selling trinkets and photo opportunities. I was able to check into to a hostel rather quickly and cheaply.

Then I walked the few blocks to the Plaza des Armes in the center of town. I sat on a bench near the spot where the last of the Inca leaders were executed, and watched the people moving along on their way to their daily business. Schoolchildren skipped by in packs of plaid skirts and black trousers. Less fortunate children were beginning to make their way to the square with shoeshine kits in hand, ready to earn a days wage. None of the stores were open yet, so I decided to walk through the streets for a little sightseeing. I walked for an hour or two up and down the steep cobblestone streets of the old city. Stray dogs jogged past me on missions known only to them. After one steep hill I had to stop and catch my breath. The air is clean and fresh up there, but the place is high, not a lot of oxygen. I leaned up against the wall of a shop and put my hands on my knees, gasping. The door to the shop opened. A man came out and propped the door. He placed a welcome sign on the sidewalk and began to hang his weavings and baubles in the doorway. He looked at me and smiled. "This town is very steep," I said to him in broken Spanish.

"Yes, but it is very beautiful is it not?" He pointed to the view of the hills surrounding the town. They were dotted with little white houses. The sky was bright and the air was crisp. I agreed with him that the town was an incredible sight. "You have to drink some coca tea," he told me. "That is good for the altitude." I nodded in agreement. "You are on vacation, yes? Where are you from?" he asked. My defenses kicked. Was he prodding me for information? I was now approaching the belly of the beast, there was bound to be more risk here than in California. Was he a plant to catch tourists who seemed a bit too inquisitive? I told him that I had to go. I walked along the street hurriedly. The shops were open now. I descended the hill down to the Plaza des Armes. There are a number of travel agencies there, all of which want to book you for a hike. I was able to pick up a fairly detailed map of the region from one of them. I also bought an instant camera. I needed proof. Then I went back to my room and started to make up a detailed plan for my next step.

There is an old Inca trail that connects many of the main ruins of the Inca Empire. People today hike along its eighty-kilometer length and enjoy the views and history. I was able to trace out the directions given in the document on the map. They seemed to point to a spot near the Inca trail, maybe ten kilometers from the famous ruins of Machu Picchu. The information implied that the base or whatever it was was located at the top of a mountain, unnamed on the map. I didn't have to follow the directions in the document exactly, I could skip right ahead by taking the tourist train to the Machu Picchu ruins. That would save me from hiking over seventy kilometers, which I must admit, would have been difficult at that altitude. I would have enough problems hiking the few miles to the mountain.

I folded up the maps and went back to the Plaza for some breakfast. I ate well and cheaply, and had several cups of the local coca tea. I don't know if that helped with the altitude sickness, but it tasted good, and it was something warm for a chilly morning. Then I went to another tourist agency and bought a ticket for the next day's train ride to the ruins. I spent the rest of the day in town, drinking even more coca tea and taking a look at the sights. I had never been to South America before, and I had some time to kill. The town was very appealing, and I enjoyed myself despite my constant surveillance for any adversaries. You may think that it was frivolous to spend the day touring when I had such a serious mission to undertake, but I thought that if I stayed in one place too long I would be more vulnerable. By walking around the city I was almost untraceable. Plus, I was supposed to be a tourist. It would have aroused more attention if I didn't look at things.

Most of the day went without incident, and near dusk I found myself standing in front of a church that was almost at the pinnacle of the hilltop north of town. The church had a yard, which was unusual for that area, and I stood looking down on the city, down on the Plaza des Armes. I was watching the city's lights blink on, one by one. There was some motion to my left, and I saw a man coming down the road, dressed in a suit. In the dusk it was hard to tell what color, but I didn't want to take any chances. I began moving the other way down the street. Then I noticed that there were two more men coming from that direction. Maybe it was just a coincidence, but I wasn't prepared to take chances. I reached into my jacket and got a hold of my gun. I had shot my way out of a situation back in Sacramento, I was prepared to do so again. I backed up and went in the only other direction I could go, I ducked into the church. There was an evening service going on. I felt that the men in black wouldn't make their move in front of all these people. I sat down on an ancient mahogany pew in the back and tried to look inconspicuous. The place was filled with true Peruvian natives, it didn't look like this church had any members of Spanish decent. Just the dark, poor people that had been economically pushed up out of the valley that was theirs by birthright. The preacher was speaking in rapid fire Spanish and I didn't understand more than a few words. After the shaking stopped and I felt safe that the men in black weren't right behind me, I began to look around. I noticed something about the main altar. It was filled with the gold and silver that most other altars in this region had, but the cross was different. It was wooden cross, ten feet tall, but instead of having a statue of Jesus tacked to it, it just had a picture of a rose, just like the cross the man at the airport gave to me. Further inspection of the walls showed that there were no pictures of any saints or apostles. No icons at all, just the repeating pattern of the rose and the cross. Many of the natives were sitting, eyes closed, hands shaking with the power of the sermon. The place began to spook me more than the men in the alley. Was this some sort of cult? I got up to leave. A large man standing at the doorway blocked my path. In desperation I pulled out the cross that I had received at the airport. It looked the same as the one on the wall. It worked. He nodded and held the door open for me. He patted me on the back as I moved past him. I immediately ran back to the hotel. I didn't get much sleep that evening. All night long I thought that I heard a faint scratching at my bedroom door.

The next morning, I got up before dawn and made it to the train station for the 6 am locomotive. It was a comfortable train, but the trip was over three hours long. I initially tried to get some rest, but between the jostling of the cars, and the incredible views, I spent most of my time just staring out the window. The peasants along the train tracks were all very friendly, waving as we passed by. Tourists threw pencils or candy or whatever they had in their purse out the windows to the children. The train pulled into a station for refueling. In the interim minutes, the windows of passenger cars were besieged by hundreds of local peasants trying to sell handicrafts to the sightseers. "Choclo, Maize, Choclo," called one old woman with a tray full of hot corn on the cob. Other women tried to sell dolls, bags, jewelry, rainforest bugs the size of your hand that had been killed, pinned and framed. Train attendants blocked the doors. The peasants weren't allowed to get on. "Choclo, Maize, Choclo." I watched the activity on the platform. There was nothing around here. No houses were in view, where were these people coming from? "Choclo, Maize, Choclo." The woman in the seat in front of me was leaning out the window, arguing over the price of a needlework handbag. "Choclo, Maize, Choclo." The people here must have hiked a ways to make it to this platform. There were a lot of them. A whole army, convinced that the only way they could make a living was off the charity of travelers from the developed world. "Choclo, Maize, Choclo." If only they just put their efforts towards building something for themselves. This place was destined to always have nothing. These people were destined to live in the mud, scrabbling a living by selling corn and baubles. "Choclo, Maize, Choclo." They were so far behind, they would never be able to catch up. They weren't even trying. They had been brainwashed well. In their world view, there was nothing but this. There was nothing but scrabbling, nothing but trinkets. My life in San Francisco was so different from theirs that I doubt that they would even be able to comprehend it. Did these people even consider the train passengers to be humans? Two cultures come into contact. On the platform stood people who knew nothing but selling trinkets for pennies, onboard sit consumers who do nothing but collect as many trinkets as they can find. A symbiosis has developed. No one cares what they are making, no one cares what they are buying. Just create and consume, create and consume. No one will question the system, no one will ask why this place exists. Questions like that are not in the vocabulary of either the peasant or the tourist. They have not been taught to think.

Behind the commotion on the platform a few people stood around. Mostly they looked like train workers. My eye spotted two men wearing dark suits. "Choclo, Maize, Choclo." They seemed out of place here. This was a place for ponchos, rags, and tattered sandals, not a place for suits. They had not spotted me in the train window, they were talking to each other. "Choclo, Maize, Choclo." A railroad worker came over and started speaking to them. The peasants were trying to sell their wares. The men spoke to the train worker. They handed something to him. He smiled. "Choclo, Maize, Choclo." Were they looking for me? Did the worker give them the information they needed? Would they see me in the window? "Choclo, Maize, Choclo." I left my seat and hid in the bathroom until the train had moved well out of the station.

Back in my seat, I remembered the cross that I had found in my pocket the other day, the one that had gotten me out of the strange church. I pulled it out. I still had the pamphlet the man in the airport had given me. I examined the cross again. It didn't seem to be worth anything. I didn't have anything else to do with it, so I put it on. Maybe it would help me if I ever met some more of the cultists, or even if I ran afoul of some Christian thieves. I read the man's pamphlet, trying to get an idea of the sect that he was involved in. It was a typical apocalyptic warning that talked about how you would only be saved by following the instructions herein. I was surprised to see that it didn't solicit money, or even have an address. It talked a lot about symbology. It explained how the cross was a physical representation of the numerical ratio 3:2, and how the rose was the symbolic representation of the perpetual series. It got into fractals and strange geometries and how the world was built on ratios, and how ratios were the language of God, and how the word of God was just a vibrational pattern that the universe was founded upon. Later I was to learn more about all of this and other principles of the secret knowledge that we've been taught to discount, but for now it was all just gibberish and zealotry, and I dismissed it within a few minutes.

As the locomotive wended its way from the high desert to the cloud forest, the world changed from dusky brown to verdant green. A few hours after leaving Cusco, the train pulled to a stop in the town of Agua Caliente. From there it was a short bus ride to the top of the mountain and the ruins at Machu Picchu. The travel company had given me a bus voucher. There was a rush as the people left the platform and moved down the one dirt street of the town to where the buses sat idling. They would leave in about an hour. I decided to get breakfast. Agua Caliente is the middle of nowhere. The town consists of a train station, two greasy hotels, a few low cost restaurants, and a several hundred peasants who sell things to tourists and wayfarers. They were very persistent with me. "Mister, mister," they called. They all had something for sale, t-shirts, pottery, one even had a selection of ritual knives that were to be used in sacrifices. They pushed and pulled me in all directions, fighting each other over the chance to sell me a bauble, to earn a few pennies. They crowded around my fellow passengers as well. It all made me nervous. Here in the jungle I was close to a power base. I could feel it in my soul. These people could be a last line of defense. A large crowd, a quick poke in the gut with a knife. Even if the police here weren't on the take there was little chance that they could catch anyone. I was alone. No one knew I was here. I needed to keep my exposure down. I pushed my way hurriedly through the crowd to the buses. It was too dangerous to get breakfast. I handed my voucher to the driver and sat on the waiting bus until it left.

Eventually the bus started off on the arduous trip up the mountain. I kept a vigil out the window for anything suspicious, but all I saw was green. The bus unloaded near the top of the mountain and the tourists began to queue up with tour guides to see the sights. Looking back on my memories I can imagine that the place was an incredible spectacle to behold, but at the time I was unable to enjoy the view. I was focused on my mission. There was a tourist map of the area painted on the wall of a ranger's station, flaked and faded. It pointed me towards the 'Inca Trail' that I needed to follow. The trail was higher up on the mountain than the bus stop, and you needed to walk through the ruins to get to the starting point. My heart was racing. I felt like I was at a pulse point for the world. Mountains towered above me. I imagined what the trailhead would look like. There were rangers all around, there was probably a ranger there, waiting and acknowledging all who passed. He might be waiting for me. Might be told to stop me. I was sure that the men in the black suits had taken precautions. They knew that I had the document didn't they? They must have figured that if I came to Peru I must have been able to translate at least the first part. Who knows what defenses they might have? It would be a sad end to my story if I wound up shot dead in the jungle.

I decided not to risk the trailhead. I climbed through the brush up the side of the mountain, coming out on the stone path half a mile or so from the rangers waiting to stop me. I was a bit wet and somewhat muddy, but none the worse for wear as I started down the trail. I noticed some tourists in this area. There was an old Inca guardhouse down this road a mile or so. The hardiest sightseers traveled back and forth from that. At the guardhouse ruin, a small group asked me to take a picture for them. I refused and moved on. I didn't want to talk to anyone. I needed to be invisible. Further down the trail there was no one. Perhaps one or two groups made the hike from Cusco each day. Hopefully I wouldn't bump into anyone else.

The air was hot, yet it drizzled all day. I put my hood up and down as I tried in vain to alternately protect myself from the rain and from the sweltering heat. I walked for several hours, stopping frequently to check my compass and the map. I was getting closer. The trail was about ten feet wide, in some places a little narrower. It clung to the side of the mountain. To my right was an almost vertical wall of dirt and jungle flora. To my left was a drop of several hundred feet. God forbid the Peruvian government install a guardrail. The stones that made up the trail were broken and slippery from the rain, but the trail was wide enough that I was able to make good progress without too much vertigo.

It took about three hours of walking to come to the point where I would diverge from the Inca Trail. I had no idea what to suspect about my access. Would there be a guard post of some sort? Would I have to hack my way through the underbrush? Was the site only accessible by helicopter? Was I even anywhere near the right place? The answer was a fork in the trail, clearly marked. A sign pointed the way to Machu Picchu. The other path was not labeled, but built with the same stones as the rest of the trail. Did the Inca build this path too? What was up there? Why didn't errant tourists go up and see for themselves? I suppose that the only ones that made it this far had already hiked seventy-five kilometers in an effort to see the famous ruins, and so no one ever bothered to see what was down this other trail. There were no guards here because there was no need. No attention would be drawn. I checked my map once more to be sure of myself and started up this mysterious trail.

There were only about three miles to go between the fork and the top of the mountain that the document had pointed out, as the crow flies. I came to a small clearing and was able to see my destination fully for the first time. It was an imposing mountain, green and very vertical. I had no climbing experience and hadn't even brought a rope. I guess I figured that if there was something up there, there would be a way to reach it. I took a minute to rest and moved on. The trail started to go up the mountain, and then around. Steep, but not too difficult. It was narrower here. The trail was only about five feet wide, and there were overhangs and boulders that blocked part of the path, so that at times I was only inches from the edge. Small tufts of grass clung to the side of the mountain up here. It must have been a 75 degree ascent. There was nothing to hold on to. No trees, just grass, dirt, the odd scraggly bush, a few rocks. If you slipped off the edge you wouldn't stop tumbling until you reached the river some two thousand feet below. There was nothing here but nature, nothing here but green. The silence was almost deafening to a city boy such as myself. A large bird circled overhead, looking for supper. I had heard that there were no large predators this high, but I was still worried. I was also getting worried because I had not seen any signs of civilization or activity. You would think that if there were a covert drug factory around here there would be signs. Guards with guns, trucks backfiring, helicopters in the sky, factory noises, but there was nothing. Just the occasional rustle of some small lizard hiding in the bush. The trail clung to the side of the peak as it went upwards. I was pretty tired. I had never been one for physical exercise, and the sheer altitude made this climb even harder. I stopped, ready to give up, wondering if I even had the strength to make it back to the bottom. I remembered something that I was once told about boot camp. I was watching a movie about the military and I asked why they subject people to that mental torture. A former marine told me that the purpose was to prove to you that no matter how tired you are, and no matter how scared you are you can always take one more step. That advice came back to me now. I stood up and took a step. My muscles ached, I was out of breath, I was scared that I would fall to my death in this desolate jungle, but I took a step. Then another one, then another one. You want to know how to climb a mountain, or run a marathon? You want to know how someone can swim the English Channel? The answer is simple. No matter what happens, don't stop, just don't stop. Just take another step.

One more step, one more step, I'll turn around after just one more step. I was trudging along, repeating this to myself as I walked along a section of the trail that followed a large dent in the mountainside. The trail curved acutely instead of obliquely. The upshot of this was that for the first time since I began my climb, a point existed where you could see the trail behind you a half mile or so. I stopped to catch my breath, and I thought I heard a noise. A rock falls. I looked in the direction and was surprised to see a small figure moving along the trail towards me. I pulled out my binoculars and took a better look. There was a single man, dressed in a clean black business suit, walking deliberately along the trail in my direction. I couldn't be sure at this distance if it was the one I had seen at the airport, but I was sure that he was one of them. Had they found me? Was he here to track my movements and stop me? Was he here on other business on the mountaintop? He was a ways behind me, and probably had not seen me yet, but he was gaining. I got back up and I pushed onward at a faster pace.

A short while after that, the trial became much more vertical. The rock path fell away and became more like a series of stepping stones. Some parts were so vertical that you could grab the next few stones with your hands and pull yourself up. There were some trees up in this area, and the branches were sometimes useful. There was even a section where you had to go through a small rock tunnel to continue. It was no longer possible to catch my breath. One more step.

I pulled myself up, higher and higher. The trail now was little more than a set of flatter rocks stuck to the side of a mountain. It meandered back and forth, left and right as it went up. Parts were mostly overgrown. Once I slipped and fell a few feet before I grabbed onto a branch. A stone loosened by my foot tumbled down, you couldn't hear it hit bottom. I looked up and all I saw was more mountain. As high as I had climbed there seemed to be an eternity more to go. I wanted to give up. I looked down, vertigo began to overtake me as my eyes tried to adjust to the perspective. A narrow trail of rocks a few feet below me, then nothing for thousands of feet. The green jungle floor beckoned from a long distance away. Your mind is not used to looking down and not seeing anything within half a mile. I heard a twig break, not a hundred feet below me on the trail. It was the man in black. I couldn't see him because the trail was winding, but I knew he was there. I knew that he was catching up. I fingered the gun in my pocket. I continued to climb, one more step, one more step.

The weather took a turn for the worse. A fog began to roll in. It obscured the view of the valley. All that existed in the universe was a few feet of mountain above and below me, myself, and the invisible pursuer that was rapidly approaching. I climbed higher, hands covered with mud. The man was closer now. I still couldn't see him, but I could hear his breath as he strained for more of the thin air. Everything was damp and slippery. He was only a few feet behind me now. I climbed faster, harder. Legs strained with the effort. I had to stop that guy. He was coming for me. He was right behind me now. He would catch up to me soon, I didn't have the strength to stay ahead of him. What would he do when he caught up to me? His brethren had already taken shots at me on several occasions, he would do likewise. It was going to have to be a fight. I resolved that if I was going to make a final stand, it would be on my terms, not his. The trail wound around a boulder to an area that was pretty flat. I crouched behind the big rock. When he caught up I would be rested. I would have the element of surprise. I pulled out my gun. He shouldn't see me until it was too late. Rain began to fall. I could hear him coming. He was expecting me to still be running, but I was going to turn the tables on him. I needed answers, maybe he could tell me. I saw his hand as he grabbed onto the boulder I was hiding behind. It was muddy and worn. These people made such a big show of being impeccably dressed, but he was dirty, fallible, just like me. Then a foot appeared. He walked right past me in his single minded pursuit. I stood up and pointed the gun at him. I told him to stop. He turned. Something otherworldly in his eyes. He jumped at me. I tried to fire the gun. He got there too fast. We grappled. Rolled around in the mud and rocks. The gun went flying. I grabbed for it in the dirt. He grabbed for me. It fell off the edge, bouncing downwards into the fog. He was on top of me, choking me. I was never a good fighter. I had my legs under him. I kicked to get him off of me. He fell backwards. Lost his balance on the ledge. If it had been a few feet wider he would have recovered, he would have come back and killed me, but as it was, he fell. His hand caught a rock as he slipped over the edge. I got up and went over to him. I put out my hand to help him up, instinctively. The rock gave way. I watched him fall down, down, into the fog. There was no stopping until the river several thousand feet below. I listened as the thud, thud, of his tumbling fell away into the distance. There was no scream. Have you heard the sound of a man falling to his death? The cracks of the bones and the thuds of the soft tissue, the scraping and ripping of clothes and skin. Your body instinctively knows the sound, is repulsed by it. Sometimes when I am lying alone at night, I can still hear it. The sound haunts me.

I lay in the mud for quite a while, rain pouring down on me, my heart beating wildly in my chest. My first thoughts were of myself. I stared at the white void beneath the ledge and imagined myself plunging into oblivion. I had come pretty close. This wasn't a ride at the amusement park. The dangers here were real. My heart pounded for at least ten minutes as I contemplated my own death and tried to recover from that mortal fight in the sparse air. We are so used to seeing death on television, we are so used to toying with it in the relative safety of the ski slope or the rollercoaster. But rarely do we ever truly think about actually giving up the ghost. Sit and think long and hard and directly confront the realistic possibility of our own demise. It is easier to quickly change channels and not worry about it. As I began to catch my breath, my thoughts turned to the man in black who had met his death on this peak. Regardless of who he had been, he was a man, was he not? Now he was dead. I saw the policeman in San Francisco get shot, but I don't know what happened to him. The image of those people in my office was lost in a blur of panic and terror. Plus, they were dead before I got there. This man though, this man had died right before my eyes (or at least in the fog before my eyes). I saw him as the stone slipped, I looked into his face, I can still visualize his hand in front of me, gripping the rock with all the strength he had. It wasn't enough. He was dead now.

That was a powerful thing. Someone that was just here was now not. An unrecoverable event had just occurred. And it was my fault. I pushed him. I was now tainted. A murderer. No, I couldn't let myself think that. I was in the right. He attacked me. Self-defense. All I wanted was answers, I wasn't going to kill him. I wasn't going to use the gun, I told myself. Didn't I try to help him at the end? No jury would convict me. I only pushed him off to stop him from killing me. When he fell I tried to save him, it isn't my fault the rock gave way, right?

Well, whatever happened, and whether it was my fault or not, it was over. I was once again alone on the mountain. A bird calls to its mate. There was nothing to do but to press onwards, upwards. The rain lifted. It was afternoon already. For the first time I wondered what I would do once nightfall occurred. I somehow expected that all of my questions would be answered at the top of the mountain. I was focused on that goal, and saw nothing past it. The trail became harder for a while. There were times when I thought that further ascent would be impossible. It was too steep. But I pushed onwards. One more step, one more step. To turn around now would negate so much of the last few months. I had to learn what was at the top. I constantly felt that I was about to slip and fall to my death, but I trudged forward. An eerie calm came over me, almost an acceptance of my fate. After a time, the trail began to soften up again. It became wider, less steep. I started to see the signs of construction on the mountainside. Small things at first, bricks piled to shore up weak sections of the trail. It looked old. The bricks seemed to be hewn in the same style as the bricks of the Inca ruins. I marveled at the thought of their construction. Here I was, barely able to survive the trek with all of the marvels of modern technology. The Inca came up here without hiking boots, without nutritional sports drinks, without waterproof pullovers. And they weren't just climbing, they were building. Obviously there was something special at the top of this peak for them.

I reached a stone staircase. The trail became easier after that. Steps instead of rocks. I looked above me, the summit was still lost in the fog, but there was evidence of buildings. Ruins started appearing. Small ones at first, then larger structures. I could see some areas that looked like they had been used for step farming. The trail ended at the entrance to a small cave. I pulled myself through. It was only about twenty feet long, but it was narrow. I had to take off my pack and drag it through after me. On the other side of the cave were more stairs going upwards. This was the main part of the Inca 'city'. There were ruins all over the place. I am not an archeologist, so I can't say what it was all used for, but it looked a lot like the ruins at Machu Picchu, although not quite as extensive. My eye was drawn to a piece of cloth that was blowing around from the ruins of one house, roof long since caved in. I looked inside. I could see amid the ruins some household items, bowls, furs, that sort of thing. This place had not been picked over by looters and scientists. What was going on here? Didn't the explorers and anthropologists come this way? I dug through the ruins of some of the other houses. There were similar items. This would be a treasure trove for a scientist, why was it never discovered? It wasn't hidden in any way.

As I walked further up, I saw buildings that were not quite as ruined. The bricks were made of better construction. I guess that this was the affluent part of town. These houses yielded the biggest treasure. Inside of a few alcoves were idols. Golden statues of old Inca gods. They were heavy too. Solid. I could see how looters might ignore the broken pottery, but I was surprised to see gold and gems, free for the taking. Maybe it wasn't drug smuggling that was going on up here, perhaps it was grave robbing. I continued onwards. I still heard no sounds beyond the light drizzle and the rustling of the winds. If this place was so important, where was everybody? If this was a secret worth killing people to keep, why wasn't anyone here to guard it? Was that lone man I pushed off the cliff the only thing stopping people from coming up here? If they were so interested in keeping this a secret they must want it for themselves right? If that is true, then why wasn't there anyone up here working?

I continued up the stairs to the top of the mountain. The view here was marvelous, despite the mist. From this vantage I could look down and see most of the settlement as it dropped off into the fog at a dizzying angle. At the very top of the mountain was a large boulder. Underneath the boulder was a cave of some sort. The entrance had once been much larger, but someone had built a wall in the cave entrance, transforming the large, rough fissure into a small, angular door. The wall was made of the same gray stone bricks that the rest of the city was made of. Maybe a little more square than some of the others, but not fancy in any way. No carvings or decorations to mark the place. It only caught my eye at all because of its location at the highest point on the mountain. I rummaged through my sack and got out a flashlight. I entered the door, expecting to find something worth hiding.

What I found inside the cave generated more questions than answers, created more puzzles than solutions. I wouldn't understand the significance of the cave for a while yet, but there was enough in it to make me question some of the things I had been taught as gospel. So many times in school you learn things without regard for other possibilities. Two plus two is four, right? Columbus discovered America. Nevermind the fact that there were millions of humans already living here, nevermind the fact that the Vikings had landed five hundred years previous. No. History was black and white wasn't it? I had never even questioned most of the things I had learned in grade school. Of course there were some minor details that were occasionally revised, but the basic, fundamental facts remained inviolate. But here, under this mountaintop, I learned that everything I had been taught, everything that I had believed about the history of the world, was at least partially untrue.

Inside the cave was a small chamber. The room had alcoves on the walls, each one containing a gold idol of some sort. In the center of the room was a statue of a man. That was very strange to see because the Inca were not known for representational statuary. What was stranger about the statue was that it seemed to be of Egyptian design. It had the head of a bird, I didn't know what type at the time, but I later decided that it was probably an ibis. It also carried the symbols of the Egyptian ruling class, the whip and the crook, in one hand. With its other hand, the statue pointed downward towards the earth. Not straight down, but at an angle. I wasn't sure what the statue was supposed to represent. What I was sure about was the fact that this statue did not belong here. It was not part of what history recorded, what I knew to be truth. It stared at me from beyond time, its presence filled me with a sense of dread and fear and ancestral Jungian loathing. On the base of the statue were some writings. There seemed to be three types. The middle set seemed to be some sort of hieroglyphics or pictograms, possibly an Inca written language, although none are known to today's anthropologists. The set lowest on the base looked a little like Indian, although I wasn't so sure. The top set of writings seemed to be of a different vintage than the rest. It was carved into the stone base in a different hand, sloppily, quickly. It was Spanish. I admit that my Spanish wasn't too good, but I was able to make out the phrase. Roughly, it said;

YOUR GODS LIVE HERE

The statue was pointing downward. Was that the underworld? Perhaps the downward direction of the statue, plus the westward facing were signs of a death cult. That would make sense. But why did it look Egyptian? What were those other two alphabets on the statue? There is no record of the Inca ever having a written language. Why did the Inca build something like this here, when no counterpart could be found in any of the other ruins in their empire? Maybe all the counterparts had been destroyed, and this one way station lay forgotten, lost. Were all the other worship sites smashed by the Spanish conquerors? Were they destroyed by the Inca themselves to keep their sacred knowledge a secret? Was this place built after the Europeans arrived, using the conquistador's knowledge?

Behind the statue was a large slab of polished rock. It was about fifteen feet long, five feet wide, three feet high. It was carved from a single piece of stone. There were dark stains across its surface. I ran my hand along the edge. It was cold to the touch. Somewhere, the sound of water is dripping. I imagined what it would be like to lie on the cold surface, waiting, shivering, bare skin against polished granite. My attention was broken by a shaft of light coming in through the doorway of the cave. The sun was setting now, and it had finally reached an angle to allow the rays to flow directly in. It gave the chamber a surrealistic quality. The shrine faced west. The end of the day. From Peru, the end of the world. The sun was setting over the Pacific Ocean. The edge of the world. This place is the end of the world, and this cave was built by the Inca to celebrate and honor the end of the day, the end of the light, the cave was dedicated to something unnatural, to the dark gods, the destroyers.

I was out of light for the day. There was no way that I was going to attempt the descent back to the Inca trail in the complete darkness of the cloud forest. I was stuck on the top of this peak until morning. The rain had stopped, but it could start again in the night. The safest place to stay would be here inside the cave. It became dark very quickly after sundown. The mountains don't have the warm glow of a nearby city to keep them lit during the night. I lay in the dark for a while, listening fearfully for any sound. I wished that I had not lost my gun over the edge of the cliff. Draped in total blackness, I strained to understand the significance of this place. It was odd indeed, and there did seem to be treasures lying around, but what was so important about it? What here was worth crashing an airliner? Blowing up an office building? Ruining my simple life? Clearly this was only one piece of the puzzle. There was still a lot of the document to be deciphered. This was just a clue, only one clue. I was sure that I could figure it out. It would take some work, but it would happen. There, at the top of the world, in the most holy place of a long-dead god, I resolved to do whatever it took to unravel this enigma.

That night I dreamt I stood in a city. An ancient city. Pillars of solid glass. It was old, older than time itself. It felt like home. It was the primal city. The dream city that all others are modeled after. It was the heart of the world. The people walked proudly through its streets. Marvels on every corner. It was dawn in the city. The first rays of day were coming over the mountainside. Old men bustle along with their belonging strapped to their backs. A woman calls for a lost child. A man runs screaming through the streets. Terror in his eyes. "The sun rises in the wrong place, The sun rises in the wrong place!" he shouts over and over, pointing towards the dawn. In the center of the square is a woman. My wife, my dead wife. She is standing, watching the dawn, watching with dead, vacant eyes. She doesn't see me. Standing with her is a young girl. My child, my unborn child. I move towards them. The streets fill with the panicking masses. The crowd closes in. I can't reach them. I cry out as the crowd pushes me farther and farther from my family. I fall to the ground. Sandals patter around my head. In minutes the square is deserted except for a few papers blowing to and fro. I am alone, all is silent. A light snow begins to fall.

I am awakened by the first light of morning. Facing west, the cave is still dark inside, but bright sunlight can be seen reflected in the mountains and trees of the Peruvian cloud forest. A new day has dawned. Even in the dim morning light, the statue looked imposing. It was good thing that it was too dark to see while I was sleeping. My dreams have been strange enough lately. I packed my things and prepared to leave. I used up both rolls of film on the cave and the surrounding ruins. I knew that it would be some effort to come back here, and I wanted to make sure that I wouldn't have to, even if further information directed me towards more meaning in the ibis-headed figure. My mind was swimming with thoughts. About my life, about meaning, parts of my consciousness were searching my brain for fragmented memories of Egyptian history. Other parts were alert for more signs of the adversary. I admit that a good deal of my thoughts were wrapped up in the marvel of God's creation here in the cloud forest. I even wasted one of my precious few photographs on the mountain vista, but you know that pictures can never capture the feel of places like that.

I did have the presence of mind to take a few items from the ruined village. Some gold figurines, some plain pottery, and a few gems that I pried out of the gleaming eyes of these dead people's holy spirit gods. I knew that I would have a hard time trying to sell the gold statuettes without attracting attention. The pottery should be easy to sell, but wouldn't bring much. Gems are gems though. They have no origin, no history. I realized that when I pulled them from the figurines that I was committing sacrilege to posterity, anthropology, and the memory of these people, but I did it anyway. I had a need. I felt that if I could use these gems to buy me the time I required to figure this thing out, perhaps I could bring this lost tribe of Inca back from obscurity. Perhaps my actions would eventually result in more honor for them, and a better version of the historical record. That is what I told myself as I pulled out their eyes. After my sack was filled, I headed back down the trail. Without the rain and the pursuers I found the trip down much easier. I reached Machu Picchu in time to catch the train back to Cusco that afternoon.

# Chapter 6:
# Glory

The following morning I sat in a Middle Eastern restaurant right on the Plaza des Armes and considered my next move. I needed time to work out more of the coded document, come closer to the truth. Maybe I had gone off half-cocked, traveling to Peru so soon. I had barely scratched the surface of the text. There was a lot more to translate. I had some money now, having sold two of the gems at a seedy pawn shop. Not for anything near what they were worth, but the shopkeeper there didn't ask any questions. My trip up the mountain had taught me that Cusco wasn't near the headquarters of whatever secret group I was searching for. It was just an out of the way rest stop for tourists and traders. Perhaps this would be a good place to bed down for a few months. I spoke a little Spanish after all, and with the constant transition of international tourists in and out of town, it would be easy to go unnoticed. After breakfast, I went up the hills to the old section of city, where the buildings are white-washed plaster and the narrow streets are old cobblestones. I was able to get a room in a small, dilapidated hostel at a cheap long-term rate. I paid my rent for two months right in cash.

Without the pressures of a job (even an insignificant one such as the coffee shop), and with renewed will and horrible curiosity, I was able to make remarkable progress. I utilized the local library, which although not great, was able to provide me with some information I needed for my studies. Luckily the second language of the document turned out to be Quechua, a dialect native to the Andes. I suppose that it was a lucky break that I happened to be in Peru. Strange, archaic, Spanish words were sprinkled throughout, so it wasn't true Quechua, it was the gutterspeak version that came about after the Inca were conquered. The text was filled with bizarre, annotated geometrical figures. This part of the document was written in a different hand, perhaps by a different person altogether. It was possible that this work was written by many, many people, each section only containing a piece of the puzzle. If none of them knew a second language, then the rest of the document would remain a mystery to each of its authors. It was possible that only a few people (maybe no one) knew all of its secrets. The new section started not with phrase like the first section, but with an equation:

$$X^{-2}:X^{-1}::X^{-1}:1::1:X::X:X^2::X^2:X^3$$

I needed to consult a mathematics textbook to understand the significance of this equation. I can try to explain its meaning, but there is no way to make math interesting, so I will just repeat what I read. The set of ratios is the representation of the progression of the Golden Division. The Golden Division is the only continuous proportion that yields a progression in which the terms representing the external universe $(X^2, X^3)$ are an exact, continuous proportional reflection of the internal progression $(X^{-2}, X^{-1})$. Basically it is a proportion. A is to B as B is to C as C is to D. This is one of the most fundamental principles of Sacred Geometry. I didn't know that at the time of course. Sacred Geometry is the science of mathematics by ratios instead of by numerals. It is the fundamental mathematics, the natural mathematics. The primal mathematics. There is no zero in nature. There are no negative numbers. In the real universe, mathematics follows this path:

1/4, 1/3, 1/2, 1, 2, 3, 4, 5

not this one:

-4, -3, -2, -1, 0, 1, 2, 3, 4

Sacred Geometry is the mathematics that the Egyptians used to build the great pyramids at Giza, it is the principle that Pierre L'Enfant used when he laid out the plans for the American capital city of Washington DC. It is the secret formula Oppenheimer used to perfect the hydrogen bomb. It is the secret intention behind the fish symbol often associated with Jesus Christ. It is all around us, every day.

How do I know all of this? It is because the rest of the Quechua text goes on to explain the basic and advanced principles of Sacred Geometry and how they are used. It gives examples, which I personally verified. It outlines some experiments that can be performed which prove the failure of traditional mathematics to explain events that can be witnessed with ones own eyes.

I have neither the time nor the inclination to go into detail about all of this. A lot of the information is available to those willing to put a little time and effort into the research. Like the ruins at the mountaintop, it isn't hidden. They have no need to hide the truth. Their ways are more subtle. They manipulate belief. If you don't believe in something, it isn't there. They know that they aren't perfect. Slivers of information will always get out. They've tried to squash the truth before, people die, heretics espouse it. Contrarians and anarchists embrace it. It will become rumored, then known, then accepted.

But, if you modify belief, then the truth can't hurt you. If the lie is well crafted and widely held, then no one will search for the truth. Scraps of information that defy dogma are ignored as 'outliers'. I challenge you to learn the truth about sacred geometry. Measure the places of power in this world and calculate the ratios. Understand the true reason why the American military is headquartered in a five-sided building. Then go out to the street and talk to the people. They won't believe you. Show your work to mathematicians. They won't listen to you. Humans have evolved to believe that they have all of the answers. They want no new questions. They are physically incapable of believing something different because it unravels their belief in the reality that they have so much invested in.

The frustrating part of my research was that I still learned nothing about my adversaries. How they thought, where they hid, what their goals were, were all still great mysteries to me. I had uncovered a second piece of the puzzle, but what did this mean? Why was this discussion concatenated with directions to an ancient altar in the Peruvian mountains? The answers would continue to elude me.

I didn't spend all of my time doing research. Even in the monomania of translation I had to perform the functions that made life possible. I had to eat, sleep, move around in the light. Cusco was a beautiful city, and it grew on me day after day as I walked its narrow streets, smelled its cooking fires, and listened to its ethereal music. I could often be found at night in any of the pubs around the city center, quietly drinking in the corner, watching the revelers as they danced, blissfully unaware of the horror that their civilization floated upon. It was one of these nights that I made my first connections to the underworld. At the start they were limited, I was able to purchase a few needed psychedelics from local dealers, but I pushed for introductions to get higher up in the chain of command. Not too high of course, as I had no doubt that the upper echelons were controlled by mysterious men in black suits, but high enough that I was able to meet smugglers and forgers and other people that could help me. I was able to sell some of my plundered pottery at a good price to dealers who specialized in prohibited works of art. I held back the gold figurines though, I didn't want to tip my hand too early. In the time I was in South America, I bought a prodigious amount of marijuana from these people. I found that smoking helped my translational skills and gave me the capability to better understand the strange, abstract principles of this new math that I was learning. Perhaps that is one of their secrets. The truth may be readily apparent, but the lack of belief, coupled with the fear of criminal prosecution, stopped the average person from going beyond a small measure of experimentation.

Through my underworld connections I was also able to sell my stolen American passport. You'd be surprised how much you can get for one of those. I was given more Soles than the average Peruvian earns in a year, plus a Peruvian passport with my picture in it. That would prove helpful a few months later, when I was ready to leave the Andean hills.

What got me moving again was the fact that I had gotten to the end of the Quechua section on sacred geometry. It ended with an example. An example in which the basic principles could be used to make distance calculations from certain well known landmarks. Those calculations implied the existence of another landmark at a certain spot on the globe. That place was a fjord outside of Trondheim, Norway. Half the world away, and then some. Although the document didn't explicitly say what would be found there, I knew in my heart that it must be the location of an important sign which would point me in the direction of my adversary. From my experience in the cloud forest, I knew that it wouldn't be obvious, that I wouldn't find anything but fresh puzzles there, but I had to go. I had to go even though I knew that moving would be dangerous, I was being pulled, pulled by curiosity, pulled by desperation. Besides, the next language in the document appeared to be Hebrew, and that translation would severely tax my research abilities in a rural area of a 95% Catholic country.

I had been in the city of the Inca, the navel of the world, for almost three months. I packed my things, and said goodbye to my business associates. I purchased a second Peruvian passport and an Ecuadorian passport, just to be on the safe side. I paid for them with one of the gold figurines. I couldn't risk smuggling the other figurines out of the country, so I wrapped up the ones I had left and anonymously mailed them under separate covers to three professors of Inca culture who worked in the United States. I don't read the research journals of course, but I never heard anything about new anthropological discoveries in Peru, so I assume that the packages were either interdicted or disregarded.

I journeyed to Oslo, Norway, by a circuitous route. I was still aware of the plane crash that I narrowly avoided on my way down to South America, I didn't want that experience to be repeated. I moved from country to country, sometimes by air, sometimes by foot. I started by going through the city of Iquito at the headwaters of the Amazon. It is a wild place there, and the customs officials are infrequent. I moved through Bolivia into Argentina, into Uruguay. Then a flight to Europe. I varied the passports I used (when I used them at all) and I was reasonably confident of the surety of the plane flight, although I spent most of the air time clutching the rosy-cross I had been given.

In Europe their surveillance of me resumed. Two men tried to grab me just outside the Paris airport. They both had the look I had come to know so well. I was able to resist them long enough to attract the attention of a gendarme who scared them off. Someone ransacked my hotel room in Brussels, and a few minor personal items were stolen. Good thing I had taken all of my notes with me when I went out that day. One night in Copenhagen I was chased by a man in a black suit. I ran down a dark alley and he lost me in a crowd of drunken revelers, waving flags from some victorious soccer team. After that incident I decided to better defend myself. I bought a rather large folding knife. I figured that would be easier to get across international boundaries than a handgun.

For about a month I had wound my way around the continent with a EuroRail pass, eventually ending up in Oslo. I had picked up a book on Hebrew and was starting to make some progress on the next part of the manuscript. I decided to lay low for a week or so in Oslo before making the final trek up to Trondheim. I had been on the lookout for men in black the whole voyage, but I hadn't seen any in Norway until my third day in the capital. I was sitting outside of a restaurant on the Aker Brygge drinking coffee and flipping through my notes when I noticed a man standing on the other side of the square. He was wearing the typical man in black outfit, and was holding a suitcase. He had dark glasses on, but I could tell that he was looking at me. He was not making much of an effort at stealth. He made no threatening moves, just standing in place, watching, waiting.

I decided to go to the restroom to give the man a chance to go through my things. I took the important papers with me of course. All that he would find was some scribbles and gibberish about Peru and a few Oslo tourist pamphlets. I always carried the important stuff with me. As I headed to the restroom the man didn't budge from his position. He knew that I could see him. He knew that I was watching. But I knew that he would make his move soon enough.

When I returned from the restroom the man was gone completely, he had finished his surveillance. I expected to find my papers pushed around on the table a bit, and perhaps to find some small item missing. These people seemed to like taking souvenirs. What I found was a bit surprising.

There was a small white card on the table. In fancy, typed writing was the word, 'Invitation'. I opened the card carefully. Inside was an address and a time. I looked up the address in my local guidebook. It was a restaurant, one of the fanciest in Oslo. Was I being invited to dinner? For what purpose? I sat for a long time contemplating the potential risks and gains of a face-to-face meeting. Perhaps they wanted to get me in a place that they could grab me. But on the other hand, maybe they had given up, decided that I was too wily for them. Perhaps this was some sort of truce. It was hard to say. I tried to list the pros and cons, but I couldn't find my pen. In the end I decided to risk it. I still had time to find a suit and to case the place out before the meeting time.

I arrived at the restaurant a full hour early, and I stepped inside pretending to be with another party that had already arrived. I looked the place over thoroughly, including the kitchen areas. Everything seemed to be legitimate. I couldn't sense any esoteric presence, and I was getting good at noticing their subtle but consistent signs. I walked across the street and sat on a bench at the bus stop. Exactly three minutes before the meeting time, A lone man in a black suit approached and entered the front door. No one seemed to be watching him, and I hadn't seen any other suspicious people enter the restaurant during my surveillance, so I figured that things were at least legitimate on the surface. I followed the man inside.

I was met by the maitre-d', who seemed to know exactly why I was there. He ignored the fact that I had just spoken to him an hour ago, and he addressed my by my name. "Mr. Sinclair," he said, "Your party is waiting, please come this way." We moved stiffly through the crowded restaurant to several booths in the back. This being a high-class, romantic establishment, there were a series of 'lover booths', which are basically alcoves with curtains. The dining party can be completely alone and shielded from view. That made me a little hesitant, but I had already come this far. I decided that if they wanted to kill me, they could probably have done so at a dozen places in the past few hours alone. There was no reason not to give them the benefit of the doubt at this point.

The maitre-d' pulled aside the curtain to reveal a darkened table, lit by a single candle protruding from an old, wax-drizzled, bottle of Chianti. My stomach dropped upon recognition of my dining partner. This was the enemy. My body tensed in a fight or flight instinct. My fingers balled up. I could see the man's outfit in the darkness, but I couldn't make out his features, which were covered in the shadow made by the brim of his hat. The maitre-d' wordlessly pointed to my seat like the Ghost of Christmas Future, and I shuffled into the chair. The curtain closed. It was remarkably quiet in the alcove once the curtains were drawn. The talk of the diners, the clank of the dishes, even the harmonies of the piano at the bar were all deadened. He just stared at me from under his hat. His face was shrouded in darkness. A bottle of red wine sat on the table. He moved forward and took it by the neck. "I'm not sure that we have given this enough time to breathe," he said flatly. "But I think that you'll be happy with the vintage. It is quite popular with aficionados." He poured some into a deep, round glass. It was the color of blood. He moved to pour some into my glass. The effort left his face visible in the candlelight. It was scarred and old. His skin was leathery and brown. His nose was large and misshapen. It was difficult to tell what nationality he was. There were traces of Asian, Indian, perhaps a bit of Arab. He poured me a full glass and then sat back. He didn't touch his. "I don't drink myself," he said quixotically.

"What do you want?" I asked. I wasn't going to give this man any quarter, I wasn't going to let my guard down.

In my pocket I fingered the knife that I had brought. He was close, close enough for me to reach out and cut him if I needed to.

"I present you with an opportunity. I want to test your resolve." He said. He smiled, revealing a mouth full of gold teeth.

"I don't understand." I replied.

The strange man pulled a revolver from a holster in his coat. I tensed up. "Leave the knife in your pocket," he said calmly as he opened the barrel. "I'm not going to shoot you." He showed me the chambers. They were all empty. He reached into his shirt pocket and took out a single bullet, which he put into a chamber. He closed the barrel and spun it around. It made a whirring noise. "How much do you want to know?" he said.

A million questions came to me immediately. What did the document say? Why were they chasing me? What was the purpose of all these games? How do I make them stop? My lips pulled across my face. I had so many questions, I had spent so much time thinking about all of the things that I wanted to know that my mind went blank with the effort of consideration. The strange man must have seen me tense up. "You want to know who we are? You want to know what our goal is? Those are dangerous questions. There are dangerous answers. I don't think that you want to play our game."

"Of course I don't want to play your game!" I blurted out. "You are the ones chasing me!"

"You have so much to learn. You have everything upside down. I can help you. I know things. I know the things that you want to know. The things that you need to know. But first, I require a test of faith. I've read the file on you. I know how you've used the rosy-cross. But you're not a believer. You have no faith. Answers only come to the faith-ful."

"What do you want?"

"A challenge. I'm sure that you are familiar with the rules. Pull the trigger, and I tell you a secret." He placed the gun in the middle of the table, with the handle towards me. "How much do you want the answers? How much are you willing to lose?" He sat back and took his wine glass in hand. He dipped his big nose below the rim and inhaled deeply. "Its up to you."

I grabbed the gun with my left hand. One in six chance I thought. Those aren't bad odds after all. What would this guy tell me? How far was I willing to go? I placed the end of the barrel in my mouth. I tried to look down to see if I could tell if the chamber was loaded or not, but in the dim light of the flickering candle, I couldn't see anything. The man put his glass back down on the table and smiled broadly. He leaned forward a little. I pulled the trigger.

'Click', the chamber was empty. I had surprised myself. Was my resolve really that strong? At that time they had only been chasing me for a matter of months. Was I really willing to die to get the answers that I needed? At the time I would have said no, but my actions that day helped to convince me that I was. That I was willing to do anything to get to the bottom of this mystery. I placed the gun back on the table. I smiled with some confidence. I was sure that they didn't expect me to have that level of resolve. The man leaned back into the shadows. I even ventured to take a sip of wine before speaking. "Now, tell me a secret," I said haughtily.

He leaned forward into the light again. The single source emanating from the candle made his features appear angular, otherworldly. "You don't understand. You have no idea what you've stumbled into. This is bigger than you.

This is bigger than you can possibly imagine. Everything you've ever believed is a lie. You have no idea what you've gotten yourself into. Do you think that the knife in your pocket will protect you? We invented that. The cross you wear at your throat? We invented that too. You think that you are a danger to us? To our plan? You are nothing. You are barely worthy of surveillance. I'm part of something bigger than nations, bigger that religion, bigger than money. Something so glorious that I doubt your limited mind could even comprehend it." He sat back, pleased with his cryptic words.

"You've told me nothing," I said.

"I've told you everything! It isn't my fault if you haven't yet developed the tools to understand me. There are levels to knowledge, there are layers to the onion. If you've learned anything in your quest so far, it has been that there are layers of truth. You start at the outside, and move inwards towards the larger truths. One in six gets you the warning, one in five may get you something of value. He pushed the gun towards me. It slid across the red tablecloth silently.

He was changing the rules on me. Like everything else, this was a lie, a sucker's game. Maybe it was time that I took the offensive, that I changed the rules in my favor. I grabbed the gun by the barrel and rotated it around so that the handle pointed the man. "We both know the rules to Russian Roulette," I said confidently, "It's your turn." I smiled and leaned back. I wasn't sure what his response would be. I wasn't sure that you could bait them. I wasn't sure how human these people actually were.

"Do you think that I am scared?" he exclaimed. "Are you questioning my faith?" He looked at me with some rage in his eyes. "I am a true believer, I have more faith than you could possibly imagine. I know the truth. I know how the world is going to end. I know my place in the universe and I know the path that I am on. I'm not afraid of death, I'm not afraid of your games. My faith is unshakeable. I am the true King of the World because I have shaken hands with God!" With that, he put the gun to the side of his head and pulled the trigger.

It is a well known fact, that when people play Russian Roulette in the movies, the bullet is always in the sixth chamber, or at worst the fifth one. The story wouldn't be nearly as dramatic if the load was in the first chamber of the gun would it? Unfortunately this wasn't the movies. The powder drove the bullet straight through the man's temple, splattering seared flesh across the darkened wall of the alcove. Surprisingly, his hat stayed on the entire time, as if it had been pinned to his head. The lifeless body slumped to one side, and the gun fell to the floor with a loud thud. At first, I sat in disbelief. This man was dead. It was quite a disturbing scene. I started to chuckle. I had won. We had played a deadly game and I had won. I began to laugh out loud, which probably wasn't too respectful, but what could I do? Once again I had come very close to death but was able to pull out of the tailspin at the last moment. I felt more alive then than I had in weeks. I could feel sweat dripping over my entire body as my autonomic system tried to handle my stress subconsciously.

I'll admit that my second thought was that I wasn't going to learn anything after all. This scene had been played out, but I walked away empty handed. Even the man's cryptic ramblings weren't of any use. My next thought was that the waiter was likely to come and take our order any minute now. I had to get out of there. I didn't want to have to answer questions about what had gone on in this alcove. I had enough of police interrogations in San Francisco. I got up to leave, but hesitated. He wouldn't tell me anything alive, but maybe he could tell me something dead. I quickly rummaged through his pockets, but he had no wallet, no identification, no money, nothing. Not even a set of keys. All he had with him was my missing pen. I picked up the briefcase he was carrying and walked out of the restaurant calmly and quietly. I even nodded to the maitre-d' on the way out.

I walked several blocks before curiosity got the better of me and I stepped into an alley to try the briefcase. It was locked of course. I smashed it against a wall until it opened, hoping to find the clues I desperately needed. It turned out to be filled with nothing but shredded paper. I smashed it into little pieces in frustration. before heading back to my hotel room. For safety and security reasons I decided not to stay in Oslo any longer, and I was on my way to Trondheim by first light.

I don't need to supply all of the details of my uneventful trek through the fjords. Suffice it to say that northern Norway is cold, even during the summertime. The important part was what I found. In a cave, in the side of a fjord was a scene very similar to the one found in the Inca cloud forest. A shrine, facing west, containing a statue of a bird-headed, Egyptian-like figure. The only difference was that the base of this statue had Norse runes on it, not the Inca pictograms. The lower, Indian like language was there as well. The statue was also in a slightly different position. The creature was still pointing downward, but not straight down, more like he was pointing to the base of a mountain to the south. I searched the opposite wall looking for a hidden door, but there wasn't any. The cave littered with things that Vikings would have. Wooden hammer symbols, furs, etc. Nothing of value like in the Inca shrine. The cave was set up and off from a coastal road, but there was no direct path leading up to it. I could see how archeologists never found this site. It was much too cold here to do any reasonable amount of exploration.

I took some photographs for future reference, but this, like the other shrine, was a dead end. I still had my untranslated document. The answers lay in the labyrinth of codes and dead tongues. I was sure of that. I left Norway rather quickly. Who knows what the repercussions of the incident in the restaurant would be? I left straight from Trondheim. I was able to get a job on a fishing trawler, which was scheduled to travel the North Sea for a few months. Most of the crew spoke no English, and I hadn't the time to learn Norwegian, so it worked out well for me. The job was hard, physical labor, but there was a lot of down time. Time I spent in my small quarters below deck, reading and translating, learning and scribing. The ship also provided food and shelter, so that wasn't a constant worry like it had been before. I felt safe in the isolation. I had signed on under an assumed name, the crew thought I was an Ecuadorian national named Diego Garcia. There was little chance that the men in black would be able to figure out where I was, and even less chance that they would be able to get to me, here above the Arctic Circle.

Despite the impeccable surroundings and constant fish smell, I was unable to make much progress, and most of my time was wasted. I only had one slim language book to learn from, and it had no dictionary. I determined that I needed more information to continue, and that meant I needed to get back to civilization. That opportunity presented itself when the trawler docked in Edinburgh, Scotland to take on supplies. I jumped ship and was on my way to London before I was even missed. I decided to rent a car instead of taking the train. My EuroRail pass was still valid, but I wanted more freedom of action than I could get with the railway system. I was still unsure how the men in black were tracking me. If they put together the apparent suicide in Oslo with the report of Diego Garcia jumping ship in Scotland, they might be able to find me. The car left no trail. Once in London, I cleaned myself up a little bit and got straight to work.

I could tell from the bits I had translated that this part of the document had many obscure and proper nouns. I decided that a standard dictionary would not suffice, I needed a more advanced reference, or even a native speaker to read it for me. I admit, I was tired. I needed help. Rabbis were generally trustworthy right? Maybe I could risk getting one to translate this thing for me. I could be in and out in under an hour. I had the car, I could disappear. The months of time it would save seemed worth the risk. I got a map and found the location of synagogue in an out of the way area of a North London suburb. I stopped at an office store and copied the four Hebrew pages out of the document. No need for the Rabbi to see the rest. I drove up to the street address and arrived at about 3pm. I pulled up and parked the car directly across the street. It was the end of the school day for the young children that were taking classes in preparation for their Bar Mitzvah. The place was too busy, with parents and kids and teachers all crowded around, saying their good-byes and hellos. I sunk down in my seat and waited for the people to disperse. A lone schoolchild walked past my car, his head down in a book, bobbing and mouthing the words to himself. He was by himself. He was going home, reading, walking, *by himself.*

An idea came to me. A child would be much less likely to be involved than an adult. Sure, he might not be as good a translator, but he would be safe, and he was studying Hebrew as he walked wasn't he? I could have asked him to come with me. There was a chance that he would have accepted my offer. But I knew that I only had one chance. If he declined he could blow my cover. I would have to leave London immediately after I spoke with him, regardless of his response. If he alerted the wrong people, things could get significantly stickier for me, wherever I went. They would have my modus operandi. This had to succeed the first time.

So, I did what I had to do. I watched as the child walked down the street. I started my car and I followed him slowly. The boy turned down a side street. There was a good chance that it was empty this time of day. I followed him down the road. I pulled up to him, stopped and rolled down the window on the passenger side. "Hello," I said, "Do you live around here?"

The boy stopped and looked into my car warily. I continued, "Please help me, I'm lost. I am from America." That seemed to interest the boy.

"Where do you want to go?" The boy stepped closer to the window. A little more, I needed a little more. I picked the name of the street I had turned off of to get to the synagogue. The boy thought hard for a second, and began pointing the way. I stopped him mid-sentence.

"I saw you were a Jew. I am a Jew also. That is why I asked you. We stick together right?" That brought the boy closer. He let his guard down just long enough. Like a flash I reached through the window and put my knife to the boy's throat. "Get in the car," I said to him. The boy did as he was told. He sat in the passenger's seat. I locked the door and sped off.

The child look confused and frightened at the same time. He knew that there were instructions he was supposed to follow in this event, but he didn't know what they were, or how they would help him, even if he could remember. He did the only thing he could think to do, he began praying. Rocking his head back and forth, eyes closed. I drove on, out of the city. I needed privacy.

We drove for almost an hour without stopping or talking. The boy remained in his meditative state. That was good, I didn't want trouble. He was about thirteen or so, not too big, but big enough to fight me off if he put his mind to it. I asked him his name. He didn't respond. I asked him his name again.

"Isaac," he replied.

"Isaac, I have a proposition for you. I need you to help me. If you can do that, I promise that I won't hurt you and I will return you as soon as I can. Can you help me Isaac?" Silence. "I said, can you help me Isaac? I am a reasonable man. I don't want to scare you. I am just very desperate. People are chasing me Isaac. I need your help to stop them. My name is Diego." I put out a hand. He looked at it. He could tell that I was scared too. He could tell that I was desperate. He kept his composure, I'll give him that.

I pulled into a motel that was just off the highway to Manchester. We had been driving for a while and it was getting dark. I explained to Isaac that I was going to go in and get a room. He was going to come with me. I would have the knife on him, so he better not say anything. We rented a room for myself and my son. Isaac did just as he was told. Perhaps I had overestimated him when I said that he kept his composure. Now it seemed more like he was just scared stupid. Isaac was just like the rest of humanity. Scared little sheep. When a crisis comes, minds go blank. They don't even have what it takes to run. They freeze, waiting for their master's instructions. Is this an ingrained, evolutionary trait? Perhaps this is what helped to keep the tribes of monkeymen together and coherent when the beasts attacked. Listen to the leader. Listen to the leader. That is what happens in the mind of most humans. That is why hostages fight for their kidnappers, Stockholm Syndrome. When the mind panics, outside input is obeyed without question. It is like being in a hypnotic trance. Listen to the leader. Isaac was young, too young to be able to break out of his trance. His whole life was spent listening to the authority of others, mother, father, the Rabbi, bullies at school. He had no independent mind. The Communists talk of one day achieving the hive mind. It is already here, waiting to be exploited by those who have broken the evolutionary mold to become leaders of men.

Was I that type of person? I ran when I was in the bloody office, I didn't go blank. Was I a leader? Did I have the right gene? Maybe I was forced into action by the fact that there was no one around to tell me what to do. If there had been a policeman (or someone who looked like a policeman) on the scene, I would have followed him unquestioningly. The rules of behavior change in an emergency. Why do you think that the world is kept in a constant state of panic? Why is it that everyone agrees that war is horrible, but they happen anyway? Does it make us more likely to listen to our leaders without question? Do the world leaders have something significant to gain by maintaining a constant outside threat? Why did the Cold War occur? What did they really discuss at Yalta?

We got to the hotel room and I locked the door. 'Do Not Disturb' dangled from the handle. I sat the boy down at the little work table and put the document in front of him. I explained to him that I needed to know what it said, what it meant. I told him that I didn't know much Hebrew, and the thing was too hard for me to follow. The child was obviously relieved that he wasn't in danger of imminent death, and was interested in showing off his skills. He began reading from the top. The first part was just three letters, Aleph, Mem, Shin. That translates to;

A... M... S...

Reading onward, "These are the three letters of our tetragrammaton. The divine name of Tohu. The Divine name of the Chaos that precedes your universe. This is our god, just as YHV is your god. The Three Mothers guide us. We feel their vibration in us. Formed from the Seferiot after the fall from grace. After the shattering of vessels. Our god is the primal god. Our divine word carries the true divine power. YHV is the pretender to our throne."

The child stopped reading. The paragraph was over. I still didn't understand. I wrote down the words, but what did it mean? I asked the child. He was unsure, but he knew that Y (yod) H (heh) and V (vav) are the letters of YHVH (Jehovah), the secret divine name of the Hebrew god.

He read onward. The next section was a complete transcription of the Saadia version of the Sefer Yetzirah, the Book of Creation. Handed down from the prophet Abraham to the Jewish people. It is the key, fundamental document behind the ancient Jewish mystic discipline of the Kaballah. For brevity's sake I won't repeat it here. It is easily available to those who are willing to look for it. Only a few paragraphs long, the Sefer Yetzirah explains how the universe was created with letters. Letters are the key to it all. The Old Testament is the written numerical interpretation of the entire universe. All things, all wisdom can be found by deciphering the code properly. It was all a code. A code for something, everything. It talked about the ten parts of YHV. The ten that are one. The ten seferiot. The ten veils through which we can see the hand of god. The ten vessels that held the word of God as he formed Creation. The word forms creation. All is just a word. A vibration. A wave of sound. The universe is built on a great wave that is represented in a word. YHV. The divine word of god. And in the beginning there was the word, and the word was God.

Translations of the Sefer Yetzirah exist, and also available are many, many discussions of its meaning. MacGregor Mathers thought he had it all figured out when he formed the Golden Dawn. Adolph Hitler murdered six million people in an effort to force its knowledge out of the last remaining Jewish high priests, who preached only in secret, and only in darkness. Famous figures from Jewish history dedicated their lives to studying but one part, one phrase, of one version of the Sefer. And even they could come to no agreement about the full meaning.

All of them were wrong of course. The rest of the chapter told of the true meanings behind the Sefer. It told of the true ways to use the word. It showed the true path, the 232nd gate. Meditation techniques that would quickly allow one to pass through the Seferiot, from Malkhut to Keter. To see the face of god itself. To understand the full nature of the limitless being. To visualize infinity, the naked singularity. I won't repeat what I learned here. It isn't germane to my story, and dangerous besides. Not many men can fully comprehend their place in the infinite void of reality without going truly mad. I would test these truths later. Learning, studying. After the night in the English hotel I would try the techniques, experiment with my perception of reality. I almost took my own life in the process. It is all there, plain as day and no one sees it. They won't let you see it. A blind spot, coming down to us through evolution. It is not possible to see what is truly there and still remain who we are, so the human race has blinded themselves against seeing the very core of reality itself, in order to live.

The child and I spent the entire night in the hotel, enraptured with the work. He read, stumbling over words. Hands beginning to shake. He understood more than I did. He was fluent in the Torah. He was able to fill in the cultural gaps that I could not grasp. He saw more deeply into the meaning than I could at that point. I would learn, but for now I was protected by my ignorance. A luxury poor Isaac did not have.

Excitement turned to fear, which turned to shear terror. But we couldn't look away. I know that you mock these words. How can four pages of esoteric writing change your point of view so thoroughly, especially when you have no faith to begin with? I can't answer that question without talking about the text itself, which I won't do, can't do. I could not explain it even if I was willing to. The text requires a reading from Hokamah consciousness, not Binah. Binah is the seferah of understanding, Hokamah is the seferah of wisdom. Binah is the singular point that reality is referenced from. Hokamah is the dark ocean, infinite, undifferentiated. Hokamah knowledge comes from within. There is no effort, there is no learning, there is just knowledge. You can study your entire life and not grasp a single minute phrase of the Sefer Yetzirah, you just have to let wisdom and knowledge, overflow you, mind a blank. This is the basis of the crude attempts of the Zen masters. Meditation, silence of the mind, nullify bright Binah and Hokamah comes from the void, filling you with knowledge. If you understand this, then you will understand why nothing I say could prepare you for the wonders held inside the document.

By daybreak, we had reached the end. Hidden inside of the text was an exercise in Kabalistic numerology that I inferred would lead me to another location. I would work out the specifics later. We were both trembling, minds overflowing with the knowledge given to us that night. Isaac was crying softly as he read the final passages. We fell to the ground together, exhausted, fearful of the future, of ourselves. Of our everlasting souls. We embraced in a spirit of brotherhood.

We slept for several hours in a dark dreamless void. When we awoke, I reexamined my notes from the previous night. They made less sense to me than when I had written them the night before. The lack of sleep had made my mind illogical, more prone to understand dichotomous concepts. My well rested, logical mind strained to understand, but of course, couldn't. I would later realize that in order to grasp these ideas, I would need to be in the proper state of mind. Meditation worked, but the fast path was heavy drug use. I packed up my things and we left the hotel. Isaac was still shaking from the night before. He didn't have the depth of my experiences in life. He didn't have the maturity of years that allow one to handle momentous news with decorum. He was a wreck, unable to speak very clearly. I told him that I could not stay, that I could not take him back to London. People were looking for me. More now that I had kidnapped a child. I gave him a large quantity of money for his effort. I pressed it into his hand. I pointed him towards a phone and told him to call his parents. He nodded blankly. I thanked him for his help. I got back in the car. My hands were still shaking. It was difficult to start the engine.

What happened to Isaac? I looked him up several years later. He had gone back home almost incoherent. He never did say what happened in that hotel room, or talk about the man named Diego. He did however become somewhat of a phenom at his study of the Torah, often coming up with new meanings for verses, meanings that his teachers could barely grasp. He had gathered the attention of some senior rabbis, and there was talk of moving him to Israel, where he could study with masters of divinity. Two years to the day after meeting me, he was killed by a hit and run driver. It could have been an accident. It could have been a coincidence. The car was never found. Witnesses were only able to give a partial license plate number for the old-style, black car. The first three letters:

A... M... S....

# Chapter 7:
# Mercy

The next few years were a blur of movement, an explosion of discovery. Complete terror, running underground, warren to warren, wonder to wonder. I got out of England, wound up in the Far East. I tried to comprehend the gravity of what I had learned, but I found that I needed the drugs to do it. When I took them, my thoughts frightened me so much that I needed more drugs just to stay coherent. I wasted almost four months lying on a mat in a Thai opium den. Smoking to forget, but finding only more knowledge and madness in the haze. The pieces of the puzzle were falling into place fast, too fast for my mind to handle. How did I get the money to survive? I stole it. I cheated people out of it. I got it any way I could. The money from the Peruvian artifacts was long gone. I sold off passports, but had to buy new ones. I stayed in motion most of the time. Traveling through the Holy Land, Africa, the jungles of Southeast Asia. Always trying to stay one step ahead. They were everywhere I went. Two faceless men in black followed me for an entire week while I was in Tangiers, taunting me. In Karachi, they tried to intercept me at a scheduled meeting with a drug dealer. I arrived to see them beating my contact silly in the alleyway, in fluent Punjabi demanding to know my whereabouts. They would have had me if I had not been delayed a few minutes. They would have beat me to death, not him.

Occasionally, I was able to lose them for months at a time. They would find me again only when I resurfaced in some way, either contacting the people I needed for information, or moving to a new location where I could get my hands on the resources I required.

The translations were happening at a regular pace. The increased use of psychedelics had an effect on my translational skills, but after my positive experience with Isaac, I had taken the liberty of 'consulting' language experts and anthropologists. The languages became harder and more obscure. There were sections in Chaldaic, Sanskrit. I went to Dresden, Germany to find one of the few living experts who could read the codex of the Mayan Quiché people. He told me that the results of his work on my document would lead to a better translation of the Popul Vuh, or could have, had he not been killed in a suspicious fire, hours after I left him.

My adversary knew my plan. They knew that there were limited places I could go. It wasn't that hard to tap a phone, to monitor a building. They knew that I would have to show up sooner or later. Sure, Hebrew, German, modern Tibetan, those I could learn in a thousand different places, but the dead languages had limitations. I needed the experts, and they knew where the experts were. I hid myself pretty well, translating chapters in non-linear order to throw them off, meeting contacts in unusual places. I had many disguises, and believable stories to make them help me. Some were excited at the chance to try their art on a new work, others were reluctant and needed persuasion. That came in the form of money, or threats. Some were scared to talk to me, having an inkling of what would happen, knowing perhaps more of the true story than they were willing to let on. It didn't matter. The end result was all the same. After speaking to me, they would show the signs of enlightenment. They would be able to translate better, or meditate better. They would tell their friends of their discoveries. Despite my warnings they would try to publish papers on their find-ings. They all slipped up somehow, and my adversary was waiting. Many were killed, some disappeared. With some, personalities changed forever, their friends, family, not un-derstanding them any more. Some were driven mad. The men in black would come in the darkness, whisper more se-crets into their ear, gorge them with more information, the keys they needed to fit together the pieces I had already pro-vided. It was more than the unconditioned mind could take.

I was changing as a person. I was learning their ways; ways of talking, ways of being persuasive, ways of being evasive that made the listener not realize that there was any-thing to hide. A lot of it is presentation. People are conditioned in childhood to believe those in authority. Au-thority has characteristics to it. Mimic those characteristics and people will follow you unquestioningly. I learned that from a section that was purported to be directly from the hand of Sun Tzu. It made it easier for me to earn my living off theft and deception. I was able to walk straight out of jewelry stores with my head held high and diamonds on my finger, the clerk not even realizing that anything was miss-ing. The techniques are simple enough. I had already learned the basics back in law school. There are self-help books that touch on different aspects. Grifters and politicians have known about the craft for years.

I don't want to mislead you about the contents of the document. I was not just learning from the text alone. It spoke of other writings, such as the Sefer Yetzirah and the Art of War. My search extended to the holy books of most cultures, to writings omnipresent and esoteric, to works pro-fane and spiritual. The information that the coded document contained gave new interpretations of these works. It spoke of their true origin, it explained how they all fit together to make a fundamental whole. Everyone, every culture, had a part of the solution, but not one had been able to put it all together. And inside each chapter were hidden directions. They only became apparent once you had mastered the discipline. For example, the section on astrology subtly pointed to a spot in Tunisia in a discussion on viewing the convergence of certain stars on a specific date. In time I was able to locate statues in Burma, southern France, Sudan, the Ural Mountains, all over the globe. All were similar. All had the same ibis-headed god, pointing downward. The words, YOUR GODS LIVE HERE, below, written in the local language as well as that strange other language. I searched in vain for clues as to what that might be. I consulted with experts in Hindi, and Farsi, and Sanskrit. Besides a few similarly shaped letters, no one had seen it before.

I didn't visit all of the sites specified in the documents. I already knew what some of them pointed to; the Imperial Palace in Edo Japan, the Dome of the Rock in East Jerusalem, the Pentagon in Arlington Virginia, SHAPE Headquarters in rural Belgium, Vatican City. Was this a list of places of power, unrelated to the shrines? Or were these places built on top of the very foundations of the shrines themselves? Whoever these men in black were, they had hidden the location of these shrines for centuries. They had watched civilizations come and go. Civilizations which tended their holy places. Was it possible that deep within the bowels of the Pentagon basement, a similar statue still stood? An unholy shrine not built for the people of some lost, dead, tribe, but for the people of modern America? And who tended these places? Who worshiped at the foot of the ibis god?

That was the big question wasn't it? Despite the fact that I was more than halfway through that tome I had inadvertently stumbled upon, I was no closer to finding any information on who my adversary was, or what they wanted. They were interested in secrecy that was for sure. They had both the will and the capability to kill as many people as they needed to protect themselves. They seemed to have some knowledge of places on this earth that shouldn't exist according to the standard definition of history. But where was their headquarters? What were their goals? What were they hiding, and why were they hiding it?

The answer to at least one of those questions would come through creative meditation techniques. I was in a tiny hotel room in Paris, France. I had decided to use what I had learned from the document. Use their own knowledge against them. At that time, I had no idea what the rest of the tome would say once I had translated it, but it was reasonable to believe that the second half, like the first half, would be filled with esoteric sciences and hidden directions to more of these strange statues. None of that helped me in my goal, which was to locate these people and find out what they were after. To somehow get them to leave me alone and allow me to get back to some part of the life I had known before, as long ago and as far away as that seemed. Sometimes we cling to a dream, even after we have moved on. All I wanted to do was to get back to that little house in the Marin hills, to have my family back, and my job in the prestigious law firm, and all those other things that everyone believes add up to a 'normal' life. Only now can I realize that I had gone too far by that point. I was tainted by my ordeal. I knew mysteries that none of my old peers would comprehend. I knew what it was like to be chased to the ends of the earth. I knew the desperation it took to kill. Looking back now I can see that I could never have returned to what I had before. I was not the same person. But at the time, desperation, frustration, yearning, all forced me into a monomaniacal burst of fury and exertion. Chasing a dream that no longer existed.

The document was getting harder and harder to translate. The first few sections were simple. Sure they were written in foreign languages, but with a dictionary, a first year text, a few leaps of faith, and some historical research, it wasn't too hard to hard to piece together ninety percent of what they were saying, which was good enough. But the later chapters of this thing became increasingly difficult. They started using dead languages, or rare dialects that didn't have textbooks. They started playing tricks. I was confused by one section in Sinhalese until I figured out that the whole thing had been written backwards. A mirror later it all became clear. Another section appeared to be written in Tamil, but it was actually French transliterated into Tamil letters. The last section I had successfully decoded was written directly in hexadecimal ASCII code. I had been working on one section for months without getting any closer to a solution. It was just a section filled with strange cross-shaped figures, row after row. It didn't match any language I could find, and as a code it defied decryption. It was becoming more obvious to me that the document might be a dead end in and of itself. I refused to play the part of Sisyphus any longer. It was necessary for me to leapfrog the information still encoded, and endeavor to come up with an answer to what was going on in a more direct fashion.

I had tried all sorts of rational theories, and tried to reason out a connection between all the things I had seen and read over the past few years, but nothing clicked. There was no logic behind any of this. So, I decided that logic and reason had failed me. I would not be able to solve this problem with the seferah of Binah, I would have to solve it with seferah of Hockamah. I would have to stop *thinking* about the problem to solve it. If what the adversary, the Sefer Yetzirah, and the Zen Masters had said was true, then I could solve this problem by looking at it holistically. Clear one's mind. You can't see the gems at the bottom of the pool because the pool is filled with froth. Stop moving and the pool becomes crystal clear. I had gotten myself a globe, and some pins. I placed them into the orb at the places that the statues had been found. I sat on the bed with the globe, the pictures I had taken of each shrine covered the rest of the mattress. I took some really high-powered acid and sat, spinning the globe, looking for connections. I stopped trying to answer the question, I just sat and looked, waited quietly for wisdom to take over, for the lost part of my bicameral mind to see the pattern and send the answer to the conscious part of my brain. Three hours later I had what I was looking for.

The key, it turned out, was in the statues themselves. Each one pointed downward, but at a different angle. It turns out that they were all pointing to the same place. They were pointing through the globe. If you followed the line from the statue in Peru, it traveled through the earth, intersecting the surface again somewhere in Saudi Arabia. The statue in Trondheim pointed mostly south, the ray also pointing through the earth, skimming right under Europe to exit also in southeastern Saudi Arabia. Of course, at first the connection was a little vague. With just a small globe and without a compass it was tough to get an exact location, but the more statues I examined, the more I was convinced that each one of them was pointing to a place on the other side of the world, the deserts of Arabia. Was that the secret they were covering up? Was that the location of the secret headquarters? What was there; riches, aliens, more ruins. YOUR GODS LIVE HERE. Something was there though, and that was what they were trying to hide. It would be possible of course to have made this discovery from the very first statue, so they would have to keep them all hidden. Why not just destroy them? And more importantly, how could these ancient cultures be connected to such a degree? How were these separate people able to know of a place, clear across to the other side of the world. How could all of these disparate people worship the same god? And how could a people whose culture had barely progressed past pounding rocks with sticks be able to so clearly understand geometry as to be able to properly align their statue towards the mystery in Arabia?

I hoped that the answers to those questions lay in the hot sands of the Arabian Desert, in the Umm al Samim, where there are no borders. In the next few weeks I was able to refine my plans. After that creative blast of Hockamah, I was able to use my analytical Binah mind to better define the location the statues pointed to. I obtained some detailed maps of the region, none of which indicated anything but sand and wadis in the region. I searched journals and legends for hints of what might be out there, waiting for me in the sands. There wasn't much. I read about Thesiger's travels with the Bedouin, newspapers talked about border conflicts in the region, National Geographic had an article about the desert nomad and how easy it is to get lost in the monotonous white sands and glaring sun. *One of the most desolate places on earth* it says. I even watched a showing of 'Lawrence of Arabia' in hopes of gaining some knowledge, but there wasn't much. Every scrap of information I could gather claimed, the entire world believed, that there was nothing out in the sands, and that to journey in that wasteland was to dance with death.

There was only one thing to do, I had to go there and see for myself. I had to go and find whatever lay beneath the desert, hidden under a veil of desolation and beyond the sands of time. I planned an itinerary. It was unwise to go into Saudi Arabia directly. They were a suspicious and reserved people to start with, plus, if my adversary had an inkling that I was close to a solution, they might try harder to silence me. No, I would go to Oman, and cross the desert, by foot if I had to. If the area is truly as barren as they say, no one should notice if I slip off the beaten path and make my way northward through the wastes.

This would be my most difficult trip. The other places I had been to in the world were close to human populations, the places I had been to didn't have extreme temperatures and lack of water. Even in the jungles of South East Asia, there were trails, and guides, maps, and landmarks. None of them had required more than a day or two outside of the comfortable blanket of civilization. By my estimation, this trip would require at least several weeks of travel by camel, if I could even figure out how to work a camel. It would be in an area that had no phones, no bystanders, no water. If I got into trouble out there, no one would find me. Without landmarks there was a chance that I could lose my way and wander endlessly through monotonous sand, past identical drifts and repetitious wadis until dehydration finally ran its course and left me a bleached skeleton for some peasant nomad to pick clean of sellable trinkets.

Despite my enthusiasm to get this whole business over with, I spent almost a month getting ready. I brushed up on enough Arabic to get by at the souks, I read several guides on how to travel in the desert, I bought some gear, figuring that quality and availability would be better in Europe than on the Arabian Peninsula. Also, I have to admit that I was loath to leave Paris, and kept coming up with excuses for delaying my departure. It was a beautiful city, filled with excitement and history and a gracefulness that was scarce in modern times. I knew that Arabia, while it might have its charms, could not approach the City of Lights. I also knew that this could be my last trip. I had hoped that whatever I found in the desert would vindicate my efforts for the past few years, but I also knew that there was a very real possibility that I would not be coming back. If this truly were something worth hiding, they would be more determined to protect it. In the lonesome desert they would also be able to move with a free hand, more overtly than they can move here, in front of millions.

I wandered to Greece, where I was able to get a job as a longshoreman on a freighter that was heading to Singapore.

It was easy enough to get the job. I had some fake documentation, plus enough ship knowledge from my time in the North Sea to be believable. We sailed through the Suez Canal and made a refueling stop in the Omani city of Salalah where I conveniently jumped ship, switching my identity from Irish longshoreman to American tourist. I wandered through the streets of the town center for a while, bright white buildings on every street. Over the roofs, the gleaming, gold minarets from countless mosques can be seen on the hilltop. Women dressed in bright multicolored robes buy fruits from street vendors. Small children stare down from intricate woodwork balconies, running back to the cool safety of the kitchen when I glance back up at them. As I do whenever I reach a new city, I spent a few hours feeling the place out, trying to understand how it feels to live here, to *be* here. I was looking for a shop that would rent me a camel. Apparently, camel rentals are not popular in that area. I didn't even know how to ride a camel anyway, so maybe it was better that things didn't happen that way. Renting a jeep or car was not feasible. I had several hundred miles of barren desert to cross. I couldn't carry enough fuel, even if I was able to make it without a breakdown. I wandered the narrow streets and crowded stalls of the main souk, connecting with individuals whose job it was to provide unusual items and services. Salalah was a port city, used to the obscure and depraved tastes of sailors of a hundred nationalities. I had become quite adept at locating and interacting with the fringe criminal element of any city. They all have the same faces, all want the same things. I carried a wad of American fifty-dollar bills, some untraceable jewelry, and almost a pound of hashish. I was able to trade those to obtain information and introductions. No one knew of anything out in the desert though, and no one was able to set me up with a reliable means of transportation. The best I could do was to find a Bedouin who was headed north. His brother was a big time qat dealer, and helped me make a connection in return for a small piece of hash. The Bedouin offered to guide me through the desert. As far as he was concerned I was just a wacky, rich American looking for a little adventure by doing something stupid.

I agreed to meet him the next morning and we would travel. He had about two dozen camels to deliver to Abu Dhabi, and the best way was still to walk them through six hundred miles of open desert. The trip was scheduled to take almost two months. In the past, these trips had been made with more camels and large groups of men, but as cars replaced camels, and young men felt the pull of the cities and not the sands, it became more difficult and less profitable to organize large contingents. He had only himself and his young nephew, a caravan of two. He agreed to take me along in exchange for some help wrangling camels, and a few trinkets and baubles that I handed him. I figured that I would be able to use my compass and other modern tools to estimate my position. Once the caravan moved close enough, I would slip out of the camp at night, taking a camel and some supplies, and I would be able to make my way to the location, the place that had remained hidden for countless years. I had no clear plan for what I would do once I got there. I had no idea what I would find. My next move would suggest itself when the time was right.

Organizing a ride had not taken as long as I had thought. I spent the next few hours moving through the crowded booths of the souk searching for signs of the Muqarribun, the Arab magicians whose traditions predate Islam. They were masters of the hidden meanings behind language. If they existed, they might be able to help me. That is, if they weren't aligned with my pursuers. You could get anything at the souk, from ancient Babylonian tablets to smuggled Persian rugs to knock-offs of American jeans. The people there immediately saw me as a foreigner, and foreigner equals money. Middle Eastern merchants are aggressive and cunning. It was tough to enjoy the atmosphere. On multiple occasions I found myself actually running or ducking down an alley, a gaggle of white-robed vendors in hot pursuit. After one of these instances I found myself in an alleyway between two old, white, clay buildings, of the kind so common on the back streets of the city. I had just beaten off a crowd of young children that wanted handouts. The children in the third world are like pigeons. Feed one and the rest come running. Word spreads through the streets at the speed of light. A few coins handed to one child can result in dozens flocking around you, hands out, eyes wide open. Some with shoe shines or ratty postcards to exchange, some with nothing but desperation. None are ever satisfied. Give a child something, and they will follow you around like a stray dog all day, looking for more scraps. They don't have begging children in the US, at least not in San Francisco when I lived and worked there. It is a disturbing sight. But I'm getting off the subject, and my time is short.

I had just ducked into this alleyway, when a dark little man appeared behind me and guided me toward his stall. It consisted of a tattered blanket lain on the dirt floor, covered with junk, trinkets, scraps salvaged from the desert. He showed me his 'wonders', which consisted mostly of pieces of metal that he found in heaps out in the desert. Probably pieces of tanks and artillery shells from the wars they fought out there decades ago. One thing attracted my attention. An old book, more of a pamphlet really. "I do not know what that is exactly," said the man. "It is from the desert. The sands have given it up to me." I picked it up, it was in Arabic. As you may know, Arabic is written from right to left, so of course I opened the book upside down, which turned out to be the key. I had committed the first line of the latest code in the document to memory. It was wise to have a bit of whatever part I couldn't crack in the forefront of my brain. Sometimes a clue comes fast and you need to be able to react to it. What I saw in the upside down book matched the symbols of the code. I turned the book right-side up and looked through it some more. It was an old U.S. issue airplane spotter's guide from WWII. The cross-shaped symbols were actually silhouettes of airplanes. The book was designed to help agents on the ground identify aircraft as they flew overhead. I purchased the guide from the man and ran back to my hotel room. I finally had a key to a mystery that I had been working on for months.

Back in my hotel room, I was able to locate some of the first few symbols in the spotter's guide. I made the guess that each letter was represented by the first letter of the plane's make. For example, A 'B-52' stood for the letter 'B'. The first line, which had been gibberish, translated to this:

Sura 89:6, *Muhammad, consider how your Lord dealt with the tribe of 'Ad, the people of the huge, columned city of Irem, whose like has never been created in any other land.*

Irem. The city of pillars. Irem, the first city. Older than time itself. The sura was from the Qur'an. It told of how Irem was destroyed by God for not submitting to his will. The Qur'an holds the oldest reference to this place, but not the only one. It is the city of roses mentioned in the Rubbiyat of Omar Khayyam. It is the city of Jinns in the Arabian Nights, a city that predated man's appearance on earth. The text was flowery and full of veiled references, but as more and more aircraft became letters it became clear what I was facing. Irem was the center of the world, only the world didn't know it. Irem was the seat of government, but not one elected by man. Irem was the most beautiful city ever built, but was cloaked by thousands of miles of desolate, barren desert. More hidden than the secret cities that housed the old Soviet weapons plants, more hidden than the true burial place of Abraham, more hidden than the secret hold of Prater John. The document spoke of the place as if it were a legend. An ephemeral dream city that existed only in the minds and hearts of those that believed in miracles. With all of the things I had seen in connection with the document though, with all of the impossibilities that were proven with this key, I knew that Irem had to be real, that it had to exist. That it had to be the residence of the 'gods' that almost every culture on the planet had once openly revered. That night, for the first time in years, I slept soundly and dreamlessly.

The next morning I met my travelling companion on the outskirts of town. His name was Ali. He had brought his nephew Salim with him. We would travel as a triumvirate through the sands of the Rub Al Kaliq. Ali was a short, thin man, seemingly too frail to have made it through the desert so many times. He wore a simple white robe and a large red turban, one that almost doubled the apparent size of his head. Salim was a boy of about twelve. His entire body was covered in the billowy folds of a vermilion one-piece robe. He led a camel authoritatively for someone so young. Reins in one hand, crop in the other. These men had grown up in the desert. They were prepared. They had brought sacks of water, tents, dried food, a few goats to slaughter along the way for fresh meat. Ali carried a late model AK-47 assault rifle over one shoulder, to ward off rustlers and bandits. I was glad to be in the company of seasoned professionals. We started north crossing foothills and green farms. We spent the whole day travelling. First on roads, past cars and streets and packs of little boys picking dates from trees, then to dirt trails in the desert, past a few scraggly shacks and misshapen palms. Finally, there was nothing but desert sands and hot baked ground, cracked and dry. The sun never stopped beating. Not the whole time we were there. Heat, oppressive, fell onto my head as we rode the camels. They were filthy, spiteful beasts, as eager to get out of the sun as we were. Our supplies were good, but the way was long, there was a lot of desert to cover.

Nights were the best times. The world cooled off, and we sat around a fire, cooking what we had for dinner. I can still faintly hear Ali singing his halal prayer as he slaughtered the goat, always facing west. They use every part of the goat in their cooking, including the Bedouin delicacy of goat brains. Why is it that the most disgusting things are always referred to as delicacies? I've tried so many of them. Ali brewed a type of coffee in a dirty yet intricately designed metal pot that sat directly on the fire. It was thick as mud, and every time I took even a sip, Salim rushed to my side to refill my cup. The boy had a flute of some sort, and Ali would sing. I couldn't understand them of course, I spoke only a few words of Arabic. They spoke no English. But we understood each other on a more fundamental level. I clapped my hands in time to Ali's voice. We laughed at things together. They showed me how to hobble a camel, which isn't as easy as you would think. I did my part to help our little caravan progress over the dunes.

We worked our way through the desert, oasis to oasis, well to well. The wells in the desert were old. The bricks must have been dried thousands of years ago. How many nomads had stopped here to enjoy the fruits of that labor, performed countless centuries ago, by unnamed hands? If I had a way to communicate I would have asked Ali if he knew the origin of the well. Odds are he wouldn't have known even if I knew how to ask. He knew the deserts, the dunes, but this was so ancient. I ran my hand over the stonework as the camels drank the briny water. Who made this? What were they like? What language did they speak? How did they dress? Under whose guidance did they dig this well? How could they know that this object would outlast their corporeal forms by millennia? What else did they put out here, hidden to all but the silent nomads?

We traveled through the desert rest stop of Mugshin, the last bit of civilization before the most difficult part of our journey, the Umm al Samim, the Mother of Poison. One hundred and eighty-five miles of blank desert. No water, no vegetation. The end of the world. The Umm al Samim is as close to hell as you are likely to get on this planet. On the fourth day out of Mugshin, a simoom blew in, and most of the day was lost, as we huddled in our tents, our faces covered by wet rags to stop from choking on the omnipresent dust. I showed Ali the map I had brought of the region, and tried to get him to show me where we were. He seemed confused. He dismissed the map. I understood that he didn't know what a map was. He had grown up in the Rub al Kaliq. He knew the paths by instinct, by feel. He had no map. There were no landmarks here anyway, what good would a map do? He knew how to get from Salalah to Abu Dhabi and back. He had been making the trip three times a year since he was a little boy, following in his ancestor's footsteps. He would be no help to me outside his preset path. That would present a problem with my quest. I needed to know where I was before I could tell where I was going. I spent some time that day trying to measure out how far we had traveled, and in what direction. The map I had listed some of the oases and wells by name, but not every one of them. Most weren't named, their location known only to handful of desert travelers. I could tell from my map that the nearest landmark to my goal was the Al Najm well. I needed to know when we reached that one, on the edge of the Mother of Poison. The place where I would begin moving towards my destiny. The time I would have to leave my travelling party behind.

The next day we traveled onward to the next oasis. One of the last before the two hundred miles of desolation of the Umm al Samim. When we got there we were in for a surprise. The oasis had been covered by the simoom. There was no fresh water to be found there. We dug for a while under the fiery sun, but gave up. There was a heated discussion between the two Bedouin, and they pointed north. The crossing would be difficult with just the water we had with us, but going back to Mugshin would mean a significant delay. It was determined that we would go on without stopping. We had some water with us, hopefully enough to make it to the next watering hole.

We struggled onward for the rest of the day. It was hot and dry. Ali wouldn't let us near our stored water, and the camels resented the fact. They were more ornery than they had been at any other point of the trip. The camels and their ancestors had been making the same trek through the desert for as long as Ali and his ancestors had. They knew when they were to be watered. They didn't understand variances in the plan.

We reached the next well near nightfall. By this point the party was on the verge of collapse. We dismounted and I began to get the camels ready. Salim was helping me. Ali went straight to the well to start drawing water. A scream of distress. Salim ran to Ali's side. They looked in the well with disbelief. More heated arguments, more desperate this time. I finished what I was doing and came over, looked in the well. The low, stone cistern was filled with sand. Both men stared out into the vast desert expanses that lay before. There was little they could do. The water was partitioned and some of the camels were driven off to die in the desert, leaving their bleached bones in the desolate wastes as a reminder to the next caravan that comes this way. Delivering half a shipment of camels to Abu Dhabi was better that having them all die. They would have to arrive late as well. We were almost out of water, and this was the last well before the start of the Mother of Poison. We would have to backtrack to the last oasis. We set up camp. In the morning we would try to make the best time we could back to Mugshin.

That evening, Ali and Salim tried to retain their high spirits. They sang and danced. We ate the meat of one camel that Ali shot. Draining its juices into ourselves. They tried to put on a good show, both to relax me and to ease their own minds. The situation was rather desperate. We were four days from the nearest water source. Even with what was left of our water reserves there was little hope of getting back to Mugshin with even a few live camels.

That night I lay in my tent, replaying the day in mind. I could hear Ali and Salim arguing over the well. One word was repeated over and over in their conversation. Al Najm. Al Najm. I took out a flashlight and looked at my map of the desert. Yes. Al Najm. It was the name of a well listed on the map. It was close to the coordinates that I was heading to. Now would be a good time for me to leave. By my calculations, it was about a day's ride to my destination. Then, about three days ride northwards across the Mother of Poison to the nearest well that had water in it. I could do it. I knew how to handle a camel (a little). I knew how to survive in the desert. I had a compass. All I needed was about four days worth of water. Four days. That was almost all that was left between the three of us. I had not expected to run into this problem with the dry wells. Was it a ruse to keep people away? Did they know I was coming? What was I going to do? If I took all the remaining water, I could make it, but that would leave Ali and Salim with none. At best they'd lose the camels, be financially ruined. At worst they would die out here in the desert. They'd done nothing to me. They were innocents, just simple people. They had been as nice to me as they could have been. How could I cross them? It was one thing to take vengeance on my pursuers, but had I now fallen so far that I could leave innocents to die in my wake?

Night. The beast moves forward, step by crooked step. They are not used to moving at night. Ali's rifle weighs heavy on my shoulder. There was some braying, some protesting. I had to move quietly. A stirring from Salim's tent. They couldn't wake up. They didn't wake up. I walked the camel out of the camp, almost a mile through the dried sands. It wanted to rest. But it kept moving. Under threat of whip, under promise of water. Moving at night would save water, save time. Here, in the unending desolation, the stars were out. I'd never seen stars this bright. No clouds to obscure them, no city lights to ruin the contrast between the shining white dots and the infinite black voids. This is how my ancestors saw the stars. This is how the stars were meant to be seen.

My thoughts were of my companions. Lost in the desert, betrayed by their partner, betrayed by my monomaniacal mission. They might survive. I told myself that they would survive. They might make it to the next watering hole before the desert sun sucked them dry. If they didn't waste time. If they left the remaining camels. If they didn't look for me, try to follow. Try to save me from the desert. At this point I could not allow myself feelings of guilt, feelings of compassion. This was about more than just a few small men scrabbling through the desert. Who knows how many more people I could save if I was able to crack this code, expose this plot, destroy this cabal

No. I'm just kidding myself. Trying to make it seem that my actions were more than they were. Trying to ennoble myself. There is no point in doing that now. My actions have spoken for me, and the past is the past, immutable, unchangable. I won't revise my own history to make myself feel better about my manner and deeds. No, the truth is that I had none of these thoughts. Looking back I can come up with justifications on how Ali and his nephew might have survived, but at the time I could not have cared less. They were nothing to me but a ride. Their connection to my life was done. They had outlived their usefulness, and when I didn't need them any more I left their empty husks to the vultures. The truth is that my thoughts were on one thing. My objective in the desert. Irem, Zhat al Imad, the City of Pillars. The dwelling place of the gods, if the hidden shrines and ancient texts were to be believed.

Dawn. I rode the camel through the wastes. Carefully checking my compass direction. Judging my speed. I looked around from my high perch. There was nothing but the serpentine dunes of sand, nothing but the vast open space. The Bedouin call this the Rub al Kaliq, the Empty Quarter. No noise save the wind and the footsteps of the beast below me. No sights except the hot sun, blue sky, and tan earth. I pulled my khalifah close to my face. My skin was burned. My lips were chapped. I tried to save as much water as I could, but my mount needed nourishment to continue. Ship of the desert my ass.

As I rode, an idea percolated though my subconscious, finally bubbling to the surface. An idea that filled me with hope. I thought about the man in the tollbooth. I thought about how he mistakenly gave me the secret document. Could it be that it was not a mistake? That the man was not an agent of the men in black, but instead some part of the resistance? Was there a group of people that were clandestinely fighting this threat? Maybe so, maybe they had given me this document on purpose. A smuggled plea of help to anyone who might listen. The information was leaked. Every conspiracy has a counter-conspiracy right? Television had taught me that much. There was always a secret resistance. There was always a place that the hero could go to for succor when the chips were down. There was always a double agent that would be revealed when things looked the blackest. All I had to do was to find these people. Locate the ones who secretly rebelled. Join their crusade. Maybe I wasn't alone. Maybe the odds weren't as bad as they seemed.

My camel and I advanced across the scorched earth for almost the entire day. Step by step. I was unsure that I was still going in the right direction. Perhaps this was all a trap. A giant pitcher plant. Step by step. You walk into the desert.

Too far for your supply lines. Then, in the middle, nothing, nothing but sand. Step by step. Quicksand all around you. No water for a hundred miles in any direction. No way to get out. Your bleached bones join those foolhardy enough to come before you. At mid-afternoon I spotted something ahead. A ridge rose up from the sands, a rocky crag. An unusual formation here in the middle of nowhere. That must be the place. I spurred my camel onward with a crack of my whip. The camel strained but moved forth, hoping for water and relief from its load. What could be in the crag? A secret cave filled with gold? A crashed alien spaceship? A more ornate shrine dedicated to the ibis-god? The crag was tall, several hundred feet at least. As we got closer it could be seen to stretch in both directions. A small mountain range of some sort. I didn't have co-ordinates specific enough to tell me where to look exactly. It could take days to search the entire area, even if I was in the right place. Buzzzzzz. A humming comes from the distance. It is difficult to locate sounds in the desert. At first I thought that it was coming from the hills, a vibration coming from the sands. But then, to the south, an airplane approaches. I can see it as it passes. Green. Through the binoculars I can see the markings. It has a familiar star, it is marked as an American military plane. A big one, a transport. It flies overhead, toward the mountains. It was low, it was landing. Its wheels were out. I hear it disappear over the hills. This must be the place.

My efforts are redoubled. I reach the crag in another hour. I hobble the camel and begin climbing. It isn't hard, not like Peru. It is dry here, it is old here. From the other side of the mountain I can hear activity, a buzz of motion. There is life on the other side of this hill. I need to reach the top. A sound in my ears. Buzzing. The drone of locusts. I couldn't tell if the noise was coming from the desert or from within my own mind. My left hand, nerves still scarred by the glass in the police station, begins to shake and vibrate in rhythm. As I climb, the sound becomes louder and louder, I can feel it penetrating my bones, my joints, my synapses. A racket so loud I wonder why the whole world can't hear. It defines itself as I rise up the slope. The drone gathers form, rhythm. It is more like a beating, a vibration, the sound of rushing blood. It is the beating of the world, the heartbeat of the world.

Just before dusk I reached the ridge, peered over the hill to see what was on the other side. What I saw defied description, but I will try. I was prepared for a base, a camp, a military installation of some sort. But what I saw could only be described as a city. The city of dreams. It had an architecture, but not like any architecture I had ever seen before. Frank Lloyd Wright had never set foot in this place. There were skyscrapers, there were towering walls, there were huge columns and pillars. The style was a little Egyptian. The skyscrapers were more like obelisks, the buildings were more like pyramids. The structures were stone, marble, gold, everything intricately carved. No faceless slabs of glass and steel here. In the center of the city was a large, pristine, blue lake. There were people in the streets. Walking back and forth in long green robes. There were cars on the roads. The city was walled, but a highway exited and went northward past the horizon. It was a modern city. An airplane took off and flew in my direction. It was another cargo plane, but this one had Chinese markings on it. What was this place? I hid in the brush at the top of the hill and watched things move for hours, through my binoculars. Well into the night. I took pictures, but pictures can't do it justice. It was a great city, maybe a hundred thousand people. Here, in the most desolate place on the globe. This was the home of the gods. It is the engine that spins the world, the secret heart of the planet.

No one came up the hill. No patrols seemed to be present. No one left the city except the transport planes that flew in and out every few minutes, and a few lonely cars straggling down the road. I checked my maps again and again, sure that I had mistaken my location and was actually staring at a Riyadh or Doha or somewhere, but it was not possible. Knowing where I had started and knowing how fast I could move, there was no way that I could have gotten out of the Rub Al Kaliq. No, this city didn't appear on the maps. Was this the city that was built with the bricks of the slave Jews, given by Pharaoh in tribute?

At night, the city became more spectacular. What was during the day the City of Pillars was at night the City of Lights. It held an otherworldly beauty. It triggered ancestral memories of what a city was supposed to be, what home looks like in your dreams. It pulled me toward it as the earth pulls the moon. I stood up and moved a few feet down the hill. I wanted to walk its streets, I wanted to hear its sounds, I wanted to feel the huge columns with my hand and my face, I wanted to throw myself on the mercy of the Ibis-God and live in the city of pillars forever. Irem, Irem, Irem, I love you.

I was able to stop myself. Remind myself that despite its beauty, this was the city of pain, the city of misery, the city of evil. These were the people that were responsible for my years of suffering. These were the people that had sent agents around the world to hunt me down, to kill me. This is the secret that needs protecting. This is what they are hiding. I can't go down there, into the belly of the beast. I need to expose this evil, but I can't go down there, not yet. I knew what the secret was, but I had yet to learn why the secret was, and how they were able to hide something of this magnitude. There were too many questions for now. There was too much of the document left to decode. Too many riddles that still needed to be answered. I would come back here one day, I would march through the streets triumphant. All of their lies exposed, all of their plans destroyed. My hatred now had a name, Irem. My anger and frustration finally had a focus. Before I was just running. I didn't know where they would be, what they would do. I was on the defensive. Now I had seen their secret, their nest. Now I could hunt them. Now I was on the offensive. But the battle would not be fought here, would not be fought now. There was work to be done, there were plans to be made.

I slid down the hill backwards, eyes still towards the city of columns and spires. My mind was full of activity, plans. I mounted the camel and rode off northward towards the next source of water. It was over a hundred miles to the next well. I had about three days of water left, so it would be a stretch for me to make it, even assuming that I could find the small pile of stones out there in the featureless desert. I decided to ride at night, and rest during the day. That might save water, or at least give me some relief from the oppressive heat that makes the desert feel like the inside of an oven.

Dawn. Another problem arose. I searched the horizon with high-powered lenses, hunting for a landmark to tell me that I was on the right track. But off to my left flank there was movement. I continued onward, northward, towards the water. Two camels followed at quite a distance. Riders. Pursuers. From this range I could not make out much, but they were clothed in black. I kept going, through most of the morning. They followed. Not getting any closer, but not backing off. They were waiting, waiting like a vulture circles the dying animal. They knew I couldn't go on all day. They knew that I needed to rest. That the camel needed to rest. They knew that I must sleep. That was when they would come for me. They probably thought that I did not see them. They were miles off, and were sometimes hidden from view by the dunes. I changed course a few times, just to check their adjustments. They followed my movements. They might have been a mirage, in the desert one often sees reflections, they might even be a reflection of my own camel. It would have been ironic if it had turned out that I was being pursued only by myself. I didn't have the stamina to make it to a populated area. They would catch me. They would track me until I was worn out, and then they would make their move. I couldn't allow them to have that advantage. I unlimbered Ali's rifle and grabbed a sack of water. Then I maneuvered my steed such that a large dune passed between my pursuers and myself. I slipped off of the camel and behind the dune. Then I gave the filthy thing a swift kick in the ass. It ran off. I climbed to the top of the dune and peered over the edge. The riders, who couldn't see that well from far away, started a gallop in pursuit of the now running camel. They would come fairly close to the dune. I cocked the rifle and waited for them.

They rode closer and closer to my ambush. My sights were set on the leader. They continued their pursuit. I knew that the rifle was not that accurate. Wait for it. Wait for it. They moved closer to the dune, turning to come along right beside it, in pursuit of the now meandering camel. Wait for it. Wait until you see the whites of their eyes. They had long, flowing black robes. They rode unadorned camels. Wait until you see the whites of their eyes. The leader slowed down. They had gotten close enough to see that the beast ahead was riderless. He put out his hand to signal his companion. Wait until you see the whites of their eyes. I fired prone, the first shot hit the lead rider in the head. A bullseye! He fell. The noise startled the mounts. His foot was caught in the stirrup. His camel ran off into the distance, dragging his driver along the sand. I stood. Fired again from the hip. The weapon kicked. Fire again. Fire again. I ran across the hot sand directly towards the man, firing wildly, screaming like a banshee. The man on the second camel did not have much time to react. They were not expecting a direct assault. The bullets hit the camel square. These shots were not aimed like the first one. It dropped. The whites of its eyes staring upwards toward the unblinking sun. The man fell off his mount onto the sand. He tried to get up but the shifting sands under his feet betrayed him. I stood over him, barrel pointed towards his head.

He looked upwards, lifted his hands in a gesture of surrender. His face met mine. He had a tanned face, but was not Arabic. White eyes. White teeth. He wore a long black flowing robe, gloves. "Don't shoot!" he said to me in plain English. I stared at him down the barrel of the Soviet weapon. "I swear, I'm not really one of them, I'm just a mercenary. I can help you. I can give you what you need," he said. Rising to his knees. "You want answers don't you? You've seen things you can't understand, you've been pursued for reasons you can't comprehend. I can explain things to you. I don't know everything, but I can tell you what is going on, what they want from you." He looked up at me. Smiled slightly. I could tell that he was sincere. That he knew the answers to the questions, that he could tell me the things that I had searched in vain for all these years. He knew how to stop them, he knew what they were after. He knew the secrets that they were hiding. He could give me everything I wanted. Before he could say another word I shot him dead where he knelt.

The two bodies lay lifeless on the desert floor, waiting for vultures. My camel had wandered off, but the other live camel had not strayed far. I took the water sacks off the two dead men and put them on the surviving camel. It was a good mount, freshly watered. I rode off into the distance, towards Abu Dhabi. I saw no one else until I reached the coast.

# Chapter 8:
# Logic

I am sitting in a hotel lobby in Selma, North Carolina. It's Christmas time. I am enjoying the continental breakfast. My car key lies on the greasy plastic table. I spin the key on its axis. It slows to a stop, pointing at the counter filled with bagels, coffee, orange juice. An old man gets up from his breakfast and walks to the counter. He is searching for something. "Norma, where are the knives?" he says to his old, fat wife, still seated at their table. "Over there," she points at the counter. To the exact place my key has divined. I smile.

I learn more of the hermetic sciences. I can turn lead into gold, I can predict the future. I can tell if a person is a friend or enemy by reading the bumps on their head. Phrenology, the study of bumps on the human head. It was discredited as gibberish a hundred years ago. Before that though, it was considered hard science. A model head sat on Freud's desk, on every serious scientist's desk. Why such a change? Why did they break from what they all knew to be true? Science was invented by men of God, by the clergy. They embraced learning. Then the break happened. Scientists were burned at the stake. What knowledge was being hidden? Why did the church turn from the study of the universe? Why did alchemists turn away from the transmutation of elements? Why did most science textbooks of the 19th century contain chapters on the paranormal sciences? Who took those chapters out of our collective memory? Why do physics students only learn some of Maxwell's equations?

I sit in a thick leather chair in the study of an American linguistics expert's home. The walls are covered in wood and books. It is warm in here. A fire is burning in the hearth, casting flickering shadows against the tomes and references. He feverishly translates the pages before him, sweat coming from his brow. I relax, close my eyes, but only for a second. His small child sits in my lap. I have a knife at the boy's throat.

I learn the true nature of time. Gnomic expansion. Time isn't linear. It doesn't *move* from one end of infinity to the other. Time *grows*. Grows like a seashell or a spiral, every second is the sum of all previous seconds before it. Gnomic expansion. Every part of time is like every other part, just larger that's all. The proportionality is always the same, always exact. That's what the Masons have been trying to tell us all these years. Past, future, it is all there, each gnomon of time building upon the past. The rose. Each level of petals growing upon the last. It becomes larger, more complicated, but doesn't change it's fundamental shape. A rose is a rose, larger, smaller, it doesn't matter. A rose is a rose. Would time by any other name smell as sweet?

Darkness. My flashlight sprays light over an obelisk covered in Egyptian script. It lay forgotten in a storage warehouse of the British Museum in London. Wrapped in plastic. Held from public view. A guard lies face down on the cold concrete floor. He whimpers quietly as his life blood flows down a drain in the ground. It disturbs my reading.

Did you know that there are thirteen signs in the zodiac, not twelve? The thirteenth one is called Teli, the dragon. It encompasses the northernmost part of the celestial sphere.

Its talons of stars have invaded all twelve segments of the sky. Teli, the master constellation, the Pole Serpent. The imaginary axis around which the heavens rotate. Draco. Leviathan. The idolatrous pagans worshipped it as a deity. It was identified with the cult of Baal. In small, unlit rooms, the true Kabballist masters still figure it into their predictions, into their astrology. Why has everyone else forgotten?

I am followed everywhere I go. The men in black are ubiquitous now. They find me wherever I hide, they seek me out whenever I rest. They push me to flee whenever I try to become comfortable. Sometimes they strike like coiled snakes, other times they just disappear into the woodwork when I get close to them, they are on the periphery of my vision at all times. I can still see them even when my eyes are closed. I don't care anymore. I move like a beaten horse, whipped forward to each new step. I am so very tired.

I have given up my search for the resistance. They don't exist. There is no evidence. I search high and low. In the cities and the country. I speak to rebel leaders in Columbia, I speak to tribal chieftains in Somalia. Even in the most anarchistic places on the planet, the hand of Irem is apparent and omnipresent. The resistance was a great dream while I was in the desert, it drove me forward when I was ready to lie down and let the sands take me. But it isn't true. There isn't anyone fighting my cause but me. I am utterly alone. People are too complacent, too comfortable. The Men in Black have done their job too well.

Thoth says: I am One which becomes Two, I am Two which become Four, I am Four which become Eight, after all this, I am One. Square the circle. The Vesica Piscis. Jesus Fish. Every one has seen it. What does it symbolize? Proportion, one to the square root of three. The Trinity, right there in a set of curved lines. The cross. Two lines, two is proportional to three. 2:3, 1:ö3. Square the circle. The cross. This is what the Templars learned from the Saracens. Proportion, ratio, this is the substrate that the universe is built upon. Relativity. Einstein knew it, but he only applied it selectively. Zero is a lie.

The simplest way is with the sniper rifle. From a distance, it is like a game. You don't have to hear their screams, you don't have to see them flailing about on the ground, attempting to stop their life essence from spurting out the gaping hole. But every time I get one, another takes their place. Interchangeable, faceless, nameless. It becomes simpler to just leave them alive.

The Rosae Crusis, the rosy-cross. That was their sign. That was their key. It symbolizes so much more than you can imagine it does. The gnomon and the proportion. I can't explain it better than that. You have to meditate on it for a while and you will see. It is their symbol. It comes in very handy. There are those people who recognize it. They might not know what it means, but they know what to do. Like that airport clerk in Peru. They know to let people with the rose-cross pass, diplomatic immunity provided by the nation of Irem. That was what stopped me from getting arrested by customs so many years ago. Joshua Vorhees' passport my ass. It was the inadvertent display of the rose-cross that saved me that day. Saved by serendipitous chance, by a man who had it all right, but for the wrong reasons.

It becomes easier every time it happens. I'm driving down a highway in the American Midwest. It is raining. It is deserted, straight. Fast. From behind a billboard a light begins to flash. A police car begins pursuit. I slow down and pull to the side of the road almost immediately. The officer sits in his car and checks the license plate against his records. Time passes. I wait, wipers sliding back and forth across the window. The officer gets out of his vehicle. I can see him in the rear view mirror. He paces towards me. Comes to the window, taps on the window. I roll the glass down and turn towards the officer. I shoot him once in the chest. He falls to the ground, immobile. I step out of my vehicle and walk calmly over to the police car. I reach inside. Turn off the lights. Turn off the car. I pull the tape out of the video recorder mounted on the dashboard. I return to my car and drive off.

Words, it is all a matter of words. Words are the key. Understand the words, understand the codes, understand what they are trying to tell you. I know that words are their game. That is how to break the riddle, the puzzle that lies before me. Nothing is as it seems. Out of necessity I learn the art of Tawil, of decoding the hidden meanings in Arab mystical writings. The City of Pillars has no pillars, not as we know them. No pillars that can be seen or touched. What is the riddle? Pillar, Imad, Arabic. The advanced Arabic student knows that 'pillar' is just slang, slang for an elder. Irem Zhat al Imad. It isn't the City of Pillars, it is the city of elders, the city of the old ones. Even the Rub al Kaliq is a metaphor. The Empty Quarter, empty, Daath, Ein. Ein is void. Ein is emptiness. Absence of thought, meditating on nothing. The Sufi mystics talk of entering a higher state by meditation, the absence of thought. You can only enter Irem though the Rub al Kaliq, through the void, through emptiness of thought, meditation. Irem isn't real, it isn't physical. It is a state of mind, a deeper level of consciousness. It is only through the annihilation of self, by devouring one's own soul and entering the void that one can enter Irem. No, that's not right. Irem *is* real, I've been there. I saw it with my own eyes out in the desert, or did I? Where am I? Everything is so confused.

The churches are everywhere, if you look for them. They appear normal on the outside, you'd think they were like churches everywhere else, but you'd be wrong. The Rosy-Cross hangs on the wall. No one ever notices them because the only ones who enter are the believers. You'll never even think about going into one. You're too distracted by the shiny, pretty things they've convinced you to collect. I was like that too, once. Now I visit their meager, nondescript cathedrals in many cities. No one ever speaks the dominant language there, only the native ones, only the ancient ones. The pews are filled with the nameless peasants. They form the outer ranks of the organization, I'm sure of that. They stare, nameless, faceless as tiny glimpses of the ancient wisdom is doled out to them. Damn, I wish I could understand the words, I wish I could read the psalms. I never have the time to stay long enough to get more than an inkling.

I retract my earlier quote from Sherlock Holmes. He is wrong. Irem is impossible yet still true. You can never eliminate the impossible. That statement is a lie, a plant. It turns us away from the truth. How could you ever discover something outside of your paradigm if you routinely discount the impossible? They want you to believe what they tell you. No questions. No worries. Ridicule and ostracize anyone who says things that are different from what you have been taught.

I can no longer tell my dreams from reality. Do the men in black actually exist? Are they a figment of my imagination? How many of those I have killed were just innocents who happened to be dressed in inopportune colors? Have I already gone completely mad? I can't tell if I'm right-side up or upside-down. I am sitting in the corner of a rat infested apartment in a ghetto in southeast Washington, DC. Empty dime bags and needles litter the floor. They are the only decorations in the room. I crouch in my underwear, cradling my shotgun in my grimy arms. John Law ain't got nothing on me man! I shiver with fright and withdrawal. They were coming. They were going to get me this time. I was going to die, cold and alone, in a strange place. Unmourned, unloved. Sweat beads on my forehead. My left hand shakes. All I can hear is a faint scratching on the bedroom door.

It all fits together, don't you see, can't you see? It's all right there if you would just open your eyes. The voice is the word and the word is god. What is a word besides a vibration of air? It isn't the sound of the word that's important, it is the vibration. It is the intersection and interference of vibration and waves that make the universe possible. Physics is beginning to understand this now. Protons, neutrons, they are nothing but swirls of energy, vibrations. Interference patterns, superstring theory. The underlying pattern of the universe, the key that makes all of existence possible. *That* is the word, *that* is the voice of god. Modern science and ancient religion interconnect. Proportion. The vibration, the wave, it is a proportion. It is large, it is small, the vibration exists in all forms at all times in all places. It is the fractal. Any part of the word is identical to the entire word, fractals, modern science is beginning to understand. The magic of proportion, the magic of waves. It all fits together. Ancient scripture give us the clues to proceed, they are backed up by the modern science. No one can see. Blind, everyone feels their way around their individual cubbyhole. Refuses to accept the possibility that they are not the leader of their field. That their entire life's work is wrong, been disproved countless centuries ago. That is the way they want it. Keep us in the dark, keep us confused and helpless and alone. Keep us from acting against them. Until the end of the fourth world, the day when YHV is replaced by AMS. When the universe is remade in their image.

You think you'd find them in the shadows, in the underworld, don't you? You think that they live in the criminal world, that they stalk the night. Boy, do you have it totally wrong. They live in the day, they live in the light. They are order, they are civilization. They are part of the system, they ARE the system. I learn that eventually. The comforting places, the safe places; police stations, government offices, shopping malls, that is where they are most likely to be found. They designed this world of ours. The very ideas and foundations behind the most comforting parts of our society are their creation. To get away from them you must fall into the night, into the seedy underbelly. To escape their influence you must go to places that they find uncomfortable, places that they can't control. Cockfights, snuff film screenings, crack houses. Oh how many nights I have spent in places like that. Reassured in the knowledge that, while something may come for me in the night, it wouldn't be them.

I am lost inside of a machine of my own creation. No, I have become the machine. No emotion, no pity, no desire. I don't even dream anymore. The death screams of those I've killed no longer haunt me in nightmares. Only the goal is left. Why I struggle for it is no concern, I can't even remember. I have walked through fire for so long I can't feel it anymore. I have gone through hell, through madness, and come out the other side. I just continue. Firefights, ancient discoveries, forbidden knowledge, hiding and running and barely surviving, these things no longer excite me. There is nothing left. My actions are perfunctory. Part of me wishes that they would catch me, that they would kill me, that they would end it all. But they don't, they can't. I have become too strong for them, too wily for them, I have learned to disappear too well.

# Chapter 9:
# Wisdom


Time has passed. Only one section remained untranslated. The final piece of the puzzle. The final pages. The final mystery. I'd learned their ways, I'd learned their secrets, but I had yet to learn who they are, why they are doing what they do, hiding the secrets they hide. The final section was written in a script I had seen before but never been able to translate. The mysterious script at the bottom of the statues. The language of Irem. The primal tongue. I traveled the world, consulted with experts in dead languages. I searched through histories and research journals. I was so close to the answer. All signs pointed to the solution of the mystery being contained in the final section. There were numerous references in the earlier segments. They pushed me onward towards the finale. I had no luck for almost a full year, until I stumbled upon a story about a French writer named St-Yves d'Alveydre.

In 1885, a French political writer and historian named St-Yves d'Alveydre decided, as most European intelligencia did at the time, that his education and understanding of history would be improved by learning the classical Indian language of Sanskrit. He enlisted a tutor, an expatriate Indian calling himself Haji Sharif, who was living in a northern suburb of Paris and supporting himself as a seller of exotic birds.

St-Yves wrote that he learned far more than he expected. During the very first lesson, Haji Sharif revealed that he was a 'Guru Pandit of the Great Agarthian School', an ancient society that had preserved the secret and primordial language of 'Vattan' and its alphabet, on which all other languages, including Sanskrit, were based.

Digging further, I was able to get some more slivers of information on this Vattan language. Legends implied that this might be the famous 'Indo-European' tongue that was lost to time millennia ago. It was rumored to be close to Sanskrit. Since the final code in my document contained letters very similar to Sanskrit, this could be the right track. It fit the M.O. of the document's creators. There was a lot of babble about the language being employed by a group of people known as Agarthians. This was supposed to be a secret cult that lived in deep caves under the Himalayas. That was probably an exaggeration, but there might still be isolated pockets of peasants up in those mountains who may recognize the script, or at least be able to point me towards the right direction. I immediately headed off to Nepal to find the final key to the puzzle. I know that it may seem to the reader that I had gone mad. Here I was off in search of the fabled city of Shangri-la, which as we all know doesn't actually exist. But remember that I had already been to places that don't exist, so I had every reason to believe that I would one day walk the streets of a myth.

All through my travels they followed me of course, on the plane, in the airport. A man in a dark suit and fedora hat followed me through customs. They are always at the edge of the crowd. They try to blend in, but you can always spot them. They stick out of the herd. They are not part of normal civilization. There is something not right about their movements. I pass customs quickly. The rose-cross medallion at my neck. My bags aren't even searched in Kathmandu. I feel the ragged papers of the old photocopy weighing heavily in my jacket. One section remains to be solved.

I spend three months in the great Himalayan cities, Kathmandu, Lhasa, Thimbu, searching for clues, travelling through bazaars and mountain passes, meeting monks and yak herders. I forged links with both the underground and religious communities. I was able to gain access and introductions mostly through gold and drugs and the telling of secrets. Almost no one had any useful information for me. Vattan was a language that seemed to have disappeared off the face of the planet a long, long time ago, when the Gobi was a lake and the King of the World ruled from his Himalayan throne. I began to give up hope. Perhaps this was a dead end. Finally, in Pokhara, in Northwestern Nepal, a fallen monk told me of a monastery located way up in the mountains. It was an ancient place that legends dated back to when the Kirat ruled Nepal and the perfect spirit was several lifetimes from being reborn into Sidhartha. They kept the old ways in that monastery, the purity of their ancient religion. The monk was only willing to give me vague directions though, and only after I had to ply him with a large amount of opium and threats of violence. The monks in that monastery were known to want their privacy, and to harbor glorious and horrible secrets. There were rumors that they could kill with a glance, and pull your soul apart with a few words. Further inquiries into the religious community in Pokhara gave me nothing but surprised looks and vehement denials.

I wear a sharp new, winter parka. Black to keep in the maximum warmth. I was able to outfit myself well in the town. It has a fair tourist trade of skiers and hikers, eager to get away from the more commercial Mt. Everest. The maps of the region were spotty, but I had a general bearing. In the mountains, there are certain paths that you can follow, everything else is a shear cliff. That limited the number of places that this monastery could be. I packed as much food as I could carry and set off to the more obscure villages of the region. It was autumn, and most people I talked to advised against traveling in the mountains this time of year. I didn't have time to wait until spring.

Off the beaten trail (if there are any trails in Nepal can be characterized as beaten) the people are simple, they have little knowledge of the outside world, and most have never even seen a foreigner. The locals spoke a myriad of obscure languages, but I was always able to find someone who I could communicate with. The people in that area speak some Tibetan. It had come full circle. Tibetan was the first language that I had to learn on this quest, now it aids me in the last part. They were warm people for such a cold climate. They gave me yak butter tea and warmed me by their fires. But none were able or willing to help me find the monastery in question. They warned me against seeking out demons.

And always, the men in black followed. I don't know if it was the same men or if they switched off in shifts, but they were always there. I am standing on a mountain trail. Parka pulled tight. Fur hood closed against the wind. The frost of my breath obscures the air. I look backwards across my footprints in the snow. I look backwards through the high powered binoculars. There, almost a dot. Far down the hill, a long figure walks, following my footsteps in the snow. The figure wears a solid black parka.

They don't follow me into the towns, or if they do I am unable to identify them. But they are out there, among the mountains, searching for me. I can usually spot them within hours of leaving the safety of the tea houses. They can't catch me though. I have evolved past them. They are too slow, too obvious, too predictable. It is a game to me now. I don't even try to cover my tracks anymore. I let them chase me. Who is hardier?

I'm dreaming again. A featureless desert plain. The sun is high in the sky. It is blood red. Slaves pull large rock cubes across the barren surface. They are building something. Dark skinned men in bird masks watch the action from a pedestal. I sit with them, admiring the view. Whips are cracked. Slaves moan under the weight, and scream their complaints to the uncaring sky. They are building something. Something immense. Where are the rocks coming from? A piece of masonry falls. Is that a Sphinx they are constructing? Is this Egypt? Where are the pyramids? The hot wind blows sand into my eyes. The slaves shield themselves from the dust. Masonry falls. Wait, they're not building the idol, they're tearing it down. I'm awake now. In my tent, the wind howls. I dust the frost from my beard and stick my head out into the morning light. Look, the snow is falling.

I was giving up hope. No, strike that. I had given up hope a long time ago. What I was giving up was the belief that this course of action was likely to present any useful results before I froze to death. Then I met an old woman on the outskirts of a tiny village adjacent to a flowering mustard field. She was sitting outside her small thatched roof hut, stirring an iron pot that was boiling over a peat fire. Although my Tibetan was not very good, I sat with her a while and we slowly talked of stew, Hindu gods, yak butter tea, life in general, the coming winter. She told me that there were no insane people in Nepal. That insanity is a function of language. The English language is flawed. The mind rebels against the inherent contradictions. It stretches against the bounds of a language that can't express certain ideas. The pressure builds, the mind is damaged. She said that in her language, there is peace, there are words that allow for concepts to be expressed. The pressure is relieved, serenity is all that's left. I took this opening to begin a discussion of languages. I asked her if she had heard of any old monasteries in the area that might harbor the old ways. She began to sob quietly. She told me a story of her son, he had been gone for many years now. He was a strong, smart boy. He left to enter the monastery. She had begged him not to go, but he told her that he needed to follow his heart. He promised to come back one day, after his training was complete, but it had been so long. She was an old woman, and wouldn't live much longer. She had wanted to make the trek to the monastery, but it was too arduous. She wished that her son would come back to her. She asked me to promise to give her son a letter when I saw him. I agreed to give the letter and to tell the son how much his mother missed him, if she would provide the directions.

The old woman was able to draw me a crude map in the snow, and I traced the route she suggested on the maps I had of the region. The monastery was located in a cleft at the foot of Mt. Machapuchare. I would be able to get there in under a week. She also gave me a sandalwood mala and mustard flowers as a gift. I handed her some cash as I left.

I was stalked the whole way to the mountain by small men in dark jackets. I used to shoot at them, try to catch them, try to get them to stop. But now it was just easier to hide, to run. They are so faceless, so nameless, so interchangeable. It is easy to think that they are all the same person, the same anonymous man, prodding along on his anonymous mission, immortal, unstoppable, a slow juggernaut. It was easier to just get out of the way. Did they know where I was headed? Was there only one source for the Vattan language? If not, then they would almost certainly know where I would turn eventually, where they should set the trap. Out here, in the open spaces, I was free and intangible, but as I got closer to my destination I would have to increase my vigilance, be more careful. Watch behind me more closely.

These are the things that I was thinking during my trip to Mt. Machapuchare. The roads (where there were roads) were dirt, full of potholes. The buses were half-dead jalopies that seemed to predate World War II. The roads were blocked by herders and their flocks, downed trees, sick yaks, other broken down buses. It was not a pleasant trip. I can't say too much about the scenery though, I was too focused on my goal. I went over previous notes, checked my gear, kept an eye for the dark men lurking just behind me. Tourists tried to talk to me, but I wasn't listening. They were interested in tales of suburban adventure. They thought that taking a guided tour of the 'safe' places in the third world made them some sort of adventurer, some sort of explorer. These people had been taken in by the delusion. To them, adventure was just another thing to be consumed. They had no real stomach for hardship. They take a few rolls of film of themselves standing in front of a Tibetan holy man or a yak and they go home to their warm houses and describe their trip in a way that would make you believe that they had found the Lost City of El Dorado. Don't these people know that the so-called holy men are just peasant actors from the village, decked out in outlandish costumes to suck a few rupee from the tourist rubes? Don't they understand that all of the hand made crafts they buy in the cities are actually made in Taiwan and shipped in? These people claim that they want to know how other cultures live. They don't want to know that. They stay in the best hotels, they go to the five star restaurants that no native could afford with a year's salary. If they wanted the truth, they would do as I have done. Walk the streets of the slums, watch children picking rags from a garbage heap, go to the markets where slaughtered dogs hang in the windows of butcher shops. That's how they live. There's no Gore-Tex or bottled water out here.

In modern civilization, everything is packaged and pre-chewed to be easily digestible. Even emotions. Even fear. Want some fear? Come see our scary movie. Only a few dollars for ninety minutes of shear terror! That isn't true fear. True fear is not being able to get out of your office because the door handle is too slippery with your secretary's blood. Life is so comfortable these days that people have to actually buy fear. You think that nefarious forces are going to take over the world? Let me clue you in on a secret, it's already happened. They are so good that when they want your money, they can actually make you buy fear! And there is nothing you can do about it either, not within the confines of your comfortable little life in the suburbs. Why? Because they have prepackaged revolution for you already. Don't actually rebel, just watch it on television! Sit on your lazy ass, and we'll beam you images of fictional people rising up against the man for your enjoyment. You'll get all the emotion of a real revolution, but your hands won't be dirty. Who cares if it isn't real, it's fun! Is your boss upsetting you? Well then, don't bother to form a union, don't bother to campaign for improved working conditions. Just hang one of our little cartoons on your cubicle wall. Stare at it every day and say, "That's so true, that's so true." Their most successful creation in recent times is the anarchist hero figure. He allows us to buy into an authentic simulation of the revolution. He encourages passive spectating, and revolt becomes just another product to be consumed.

After several days of avoiding the inane chatter of the tourists, surviving the reckless driving of the bus drivers, and enduring a five-day walk up snowy paths, I found myself at the end of the trail. Blocking the mountain pass was a large wall. It must have been forty feet tall, red brick. It stretched from the shear rock face on my left to the shear rock face on my right. There was a large wooden door, banded with iron. It is a physical representation of the secret gate of Daath. The secret door to the void, to Irem. A small gong stood to the left, and an offering bowl. It was filled with fresh flowers, which seemed odd, as it was almost winter here. Snow was falling lightly. I rang the gong. I hear the sounds of rushing water. A face appears at the top of the wall. A bald head, red robes. He has Sherpa features, he could be Tibetan. The monk tells me in Tibetan to go away. I lie. I tell him that I have come to give tribute, and that I would like to speak with a master. The monk tells me that the masters here have no wisdom that I would accept, and that he has nothing for me. I tell him that I am a cold traveler, would not the Buddha advise giving succor to one such as myself? The monk tells me that there my gods aren't here, and that I had best go back to the town if I wanted a nice hotel. Then the head disappeared from the wall. Repeated banging on the gong produced no further result. I sat on a large rock for a while and I thought about my next move. I can hear rusty prayer wheels spinning behind the wall. They had the information I needed inside. The fact that they refuse to open their doors to a traveler in need is proof that this was not the typical monastery. I was sure that they would have the knowledge I needed. Of course, there was no way I could get in. The place was sealed like the fortress it was.

It was probable that this was the only entrance. Whoever lay behind this gate would have no other egress, unless they had tunneled all the way through the mountain, which was not something I was prepared to believe. That meant that they would have to come down the trail I was standing on in order to get anywhere. They were monks and hermits, sure, but they would have to have some dealings with the outside world. They would have to send somebody somewhere, sometime. All I would have to do was wait, and when someone came along, I could just grab him. It was likely that if any of them knew Vattan, then all of them knew Vattan.

It was only then that I realized I had forgotten to prepare myself for a trap. I guess that I was too excited about reaching my goal to think of anything else. Stupid. Careless. This pass was a great place to set up an ambush. It was windy and narrow, with many places to hide. But they weren't here, were they? Maybe they didn't know where I was headed. Maybe there are multiple monasteries out here in the mountains. Maybe this was the wrong place all together. The fact that there was not an ambush worried me a little, but I decided that sticking to my original plan and finding out what the monks really did know was the best course of action.

I set up a camp about a half mile down the road, around a bend. There wasn't anywhere else you could go once you came out of the banded door, so I thought that this would be a good site to stage an ambush. The acoustics were good, I could still hear the prayer wheels turning. I should enough time to prepare when I heard the door open. In the other direction I had some good visibility through the thin trees. At least on the first day. The light snow continued to fall all through the afternoon and into the night, and the brush became obscured with a white blanket. The full force of winter was rapidly coming to the mountains. The temperature was falling. But I knew that they would have to come out sometime. I watched and I waited.

I filled my days with meditation and research. I went back over all of the papers that I had, reviewing the document for further clues as to what my adversary was up to. My eyes were now much more open than they had been when I had decoded the first few sections, and I poured over them again, looking for things I might have missed. And I waited. As I suspected, there was much more that could be read into the texts than initially met the eye. There were hints at truths that I had inferred, but hadn't been able to conceptualize until now. Truths that made me shiver even more than the drop in temperature. And I waited. I put together different parts of the text. Each segment held a piece of the puzzle, hidden between the lines. It was easy to overlook subtle yet vital pieces of information. Each section seemed so separate, each code so independent, but there was an underlying theme. A dark theme that need not be repeated here. It wouldn't matter even if I did try to express the horror that I was discovering. I couldn't do it, not in words. I initially undertook the writing of this confession to see if in some way I could express what I now know to be true about the world, but here, near the end of my tale, I can see that it is not possible. You have to have had the experiences that I have had, you have to have seen the things that I have seen, you would have to explore your inner soul down to its fundamental core. Only there does the answer lie. I could no more explain to you what I now believe than you can explain to me your feelings on the meaning of life. You can't do it. It is fundamental to your existence, but it is not something that can be squashed down into a few paragraphs. Not something that can be explained without a full accounting and deep understanding of what you felt when you were beaten by the school bully, how you felt when your mother died, how it still hurts every time you think of your first love, and how she is lost to you forever. You can talk about the events yes, but you cannot express the feelings behind those events, and how those feelings make up the person you are today. I won't even bother to try to describe to you the person that I had become at that point. You can imagine what I was like, but your own preconceived notions of how a person reacts to events, events you yourself have no experience with, will color your conception. You can't understand me. You can't understand what I have been through or what I discovered as the snow fell in the Nepalese highlands.

No one came or went for days. The trail became covered with snow. Winter was coming. I waited in ambush around the bend for almost two weeks. My supplies were running low. It was almost a week of hiking to get up here, with the snow it might be a lot longer to get back. The solitude didn't drive me insane, despite what you might think. I just sat and waited. I waited because waiting was what I needed to do. My actions had become inertial. I just did what needed to be done with no consequence of the future or emotional attachment. Gone were the days when I would feel elated from some slight success in translation, from some daring escape from almost certain death, from the majestic beauty of the peaks that surrounded me. I performed all actions in a simple perfunctory manner. I did what I needed to do to survive and to continue. If I was killed, I was killed, that was it. Whatever the future brought, I would be ready for it. Finally, after such a long wait, there was some motion.

In my tent that morning I heard the prayer wheels grind to a stop. The sound of a door opening. My opportunity had arrived. I was ready for them, I moved quickly. Three men, walking barefoot through the snow came around the bend. Their heads were bowed in prayer as they walked. They expected to cross no one on their descent. I shot the leader once in the head. He fell to the ground motionless. There was a disturbing crack as his neck was broken by the fall. The second monk stopped, horrified at what had just happened, and paralyzed with fear. I put two bullets into his chest. He fell to the ground. After the report of the gun, the next sound heard was the monk screaming in agony. The next sound after that was the sickening thud of another bullet hitting him in his back as he rolled in pain. Then silence. The third monk spun around and tried to get back to the monastery. I was on top of him before he could get far. I tied his hands together with a piece of rope and dragged him into the tent. I spent a few minutes and pulled the bodies off the road. After a short time the falling snow returned the red ground to pristine white. In the remaining time I spent on the pass, no one came out of the monastery to look for their lost comrades.

I returned to the tent. The surviving monk was a younger fellow, red robes, shaved head. He looked at me with disdain. I wonder what it is like to live in Shangri-la, to

191

spend your days in an earthly paradise. I sat him up and threw the first page of the Vattan document into his lap. I told him in Tibetan that I needed him to translate. He refused at first. He played as if he didn't know what the document said, couldn't speak Tibetan. I knew better than that. Decency prevents me from describing the horrific things that I did that day to convince him to help me. This was the only way. The people on this mountain possessed a lost knowledge that was unavailable anywhere else, except perhaps Irem. This was the last section. This was the last clue. I had waited so long, I had had so much taken from me, I had sacrificed so much of my soul for these answers, that I couldn't accept defeat at this stage. That isn't an excuse for my actions, but hopefully it is an explanation.

After much effort on my part, he translated the paper from Vattan into Tibetan. My Tibetan was still pretty poor, I knew only a little outside of how to order food, ask directions, and make threats. I couldn't understand the complex and archaic terms he was using. I forced him to write it down, word by word, which he did, slowly, methodically. I could understand but a small fraction of the thing. I would have to go back and research more Devenagari at another time. It started with Tibetan, and now it ends the same way. Orobourous. The circle was about to be completed.

It took him most of the day to finish the script. He laughed and cried throughout the entire thing. I didn't let on that I couldn't understand much his speech as he spoke the translation. By the time he finished he was shaking. He had learned the end without the beginning. I had once thought that these people up on the mountain were in on the whole joke. That they had been connected with the people of Irem, and even possibly harbored a bird-headed god of their own deep within their underground fortress. But, seeing the monk's reaction, I knew that this was something he was unprepared for. Perhaps they had not let him in on their inner mysteries, but he was clearly not expecting what he read. It effected him deeply. At times, he even stopped reading entirely, began praying to the Buddha or Shiva or whatever creature they worship in the bowels of their secluded sanctuary. It was only when I broke his concentration with the butt of my pistol did he come back around. He was terrified. Scared of what I might do to his body, but also of what the hidden knowledge he was uncovering would do to his soul.

I guess that the threat to his physical being was greater, or at least more immediate, to him. He finished the translation. The last few words were very difficult for him. His hands were shaking so badly. At the time I thought that it was due to the intense cold of the Himalayan winter, but now I realize that after reading that document, one would never feel protected against the cold again. When he was done, he backed off of the thing, knelt his head in prayer. As I said, I don't know much Tibetan, but I could gather that he was speaking a prayer for forgiveness.

I pulled him from the tent and threw him into the snow. He fell face down. I asked him what his name was. He told me. Through perhaps serendipitous chance or moralistic irony it turned out that this was the monk whose mother had asked me to deliver a message. I put the scrap of paper in his hands and told him that his mother had words for him. He didn't want to read it at first, assuming that more horrors awaited him with this paper, but I told him that his mother cried for him every day and begged me on her knees to make sure that he received this. He began reading. Once he recognized his mother's handwriting he began scanning the note voraciously. He knelt there in the snow, eyes streaming tears as he read his mother's declaration of love for her son, and her desperate appeal for his return. It stirred something inside me. I allowed him to finish the entire letter before I put a bullet in the back of his head.

I watched the all too familiar yet still disturbing sight of a dead body flailing about. The heart continues to rhythmically pump for several minutes. Blood flows from the wound intermittently, in step with the final beats of the heart. The snow was stained red again. I packed up my things and left. I hadn't expected my trip to have taken this long, and I was running low on some supplies. I needed to get back to the last village.

As it turned out, the voyage back took much longer than I could have ever expected. It should have only taken a week or so, but on the third day there was a storm, a big storm. Snow had been falling off and on for most of the time that I had spent up here at the top of the world, but now it came down in buckets. I was able to find a small cave and take shelter from the winds, but by morning there must have been ten feet of snow on the ground. The entire pass was snowed in. I had prepared for some snow, but I didn't expect to have been up there that long, to have had to deal with the effects of true winter. I would have to change my plans, re-route and see if I could get somewhere before my supplies ran out.

That took longer than I anticipated, much longer. I rapidly became lost in the white, monotonous foothills. With the deep snow it was not possible to tell where the paths led, if any were even there. It was not possible to locate rivers or fields, or anything. The place was a barren, white wasteland. No one came this way during the winter months. The locals were all holed up until spring, and even the tourists weren't stupid enough to be out here. I can follow a map, it is not that hard to tie snowshoes on my feet, but orienteering isn't something that I was particularly good at. I barely made it out of the desert some years ago, and in the desert you don't have to worry about mountains and cliffs disrupting your route.

I walked and walked through the valleys and over the hills. Several times I thought that I was getting close, only to be frustrated by another long, barren field, or another un-climbable wall of ice. The food ran out on the tenth day. I thought that I had prepared, I thought that the trip was only going to have taken maybe two weeks, with the possibility of resupply at the monastery. It was now over four weeks since I had last seen a village or other place of succor. I had become more lost than I had though, because after the third week I found myself once again at the gates to the mysterious monastery. That sent me running. By now they might know the Cimmerian sins I had committed against their brethren. I didn't have enough bullets to stop all of them.

I was hungry, tired, and cold. I was so close, all I had to do was get out. I was lost in this maze. I was frozen in this rocky, white graveyard. The air was thin. There were no animals to be seen. It was winter, the leaves were off the trees, and there were no berries to be found. Twice I saw animal footprints in the snow, but I was not able to track them to anything I could catch and eat. None of the hardships stopped me. I was on a mission. I had a goal, namely to get out of the mountains and to learn the secrets of Irem. Nothing was going to stop me from accomplishing that goal, not the weather, not the unSinclairative monks, not the men in black that were always just around the corner, nothing.

Almost five weeks had passed since I had left the small village with the old woman. Almost a week without food. I was getting weak. I blamed my slow movements on the thin air, but it was more than that now. My belly had stopped aching after a few days. Had delirium begun to set in? Was this the vision quest that the shamans talk about? Was this the suffering that was supposed to bring spiritual enlightenment? Was my spirit animal just around the corner, filled with advice and guidance? I prayed that it was and I prayed that it was edible.

My journey almost ended on one mountain pass. Delirium takes its toll on the senses. Was I really climbing this mountain? Was what I saw real, or was it all happening internally, in my mind? Was I only climbing this mountain figuratively? Scaling walls of self doubt, overcoming mental obstacles, growing stronger and better and larger as a person. Who was chasing me really? They were so faceless, so unidentifiable. Were they real at all? Was any of this real? Maybe they were just expressions of my self pity, of my inner demons. What was I running from? What part of my inner conscious did I not want to face? Would I get to the top of the mountain, would I conquer my demons?

Then I was falling. I regained my perspective fast enough to grab on to the nearest outcropping. Things fell; rocks, equipment, my gun. Downward, off the cliff face. Down into the mists. Down like that man in Peru fell. I was holding on with one hand. My sack was slipping. I couldn't let it go. The equipment I could do without, but the sack contained my notes, my evidence. It was my whole life, the sum total of my existence. To let it go would be to let go of myself. To lose all. My grip was slipping. I needed my other hand to pull myself up, but that would require letting go of my sack. The miser's dilemma. You see this all the time at the movies. Some greedy bastard is falling off a cliff, and he can't bring himself to let go of the gold figurine that weighs him down. Then he falls, booty in hand. I couldn't let that happen to me. It would be too poetic, too trite. But I couldn't let go of the document, couldn't lose the one thing I had traded everything for. There was only one possibility, only one destiny for me. I used the strength I had and lifted myself up with my one free hand. Once safely back on the trail, documents intact, the veil of delirium temporarily lifted by the shock of imminent death, I stood up, dusted the snow off, and continued on my way.

I had made it to a long, featureless valley. A small river flowed at the bottom. A river meant fresh water. A river meant steady flat ground, a river meant settlements and civilization and life. I knew that if I followed the river I would eventually get somewhere. It was just a matter of how long that would take.

I had another problem though. There was little snow down by the banks of the river, but there was mud. Boot tracks were visible, heading off into the distance. They didn't match my boots, but they were fresh. Who but the men in black would be out here this time of year? They were getting closer.

I kept walking through the valley for the rest of the day. Step by step, minute by minute, hour by hour. I hoped that I wouldn't be spotted by anyone as I trudged along. I crossed a second set of footprints in the mud. I shivered instinctively. The valley stretched out before me for what seemed like an infinity. To my right and left, mountains towered in the distance. I didn't have much room to work, I didn't have anywhere I could run. The valley was about a mile wide, but featureless except for some hearty winter grasses. There was nowhere to hide. It was a race. Could I get out of this frozen hell and to a warm tea house, or would the men in black catch up with me? I pushed onward, fighting against my enemy and my hunger.

Night comes. Black. You think that you know what night is, but you don't, you can't, until you experience night in the middle of nowhere. Far from the noise of cars and comforting lights of cities. Night in the Himalayas is sheer total blackness. I had no choice but to stop. So did my faceless pursuers. I sat in the silent darkness and waited, listening, straining to hear when they came for me, chilled to the bone with no fire. But the blackness was a shield, a comforting shroud that protected me. I couldn't run, but they couldn't chase, at least not until morning.

The march through the valley lasted three days and three nights. The place was endless, lonely, featureless. I'm sure they were watching, I'm sure they could tell that I was on my last legs. Was I in rifle range yet? Why didn't they make their move? Why did they taunt me with muddy footsteps? I knew that time would win their battle for them. It would only be a few more days before I fell into the snow. Covered by the fresh fallen snow. My body would not be found for decades, if ever. I had left no heir, I had left no sign of my progress. All my work would be for naught. Everything I had learned would sink back into the misty darkness in which it had lived for eons. Irem would continue to thrive as a leech on humanity. There was little I could do. I had little strength left. Perhaps it was better to end it now. Dive headfirst into the cold, cold water of the river. The ultimate act of freedom. A self-determined life span. Wasn't that better than dying in the wastes? Thin, frail, would I fall from hunger? Would I freeze in the dark of night? Would they come for me in the night? Oh God, would they come for me in the night? End this thing. Tears froze against my cheek.

My footsteps fell slower and slower against the snow and mud of the valley floor, I could almost hear them now. Hear the rhythm of their boots keeping pace with mine. Hear their heartbeats in rhythm with mine. I sensed they were almost close enough for a shot. Step by step across the plain. As night began to fall I approached what appeared to be an old abandoned farm. The house was ruined, but a small prayer wall remained. A three foot high pile of stones, inscribed with prayers for the dead. It was one of the only things in the valley besides the grass, snow and river. There, behind the wall, can you see? Movement. I took out my binoculars and had a closer look. It was one of them. A faceless man dressed in darkest black. Waiting, working. Was he on guard, a sentinel? Or was he just cold, searching through the old farmhouse for something to burn, something to keep warm. I turned to run, make a wide detour around the farmhouse and the river, but I stopped. I knew that I didn't have much time left. That I would have to make a stand soon, or I wouldn't have the strength to. I had already accepted the inevitability of my own death, but I refused to go down without a fight. At least let this opponent of mine know who I was, force him to have the guts to kill me with his own hands, force him to do the dirty work himself. Let my death screams haunt him in the night like so many of my victims haunted me.

He hadn't seen me yet. The grass here was high, but not that high. I crouched and moved closer, closer. I could hear his heart beating. I could read his body language, I could read his mind. He was scared. He was lonely, he was human. They are just human, just like me. They need to sleep, they need to eat. Eat, he would have food, he would have supplies. Maybe he would have the things I needed to survive. Visions of k-rations danced in my head. Soon I would eat.

I slid closer and closer, slower and slower. He was on the other side of the low prayer wall, tearing down some timber for a fire. He wasn't looking in my direction, he wasn't as wily as I was, wasn't as trained as I had become. That would be his downfall. They had taught me well, but now the student surpasses the teacher. They had forced me to learn their ways so that I could avoid them, defend myself from them, now I use those same techniques to enact my revenge.

My approach was not perfect. He turned towards me as I made my last move for the cover of the prayer wall. He could see me do it, he knew where I was, that's for certain. But, behind the wall, he couldn't get a clean shot. He would have to come around, close. As I said, my gun had been lost up on the high slopes, I couldn't compete with him in a firefight. I needed him close. I gripped my ice axe tightly as he approached. My heart was beating in my chest.

I could see through a crack in the rocks as the man drew near. Beat, beat, beat, my heart beat in rhythm with his footsteps. He was walking carefully, cautiously. He had his rifle drawn. Waiting for a shot. Waiting for a chance. My heart beat. I could feel the blood pump though my wrists, pulsing around the steel weapon I held so tightly. Too tightly. Beat beat beat. The man approached. I could see his eyes. The whites of his eyes. He didn't know where I was behind the wall. I would have to get lucky. If he came around the far side he would be able to get a shot off before I could get to him. Beat beat beat. He came closer, closer. His steps slower, slower. His ears strained to hear my breath, my movements, anything that would betray my position. I was sure he could hear me, that he could hear my heartbeat, it was so loud. Luck, he came near me. He reached the wall, mere feet from my position. He waited, he was steeling himself. Beat beat beat. Beat beat beat. In a movement he reached over the wall, aimed his gun over the wall. He guessed wrong. I hit him in a flying leap from the other side. We were rolling on the ground, rolling in the mud. It was getting dark. I knew I was weak, but adrenaline pumped through my veins. I was stronger than I should have been, stronger than he expected me to be. I was feral, primal. I moved the axe to hit him, but he blocked my arm. We rolled. Evenly matched. Then his head hit a rock lying on the muddy river bank. He stopped moving. I got up. He wasn't dead. Not yet. Just unconscious. I had won.

I started to get up, to run, to lose myself in the wilderness before he woke up. But no. I fought the urge to flee. I turned back. He lay unmoving. I rolled him over. Blood dripped from the back of his head, but I could hear his labored breathing. I could still feel my heartbeat pumping through my chest. Beat beat beat. I felt dizzy, nauseous. I needed food. I needed supplies. I pulled open his backpack and began rooting through it. Beat beat beat. I could feel my heart subside as I sat in the muddy ground, resting. I would take his food, take his supplies. Then I would be all right, then I would make it. Then I would solve this three thousand year old puzzle that had cost me so much. The man moaned softly. I knew he wouldn't make it, that by taking his supplies I was sentencing him to death out here. That didn't bother me. Let the vultures pick at his bones. He had what I needed, and I was going to take it. I was going to make it. I smiled instinctively, I was going to make it.

Elation was short lived however. The man's pack contained almost nothing. A few scraps at best. I ate all of it sitting there on the prayer wall, and I was till hungry afterwards. If anything, the introduction of a little food once again woke my stomach to its situation. No wonder I was able to match my pursuer despite my weakness. He was weak from hunger as well. He was as lost as I was, as unprepared as I was. Snow began falling. I wouldn't make it. Even though I had won this battle I wouldn't make it. I couldn't march much further before collapsing. With the snow falling like this I doubted that I could make it another mile. Night was fast approaching.

Another idea entered my head. Small at first, one tiny note against the cacophony of self destructive thoughts that ran through my fevered brain. A dark thought. Unthinkable. My mind refused to except it. It was a light. It was a ray of hope. It was the summation of my worst fears. It was the final pit into which I must sink. Must sink to continue, to survive, to live. As the hint became thought, and the thought grew and flowered in my delirium I became ill, actually vomited just from the idea, or would have anyway if there was anything in my belly. I knelt in the snow, dry heaving, shedding tears. I had suffered so much to reach this point. I had done so many things to so many people. So many had died because of me. What was one more act? What was one more stain on my already ragged soul? It was nothing really, nothing that I hadn't already done before, a sin that I had already conceptually committed. It would soon be made flesh. It would soon become a reality. I knew that. I didn't want to do it. I didn't want to commit the final sin of my pathetic existence, but I knew that I would. I knew that desperation drove me. I knew that I would do what I had to do because I had always done what I had to do. Semper Fi, do or die. It was like that time on the mountain in Peru. Every step was torturous. I knew that I could not go on, but I did. Step by step, stair by stair. Now I was to take the final step. Perform the unthinkable. Perform an act that I would have been unable to comprehend in my former life, even in my darkest nightmares. Nothing could have prepared me for what was to come next. They say that a man grows hardened to violence, grows inured as he sees his friends and enemies fall before his eyes. That isn't true. Every act follows you in your dreams, every sickening splash as blood hits the floor echoes in your ears for the rest of your life. What happens though is that you learn to continue. You learn that even when the bile is pushed to the top of your throat, and the horrors you see make you never want to open your eyes again, you can still act, you can still move. You can still do what needs to be done to survive. I was hardened inside, I was inured to the horror, an iron box had been erected over my soul.

The idea took time to root of course. In the Shakespeare play, Macbeth says that he stands waist deep in a river of blood. That no matter which direction he goes, forward to glory or back in defeat, he cannot help but get more blood on him. Since this is so, he chooses to go forward. Justifies the killing as a necessity. He has no choice. I too had no choice. As night fell I sat on the wall, watching the unconscious man's labored breathing, telling myself over and over again that I was not going to do what I knew I would. But under the blanket of night, under the dark cover that obscures sin, I played my final card.

Adrenaline takes over, aggression takes over. My axe moved with the force of all of my suffering these past few years. They say that a man in desperate situations can have super-human strength, can lift a car off his crushed child with one hand. I experienced that inner fire that night, but it was not love that moved my hand. It was shear horror, horror at my thoughts and actions. It was shear rage, rage at my adversaries for what they had made me do. Hatred, hatred for myself for what I had allowed myself to become. The axe came down on the man's chest as he lay unconscious. I heard the sickening thud that sounds like someone beating muddy ground with a bat. I heard the repulsive snap of human bones breaking. I heard the loathsome wheeze of air entering lungs, but not from the throat. I heard the repulsive sputtering of a man trying to clear his mouth of blood.

Then silence. Then nothing. The only heartbeat I could hear was my own. It was over. The body grew cold before me. The evidence of my final transgression lay steaming in the mud. I hadn't killed this man out of frustration, I had no need to kill him to steal his food, I had killed this man because he was food.

That may sicken you. That may destroy the last vestiges of pity you may have left for my wretched self, but that was what I needed to do to survive. These people had taken everything from me. They had killed people for no other reason than to protect their secrets. That is a pathetically small reason to kill isn't it? My reasons were much better. I needed this to live. I needed this to continue the fight and avenge all of those who'd suffered at their hands. Isn't that a better excuse? This was the only source of sustenance around. Looking back, I am sure that if I had not taken that desperate action that night that I would have died up on the taiga. Doesn't that make it better?

I apologize. I am seeking validation from you, and that isn't my goal. This is my confession. I know what you will think of me at the end, and you think rightly. My actions have no excuse, I shouldn't keep trying to defend them. I shouldn't keep trying to justify myself. It is too late for that now. Of my need for acceptance, need for forgiveness for my transgressions, only these vestiges remain. I neither require nor want your understanding, not where I am going. I am beyond that now This diary is an attempt to purge myself of my last bit of former humanity, my final break from civilization as I was brought up to understand it.

I sat in the darkness, axe in my hand, blood congealing on my boots, for a long time. Quiet. I was moved to action by the approach of dawn, the light of the new day. It was an easy matter to take what I needed from the dead man. To start a fire, to cook chunks of flesh. Human fat gives off a peculiar odor when it burns, it's like nothing else. The body has a natural aversion to the scent. Out of a sense of decency to the corpse, I will leave out most of the gory details of that morning. Suffice it to say that by mid-day my pack had been refilled, and what was left of the man was properly disposed of, along with the equipment I couldn't carry.

I had the final solution. I held it warm against my chest, under my jacket. The final part of the strange manuscript was decrypted. Its secrets would soon be laid bare. Somehow I knew that once I was able to read the final section, my path would become clear. The journey that began on the Golden Gate Bridge all those years ago would be over. I walked deliberately, mechanistically down the slope of the mountain. There was no joy or elation. There was no sense of accomplishment. There was only the end of the mechanical journey. I was like a toy whose spring was winding down. It was almost over, but then what? I had long ago lost the ability to contemplate the future. My life had been about the present, about satisfying my own needs, about survival. It would continue to be about survival. More information would probably not change that. Even if I had the ultimate secret, been able to put my finger on the button that could bring down all of those bastards that had chased me all these years, it wouldn't matter. There was nothing left. I moved down the mountainside because there was no reason not to move down the mountainside. I continued to survive because there was no reason to die. I continued to go because there was no reason to stop. My life had become the absence of negative, not the presence of positive.

It was all symmetrical wasn't it? Orobourous. The end is the beginning is the end. That is why the last section was written in Tibetan. It has to be. The end is the beginning. This whole thing started with Tibetan, of course it would have to end that way. Had I only seen that before, had I only been able to comprehend that before, I could have saved myself so much time and effort and hardship.

Every night that I spent in the cold I had the same dream. I was rampaging through the black veil of night. Axe in hand. Chopping and stabbing and killing, like an animal. Just like in real life, just like the way it truly happened. But this time I unmask the corpse, a light shines upon us, blood everywhere. The face is covered in blood. But I can make it out, I can recognize my pursuer, my stalker, my victim. The face on the body is my face, distorted by the pain of death, but it is my face. In the dream I have killed no one but myself.

I would translate the last part of the document from Devenagari to English. I would do it because it was the next thing to do. I would do it because I had spent so much time getting to this point, because it was the next chapter in my saga. I had no curiosity left, I had no joy of discovery left. The mysteries of the universe could have opened themselves up to me there on the mountaintop and I would have greeted the knowledge with a simple shrug. I was tired, I was drained. I needed to get to a place where I wouldn't be bothered for a while. A place where I could have time to finish the translation. I completed my trek along the top of the world blankly. No thoughts moved through my head beyond those that I have listed here. A few weeks after I returned to the world, I found myself in a small cabin, in rural Ontario. I had collected some of the resources I needed to work out the script written by the doomed monk. It would only take me a few days to finish rendering the words into understandable English.

# Chapter 10:
# Crown


I have been here in this cold drafty cabin on this snowy windblown plain for over two weeks now. Warmed only by the small fireplace and my own burning desire. I worked almost non-stop, nighttime hours filled with strange dreams interspersed with candlelight flickers over forgotten texts. As the first rays of dawn entered my window this morning I finally finished my work. I am cold. Has the fire gone out? Can any fire warm me now? The final chapter has effected me the same way that water effects a blaze. It has put me out. It has made me cold. I feel as though my body no longer generates heat, that my heart no longer beats, that I am no longer alive.

I sit in the same wooden chair, in front of the wooden desk covered with my work. I drink the last of the absinthe and try to forget. My mind had become quiet. I don't think about anything for hours. There was little left to think about. I had searched years for an answer, now I had it. What to do next would come naturally. This was big, bigger than I had thought, bigger than a few drug dealers growing cocaine in the Andes. Bigger than a spy ring operating on the streets of San Francisco. This was a global conspiracy, an ancient conspiracy. The buildings of Irem were old, some seemed thousands of years old. This was immense, something that was never meant to exist on this earth lay out there, beneath the desert sands, forgotten by all but the initiated. A viral organization that existed for no other purpose than to replicate itself into future generations. A cancer, eating humanity slowly, spreading its tendrils into the lives of everyone and everything. You may not know it, but they are in your life too. They are everywhere, their black hand is in every aspect of your existence. In ancient days, when the bicameral man believed gods directly ruled every component of the universe, everything was deliberate. Nothing happened by chance. Everything was an omen, a sign. Everything in the primitive man's world was there for a purpose, one only needed to divine what that purpose was. Nothing has changed since that day. Just the names, just the thickness of the veil. Irem controls all. They control the government. They control the media. Every event in your life, however seemingly insignificant, is performed under their guidance.

You may ask why I continued as I came to these revelations. I knew that as long as I stayed in one place and didn't pursue my research, they were content to leave me be. They seemed to only reappear when I moved in their direction. I know now that I could have given up at any point. I could have dropped out of sight. To a cabin in the middle of the wilderness somewhere, to a small apartment in the big city. Lived a life. They couldn't be stopped. They couldn't be revealed. They were too big, too encompassing. I shouldn't have tried. I was foolish to continue. But I kept going. I continued to pursue them. I continued to look through the forbidden door. I continued to follow their trail, to decode their secrets. At first I did it because of fear and revenge. Then out of need for excitement and glory. But at the end I kept going because it was easier than stopping. Inertia. I did it because that is what I did. That was who I was. I was no longer the young attorney with the nice car. I was no longer the guy in the business suit with the trophy wife and the high powered job. I was now the pursuer, the challenger, the anarchist hero. I said before that I felt exhilaration at the breaking of bonds, at the crossing of taboos. I broke down the constraints of my previous life, did what I wanted to do, felt how I wanted to feel. Performed acts that I never thought possible. I realize now that it is never possible to be truly free. It is not conceivable. You cannot break out of your cage. You can only exchange one cage for another. When I left my life, when they drove me from my life, that didn't make me free of rules, all it did was exchange one set of rules for another. My behavior can still be accounted for with a simple set of regulations.

Within days of my departure from what you call civilization, I had assumed my new role. I played it for all that it was worth. It was a stretch, it was difficult, but I played the game the exact way it was meant to be played. I didn't do anything innovative or unique. All of my actions were easily followed. That's how they knew where I was, where I would travel to next. They have no psychic powers, at least not in this sense, they just knew who I was, or I mean who I had become. I can see it all so clearly now. I can see how simple it would be to gauge my reactions, to feed me the proper information, to nudge me in the direction they wanted me to run. They were like the contestants in a frog jumping contest. They slapped the ground behind me and I hopped, right where they wanted me to go. So simple to get me to play along. I thought that I was so ingenious so resourceful, that I would outsmart them, ha! They knew exactly what a man would do if he thought he was ingenious and resourceful. It is all pretty obvious if you think about it, isn't it?

I was so mistaken, about everything. Everything that I thought, every theory that I espoused, is untrue. Everything they told me is a lie. Everything I believed, every reason I inferred, was all part of the scam. Why do they enforce traffic laws? Control. It has nothing to do with safety, that's the outer lie. It has nothing to do with identifying trouble makers. That's the inner lie. The true reason they enforce the laws is control. They want to be able to stop anyone, anytime, for any reason. Why traffic? It's so public. How many times have you seen a cop's flashing lights on the side of the road? Did you ever stop and consider what is happening to the man in the car on the shoulder? No, you just assume that it has something to do with some minor traffic violation and you drive on, forgetting that you ever saw anything. Meanwhile those in control have a mechanism to edit out anyone they like, anytime they like. We all drive cars don't we? We are all available to be pulled over. No one will question. No one will ever know. They have complete control. They have the enforcement mechanism for a police state without anyone suspecting what is really going on. Brilliant isn't it? I wonder how you will react the next time you see the flashing lights in your rear view mirror.

I used to think that drug use was illegal because it opens doors to new thoughts. Thoughts that they don't want you to have. It is true that psychedelics can have that effect, that they can open doors, that they can cause you to see things in a different light. A light in which their ugliness is exposed in its full glory. But they don't fear that. They don't fear you, you small insignificant peasant. They know, as I now know, that the average human is incapable of comprehending even the smallest part of their methods and goals. They know that people don't want their minds expanded. People specifically do things to shrink their minds. Alcohol is the most popular drug because it lowers your awareness. The average drug user is more concerned with dancing until dawn and scoring some chicks than they are in the secrets of the universe. And the small minority that is interested in expanded thought patterns are watched very carefully.

So, why do they do it? Why have they created such a jumble of laws and ruined so many lives? It is the same as speeding. They do it because it makes control a simple matter. It is a crime of possession. You don't have to *do* anything, you just have to *have* something. It is very easy to set someone up on a drug charge. Just put some drugs in their house/car/person. If you try to frame someone for burglary/murder/etc, you have to have a victim willing to testify that they have been victimized. But with drugs, you don't need any evidence beyond the drugs themselves. There is no defense. You can't be somewhere else, you can't have an alibi. You can't have witnesses that can testify that you couldn't have done it. Possession is nine tenths of the law, right?

But I digress. My time is growing critically short. It will all be over soon. I had intended to tell more about what I learned, I wanted to put all of their secrets down on paper before the end, but I know now that I couldn't do that. It would take months just to sort out what is in my mind. It would take thousands of pages for me to try to explain even a tenth of what I have learned in the last few weeks. It isn't just what the manuscript said, but what it implied. There is so much that falls into place after reading their words, penned so long ago in a dead tongue. It all falls into place. Pieces of the puzzle. Unconnected events, they all make sense now. This document is like a filter. Looking through it everything is clear. All of history falls into focus as a single directed act. I know that you don't understand. I know that you think me a coward for not giving you the punchline to the joke. For not letting you in on the miraculous knowledge I now have after praising it for so long. But I can't do it. I don't have the skill, but that is no excuse. The real reason is that you are not ready for it. It has driven me to the brink of insanity (and I fear soon over the brink as more sets in), and I was prepared for it. I have had all of the background information. I have had years to digest the truth in little pieces. To try and give you the sum total of what I now know to be true in a matter of a few paragraphs would be preposterous. It would be like asking you to describe the history of America in one sentence. You can't do it. Even if you had the skill to do so, it wouldn't be understood. All of the implications and hidden double meanings would be lost. It would just come out as a short group of words with no value to the reader. It is the process that leads to enlightenment. It is the process that is necessary. It is the reason the za-zen masters use koans. What is the sound of one hand clapping? There is no answer to that question, and even if there was, it is not the answer that is important, it is the meditation on the *question* that matters the most. I can't give you the translation here because it is only the meditation on the translation, it is only the gradual process of opening one's mind to the point where the translation could be understood that is the important part. And I can't do that here, now, with so little time left. It is a process that everyone must go through on their own. It is a process that takes years to accomplish. It is a long hard road, and the end is more terrifying that the sum of all the other parts. It is something that I don't recommend you even attempt, and I curse myself for not having the foresight to stay fat, dumb and happy in the little life that they had prepared for me.

Did you know that they use a lot of contractors to do their work? That was one of the things that surprised me most about them. Did you think that every man in black that I had interacted with was one of them? Knew all the secrets? There are so few of them, I doubt I even saw one true initiate. Detective Smith and the man who gave me the cross in Peru are the only ones I suspect were truly in on what was going on, who truly understood the secrets of the City of Pillars. The rest were mercenaries, adventurers, security specialists. They had no idea what was really happening. They were just manipulated by the proper front agencies to do what they were required to do. Most had no idea who they were even working for I bet. Irem has so many faces, so many fronts. The poor bastard I took in Nepal probably thought he was a CIA agent. The suicide in Oslo was just a zealot of the outer church who had a far poorer understanding of the inner mysteries than even I had at that point.

What *can* I say about the document you ask? What was the 'Master Plan'? Well, I can say this. It isn't anything that I thought it would be. Over the years I had alternately assumed that it was some sort of secret plan for global domination. That it was some sort of manifest for drug smugglers. That it was some coded bit of classified data that was being slipped to America's enemies. That it was a smuggled plea from the secret resistance. I couldn't have been more wrong. It was none of those things. It was so much more. Do you want to know what the secret is? It is a training manual. Yes, a simple training manual. Oh, not a manual in the way you think of. It doesn't have rules and tips and test questions, but it is a training manual nonetheless. You see, the whole thing was a set up. It was all part of their test. The man in the tollbooth so long ago didn't make a mistake. The document was never meant for the man in the identical car behind mine. It was meant for me. It was always meant for me and me alone. They never wanted to shut me up. They never wanted my silence, they never want their secrets back. Ha! That is the funny part. That is the part that I didn't understand until just now, until just before I started this last confession as a eulogy to my humanity. They wanted *me*! You see, they need replacements. They don't live forever, despite what you might think. They are humans too, at least biologically. But how to choose replacements? You can't just pick genetic descendents. Most of them suffer from the same stupidity and small mindedness that afflicts the rest of humanity. No, candidates have to be carefully selected. That's part of the reason they watch everybody, part of the reason they are watching you. They are looking for their next generation. They poke and probe and tickle civilization and see what floats to the top. I don't know what brought me to their attention, but somehow I caught their eye. They didn't accidentally pass me something that I shouldn't have seen. They gave it to me for a reason, they wanted to see what I would do. Then they made me run. They shook up my life. They opened me up to possibilities that I have never seen or even thought of before. They made me question authority, my place in the universe, the true meaning of existence. And they sat back and watched. They sat back and waited for me to make my move. I always thought that I was too clever for them. That whenever I lowered my profile they would lose me. They never lost me, they were just giving me a chance to drop out of the game. They were just giving me a chance to prove myself unworthy of them by giving up. Oh, why didn't I give up? Why didn't I say 'Enough is Enough!' But I kept going. They threw obstacles in my path to see if I could surmount them. They kept passing information to me through the chapters of the document. Don't you see how they did it? Don't you see how they manipulated me every step of the way? How they made me into one of them, slowly, piece by piece removing my humanity.

That is all I the time I have left. I can't hear my heartbeat anymore. All I can hear is the droning. The vibration. The heartbeat of the world. They call to me. I will sit and wait. I know what happens next, I think like they do now. I know that in a few minutes there will be a knock at my cabin door. I will rise from my seat and walk the length of the room. I will open the door. No one will be there, only a package, wrapped in plain brown paper. I will take the package inside and open it knowingly. Inside will be a black suit, white shirt, black tie, black hat, black shoes. It will all be my size. I will put on the outfit. I will place the hat on top of my head. Then I will make my way to the only place I belong. Not San Francisco or Eugene or Cusco. The only place where I can exist now. I can't go back to humanity knowing what I now know. There are things I've seen that I can't unsee. I can't do anything but continue to play the role that they have selected for me, in the same way that you have no choice but to continue playing the role they have selected for you. I will leave this snowy cabin and make my way to the City of Pillars, the City of Glass Dreams, the last outpost of the once great civilization of Atlantis. I will walk through the front gates with tears in my eyes. Tears of joy and horror. I will walk through the gates of the only place that is my home, the only place that has ever been home. I will feel the beating of the earth beneath my feet. I will walk through the gates shouting, shouting IREM, GLORIOUS IREM, City of Pillars, City of Lights, holiest of holies, glory of glories, IREM, I love you, I LOVE YOU.

## About the Author

The name 'Dominic Peloso' has a Kabbalistic value of 284.

Despite being very well rounded, he is usually obtuse and is rather pointed despite not being too sharp. He holds two MS degrees from Berkeley, and is working on a third at JHU. He knows how to build a nuclear weapon, and has taught classes in the subject at the Joint Military Intelligence College. Due to what can only be attributed to a clerical error, he has been allowed to freely roam the halls of the Pentagon, CIA, NSA, and a few places that don't even officially exist. He is currently developing environmentally friendly ways to dispose of chemical weapons left over from the Cold War. Besides writing subversive novels, his hobbies include; esoteric gnostic religions, hermeticism, tribal art, ethical philosophy, particle physics, environmental extremism, 20th century literature, feng shui, international politics, '80s dreampop, and several other things that absolutely no one else seems to be interested in. Although he sometimes wears black, he adamantly denies being affiliated in any way with the Knights Templar, Illuminati, or the Rosicrucians.